WOLF'S GAMBIT

USA TODAY BESTSELLING AUTHOR

EVE L. MITCHELL

WOLF'S GAMBIT

Foreword

This story began as chapters that I released in my newsletter. Only six chapters were ever released and this is a continuation of that story.

This is Book 1 in a three-book paranormal romance series. This book is not a standalone.

Book Description

My whole life, I've been the outsider. The wolves of the Anterrio Pack took my brother and me into their pack after our parents died.

To the pack, I remained the wild, untamed misfit despite my efforts to belong.

My first heat loomed ahead of the Luna Ball, and once again, I found myself attracting unwelcome attention, not just from my pack but also from the visiting Blackridge Peak Pack.

When my brother suspected their new alpha might hold answers about our past, he refused to put me at risk while he searched for the truth. Instead, he set me free from a pack that never truly accepted me.

Running from the only home I'd ever known, I longed for a fresh start. But in an unfamiliar human world, finding my place proved to be another challenge, as trouble followed me relentlessly.

Until I realized it was not *just* misfortune that was dogging my heels.

It's an alpha.

Content information: Wolf's Gambit is a paranormal romance, the first book in The Blackridge Peak series. Recommended reading age is 18+ due to sexual content, mature language, violence, and some mature themes. This is Book 1 in a continuing series and ends on a cliffhanger.

CHAPTER 1

Kezia

COOL WATER LAPPED AT MY FEET AS I MOVED carefully through the river, a wooden spear held tightly in my hand as I stalked my prey. The fat trout swam lazily ahead, taunting me with their leisurely afternoon swim. Grinding my teeth, clutching my spear tighter, I brought it down in a smooth, practiced strike, ready to impale an unsuspecting fish.

I missed Mr. Trout by a country mile.

The loud laughter from the riverbank made me close my eyes and count to ten before I turned and faced my peers. My best friend and accomplice in all of my crimes, Cass, sat on the grassy banks, her head thrown back as she laughed loudly. Beside her sat her brother, Landon, who was grinning at me as I stomped out of the water.

"You're both dicks," I grumbled as I dropped down beside them on the bank. I refused to look at their two overflowing baskets of trout.

"Why is it, when you shift, you're practically perfect, but you're just..." Landon floundered as I raised an eyebrow at him in a silent challenge. "This? You're so bad like this," he finished lamely.

"I'm bad?"

"Kezia, you're a terrible hunter in human form. You know it, we know it, and the whole of Anterrio Pack knows it." Cass exchanged a look with her brother, and they started chuckling again as they filled my empty basket with some of their catch.

"You don't need to," I told them quietly. Keeping my eyes averted, I looked out over the river toward the peak that sat to the west. "As you said, everyone knows I can't hunt when I'm human."

"Who cares?" Landon said as he bounded to his feet. "We won't tell, and who the hell is asking *us* anyway?" His smug grin earned him an eye roll from me as he helped his sister to her feet.

Dusting off the back of her shorts, Cass bent down to hand me my basket. "Stop moping. We caught lots. Trout is still on the menu tonight. At the end of the day, who cares who caught what? The fact we have the food is all that matters."

"Teamwork makes the dream work," Landon cried out with his arms wide and his head tilted back as if he were a showman.

As Landon always did, he made me laugh. His bright blue eyes twinkled with glee as he looked at us both. "You're such a clown," I told him with a smile as I took the basket off Cass.

"Which is why you love me."

Pretending to think about it, I rubbed my chin. "Love? It's more like...tolerate. I *tolerate* you."

"Cassandra! Do you hear how she wounds my pride?"

"You're an ass." His sister elbowed him as we set off back to town.

With a final glance back to the river and a look down at my

half-full basket, I shrugged off the day's fishing failure. When it was time to hunt in my wolf form, I would be victorious. My wolf never failed in the hunt. I may have been crap at most things in human form, but when I was one with the wolf, I was almost invincible.

"She isn't listening again."

Hearing Cass complain to her brother got my attention. "I was listening."

"You're such a rotten liar, Kezia," Cass said with a scowl. "You weren't listening, because if you had been, you would know I was talking about the Luna Ball."

Shit. I hadn't been listening. "I was listening. I've been listening for two months, because all you've talked about is the ball. I know, *we* know"—I indicated to Landon—"that it's the biggest event of the year. We understand that your dress will be the best and most beautiful, and we appreciate you're hoping to meet your mate."

"We also *know*," Landon started, as he grinned with me, "that you will *not* meet your mate. We recognize it is *the* most boring event of the year, and we know that your dress will *only* be spectacular until the next one. And that, my fair-haired sister, is exactly why we don't listen."

Cass looked between us for a moment and then stuck her tongue out. "I hope you both get pimples."

As I slipped my arm through hers, the three of us walked back. The siblings fell into an easy banter, talking about everything and nothing as I walked beside them, content to be quiet.

We'd been friends from a young age, not long after we'd joined the pack. My brother, Kristoff, or Kris as he was known now, and I were taken into the pack when my brother realized he was too young to raise me alone.

Especially since I'd shifted into my wolf form as a babe and hadn't shifted back.

Our parents had been nomads. Packless. They'd chosen not to conform to the ways of the larger packs, preferring to be their own pack, so when I shifted before I was even one year of age, they never made me shift back. They'd been so delighted at how in tune I was with my inner wolf that they allowed us to run free. Encouraged it.

When our parents were killed in an accident, there was no alpha or pack leader to force the shift on me, and instead, Kris forced himself to stay in wolf form to take care of me. But even as a young boy, my brother knew he was too inexperienced to raise a sibling.

He may have been a child himself, but my brother was methodical. Kris watched and studied the Anterrio Pack for weeks before he approached the pack's leader and told him our story, seeking shelter and refuge, but really, he was asking for help.

Guiding the pack leader and the shaman to where I was hidden, he explained I had been in my wolf's form for nearly five years. As an acknowledged pack leader, Bale had the power to force my shift. It took weeks of being forced to submit to him before I didn't automatically change back to my wolf and learned to embrace my human form.

The shaman advised I should remain human until I was of the age when most children embraced their wolf for the first time, normally between ten and twelve years of age. He said I needed to learn my body and mind as a human. My wolf already knew me, but the human side of me needed to be just as dominant.

I was six when they took us into the pack. They refused my shift until I was fourteen. For *eight* years, they forbade me to let my wolf come forward.

I knew why they did it. There was little to distinguish me between a shifter and a wolf cub born in the mountains.

I had been wild. Untamed. *Feral.*

Even now, almost twelve years later, I preferred to be in my wolf form more than my human one.

Four legs were better than two. Short legs were better than the gangly things I had as a human. A wet nose close to the ground was better than being stuck in a book like Cass usually was, believing that her prince would one day come. A white-furred wolf was more acceptable than a white-blonde eighteen-year-old girl with pale blue eyes and skin as light as her hair, which still caused some pack members to look away instead of meeting my eyes.

Being human sucked.

Being a shifter was better.

Being a wolf? Nothing would beat it. Ever.

"Earth to Kezia," Landon murmured from beside me.

Looking up, I saw Kris waiting for me on the outskirts of town, and all three of us naturally slowed our steps.

"Kezia," he called to me brusquely, the warning in his tone that he knew I'd slowed as we approached was clear. His gruff voice was at odds with his handsome face. Kris had light brown hair that reached his shoulders, not my white-blonde coloring. His eyes were deep blue rather than the pale blue I had. But the constant frown line on his forehead, on an oval face like mine, with the same sharp cheekbones and thinner upper lip, and the way his fingers twitched at his side as if he were constantly restless, gave away our familial resemblance.

My brother may be more comfortable in his skin than me, but we both shared the same wildness that the other shifters of the

Anterrio Pack lacked, and when Kris scowled at me as he was now, it was even more prominent.

"*Kristoff*, lost your reindeer?" Landon jibed as he walked past him. We should never have let Landon watch that movie. That one character shared the same full name as my brother and was a constant source of delight to Landon. He took every opportunity to refer to it when Kris was within hearing distance, and my brother had *exceptional* hearing.

"Landon, lost your dick?" my brother bit back at him as he turned his attention to him. "Seems you were playing in the water with the women when you should have been training."

I bristled at the tone and the statement—my brother is an ass. He's also one of the pack's betas and head of pack security, so they respected him within the pack. But he was still an ass.

"He was helping me." I cut off whatever retort Landon was about to give. We didn't need him and my brother bitching at each other right now.

Kris glanced at my basket. "Nothing?"

Looking at the seven fish in it, I looked back at him. Yup, I knew it—we'd fooled no one. "If you let me hunt without the spear, I would have caught more than fish."

"Not everyone wants your saliva on their food," he chastised me. Stepping forward and taking the basket off me, he tipped the contents into Cass's. "Stop cheating for her," he softly reprimanded. With a hard look at me, he turned on his heel. "Come."

Giving my friends a weak smile, I hurried after my brother.

"I wouldn't mind if he commanded me to come."

Hearing Cass's soft whisper to Landon made my eyes widen in shock as I turned to stare at her in disbelief. If I heard her, that meant my brother did too, and also, *what the hell*?

With a cheeky grin, she blew me a kiss and grabbed Landon's

hand, ignoring his disgruntled look at her remark. They both headed to the kitchens with today's haul.

I walked behind Kris as I followed him to the shaman's house. This routine was well-known to me. If I left the town's boundary, despite being with the pack leader's children, on my return, I was to be taken to the shaman who would ensure I hadn't shifted.

For eight years, this pack denied my wolf, and from the age of fourteen, I could not shift unless it was at the command and supervision of the pack leader.

The Anterrio Pack may accept my brother, but making me do this every time I left the town confirmed that they still didn't trust me. I'd been wild and *free* for so long, how could someone like *me* conform to their pack ways?

What I resented even more was that my brother went along with it. Kris never once took me at my word. He would always chaperone me and then, more often than not, wait for the shaman to tell him if I had shifted so Kris could tell Bale I'd remained human.

As I said, he was an ass.

"Did you hold the spear the way I taught you?" he asked me over his shoulder.

"No, I held it with my feet while I stood on my head."

"Quite the feat to stand on your head while holding a spear."

I stopped walking, my mouth falling open. "Feat? Was that a pun? Did you try to make a *joke*?"

Kris snorted as he turned to look at me. "I don't care if you're almost eighteen. You're not too old to be sent to bed without supper, especially a supper you didn't catch."

He would do it too. *Asshole.*

"I held the spear as you taught me. I moved through the water as you taught me. I threw the spear as you taught me. I missed the fish—"

"Because no one can teach you," the shaman said as he emerged from his home. He was blind in one eye and had reduced vision in the other. Even so, his smile was wide as he looked straight at me. "Kezia, my child, you've been hunting?"

"Yes."

"No," my brother answered at the same time. Turning, he looked at me with a raised eyebrow. "To *hunt* means to *kill*. I see nothing you've killed from today."

With a tight smile, I looked him over swiftly. "The day's not over yet."

Kris merely ignored my implied threat, but the shaman's chuckle brought my attention back to him. "Come, pup, let's finish this inside. Kris, she knows the way home."

The shaman was the only person other than Bale who could easily dismiss my brother. It gave me perverse satisfaction watching my tall, broad-shouldered brother being dismissed by a small, thin, wiry old shifter.

Kris, of course, had nothing but respect for the shaman, and as his head dipped in acknowledgment, I didn't miss the quick flick of his eyes to me with the unspoken order to behave.

"Come on, you," the shaman said as he turned to enter the house. "The afternoon is waning, and I heard trout is on the menu tonight."

"You hate fish," I reminded him inside as I sat on his couch, leaning back with my legs kicked out in front of me. A pose so casual that my brother would die of shame if he saw me like this in the shaman's house.

"I do, which is why you and I are having burgers."

Sitting up straight, I looked at him in excitement. "Tell me you're not joking."

"About food? Never."

"You are the best," I told him as I leaned forward and picked up the small knife and wooden bowl. "Left or right?"

"Hmm, oh, the right one, if you must. You know I don't need to taste your blood anymore to know you didn't shift."

"I know," I answered softly. The shaman, unlike my brother, took me at my word. "But he may come and ask, and I don't want to put you in that position."

As I made the small cut across my wrist, I let the drops fall into the bowl. When there was a small amount, I selected the herbs that were on the table, and with a pestle, I mixed my blood with them. Holding out the bowl to the shaman, he took it, then with a deep sniff, his tongue darted out, and he licked up the contents.

"Hmm," he murmured as he placed the bowl down. "Interesting. Your first heat is coming."

"Is that why I'm so snarky?" I asked him, even as my cheeks flared with embarrassment. There were things a female didn't need to hear from an ancient man, even if he was a shaman.

"No. You're snarky because you're an eighteen-year-old shifter with a bad attitude."

"Wow, I must be feisty today," I muttered as I watched him take a long drink of water to wash any remaining influence of me from his mouth.

"The flavor of your blood is strong," he told me easily, smiling when I said nothing. The shaman knew that the act of tasting blood made me queasy. "It packs quite the punch," he added. Sitting back, he considered me. "Your heat is a problem."

"I'll be eighteen soon."

"I know."

"Isn't it less of a problem because I'm almost an adult?"

"We're not animals," he began but stopped when I snorted. "Okay, we're partly animals. A virgin's heat is more potent. Your age is irrelevant in our world. Humans need an age of consent. Our wolves only need the first heat to descend, and maturity is theirs."

"He's going to lock me in a cell and throw away the key, isn't he?"

The shaman chuckled. "In Kristoff's case, I think that may be fairly accurate. It's his duty to protect his sister."

"It's his duty to smother her, you mean."

"He loves you very much, young one," the shaman admonished me quietly.

"Meh." Looking down at my lap, I thought about what he said. "Do you know when?"

"Hard to tell at the moment. I'll keep a close eye on it, though."

"If it's soon, I might miss the Luna Ball..." I tried to sound nonchalant despite the hope surging in my chest.

His face fell, and he nodded in confirmation. "You could. I'm sorry you'll be disappointed."

On the contrary, I would happily miss the ball. For once, Mother Nature might do me a solid.

"Kris will be gutted," I said instead, knowing he would also have to miss the ball. But as head of pack security, he would be sad he wasn't throwing his weight around in front of the visiting packs.

"He may entrust you to another," the shaman said absently as he checked the pouches of herbs on his table.

Yeah, me in my first heat in the middle of a ball and lots of visiting packs? My brother would not leave my side. There wasn't a chance in hell, and I was genuinely grateful *this* time that he was an overbearing oaf.

Now, all I needed to do was hope my heat came before the ball and then break it to my best friend that I couldn't attend the event she was so looking forward to. But after that...well, I could officially class this year's Luna Ball a success.

CHAPTER 2

Kezia

LATER THAT NIGHT, I TOLD KRIS WHAT THE SHAMAN had told me. He reacted much as I expected, meaning he nodded, told me to get a good night's sleep, and went to bed.

The morning brought the rain I'd been expecting, and Kris had left me a list of chores for the house, as well as a note to tell me we would eat at home until my heat was over. As I scrubbed the kitchen floor, I ran through the list of why it was wrong to kill my brother.

Even in a wolf pack, family is everything, and they frown on murder.

The pack had so many positive things going for it that it made me feel guilty about how much I resented being here. The town was small, once an old silver mining town. The humans had left when the minerals were depleted from this part of the mountain.

The pack moved in, fixed it up, and built more houses, making a small mining town a community.

A community that lived in the past.

We were wolves. Hunters. *Fighters*. An intelligent, evolved species. We were *shifters*, for Luna's sake. In this pack, though, the women were part of the pack hunts and nothing more. They expected us to maintain a pleasant home, do the housework, raise the children, and pretty much live like we were grateful for the men being the providers.

The men hunted the most. They fought and defended our pack—that was men's work. The pack trained their women to defend themselves, but not the art of combat or fighting. Most of the important roles in pack life were a man's job.

I knew Kris didn't like it any more than I did, but he was more subtle about his aversion to this archaic life.

However, I protested loudly and often about what utter bullshit it all was. It didn't win me any friends within the pack. My training in our basement was no secret, and they didn't like that my brother didn't stop it. Had they known he encouraged it, they may have been more vocal.

I'd heard their whispers over the years. What did you expect of someone raised wild like an animal? I knew Kris was the only reason the pack tolerated me. That and apparently the fact the pack leader had a soft spot for me because I was close to his daughter.

Which was funny. Bale tolerated me even less than his pack did.

With its not-so-quiet whisperings, veiled looks, and backward ways, this pack was not my home.

But as I finished my daily chores and with a casserole in the oven for our dinner later, I knew I shouldn't be so harsh.

Our pack was stable. There was hardly any in-pack fighting. Bale was a good pack leader. He was fair and reasonable in any raised disputes, adored his children and wife, and strived to be an example in every way. He had good relations with neighboring packs, and we hardly had any issues with humans.

I'd heard many tales where pack leaders were terrible tyrants, so I was glad that Bale was not one of them. I'd also heard tales where the pack females also defended the pack, and felt envious of their recognized equality.

Leaving our small two-bedroom cottage, I headed to the small bakery north of the village. I'd made lamb stew for dinner, and while I could cook, I couldn't bake worth a damn unless it was bread.

If asked outright, I would deny that I was perhaps feeling bad that my brother may miss the Luna Ball because of me, and buying him an apple cinnamon pie was not out of guilt. I was just being a dutiful sister.

It happened. Sometimes. Rarely, but sometimes.

At the store, I tried to ignore the fact that three girls my age turned away when they saw me enter. Kris encouraged me to make friends when I was younger, but I already had resting bitch face mastered, and I would rather be ignored than be fake.

I wasn't popular in our small school, and when they realized I preferred it that way, it didn't ease my social status in the pack.

"Kezia?"

The store owner, Belle, called me forward, and I greeted her with a smile. Belle was always nice. "Hi, do you have any apple cinnamon pies?"

Belle narrowed her eyes at me, but I saw her small, teasing smile. "What did you do?"

Behind me, I could hear the other girls stop talking.

"Nothing," I told Belle, forcing my smile to stay on. "I just thought he needed a treat."

"Mm-hmm," she said with an arched eyebrow. "I've got one in the back. Give me a minute."

I watched her retreat with dread, and sure enough, as soon as the door to the back kitchen swung shut, they were around me.

"Supposedly, you're banned from the Luna Ball," Melanie said to me from my left.

"Yeah? Bonus for me," I replied dryly. I hoped the town didn't know this, because I hadn't told Cass yet that there was a possibility I may not be attending. I didn't want her to hear it from these idiots, either.

"You really don't want to go?" Lisa asked me incredulously. She was the more tolerable of the three but still annoying.

"I really don't mind," I told her honestly.

"Is it because you can't afford to go?"

Turning my head, I smiled at Melanie, experiencing a small thrill of delight when she stepped back. "Did you just say that Pack Leader Bale doesn't provide well enough for his betas?"

Melanie's face drained of color. "No, I...no!"

"Really? Because you asked if my brother was poor, and to ask if my family is poor is to imply he isn't well paid. But..." I shook my head as I pretended to think about it. "My brother works directly for the pack leader, so..."

"Why are you twisting my words?" Melanie wailed. "I said nothing like that."

"Really? Lisa, what did you hear?" I asked, turning back to the other girl.

"I..." Lisa looked between us, and then, with her head lowered, she murmured, "It's what you said, Mel."

Belle came back out to the front, suspicion clear in her eyes as she looked at the four of us. "All okay here?"

"Never better," I said smoothly, taking the boxed pie from her. "Melanie was just telling me how unfair it was of Pack Leader Bale to pay his trusted advisors so poorly for their pack work."

Belle's gaze sharpened on Melanie, who squirmed beside me.

"I'll tell Kris over this delicious pie tonight that the pack has concerns about this," I added with malicious glee. "After all, the pack comes first."

Belle gave me a long-suffering look as I handed over my money for the dessert. With a smile even wider than before, I left the bakery as she started berating Melanie for her foolishness.

Whistling on the way to the pack leader's house, I said hello to some of the pack and ignored the ones who snubbed me. At his house, I waited patiently to be let in. There was no open-door policy for his home—he had two males guarding his door at all times.

I always thought it was pretentious, but Kris scowled when I said it out loud, so I learned to keep my thoughts to myself.

"Kezia," Grant greeted me when he opened the door. Grant was a good guy. Tall, blond, and a trusted advisor of the pack leader, he also balanced out my brother. Where my brother was usually frowning, Grant was usually smiling.

"Hey, is Cass upstairs?" I asked.

Grant looked over his shoulder at the wide central staircase. "Should be..."

His response made me smile. "You have no idea, do you?" I teased him.

He grunted out a laugh, closing the main door behind me. "No, we've had a busy morning. Seems there was a coup a few months back in one of the neighboring packs, the old alpha's been replaced, and we've spent the morning strategizing."

"Sounds boring," I told him quickly, already making my way up the stairs. "If you need help fighting..."

His good-natured laugh followed me. "Always a trier, aren't you?"

"Yup, that's me, the overachiever for equality," I muttered as I jogged up the stairs. Taking a deep breath at Cass's door, I knocked once before I entered.

She was sitting on her bed, cross-legged, head bent, engrossed in a book. She didn't even lift her head as I walked in, closing the door behind me.

Honey-blonde hair lay loose over one shoulder, and her favorite purple T-shirt had slipped off her shoulder, exposing her golden-tanned skin. Even in scruffy shorts and a well-worn shirt, Cass looked effortlessly beautiful.

Looking down at my pale legs, made even whiter by my dark jean skirt, I looked like a washed-out version of *something*.

"Stop biting your nails," I admonished Cass, causing her to jump.

"Luna, Kezia! I just had a heart attack!" she yelled, glaring at me. "I was at the *good* bit," she chided, closing the book with a sigh.

"The sex, you mean?" Dropping onto her couch, I watched her flush.

"Shut up, it was *hot*."

"Sure it was." Personally, I didn't see the need for sex in books. Wasn't the whole point of reading to use your imagination? However, it was an argument we'd had before and not one I wished to have again. "So, the shaman told me something interesting last night."

Cass rolled her eyes. "Is it about the hostile takeover of the Blackridge Peak Pack? Because Dad's been muttering about it all day."

"No. The shaman would never talk to me about pack stuff," I said stiffly while wishing that he would.

Cass perked up, knowing she wouldn't have to listen to boring pack gossip. "Ooh, what was it then?"

"My heat is coming."

Cass squealed and threw herself off the bed and across the room to me. Engulfing me in a huge hug while talking about me becoming a woman was appreciated, and I took a moment to share her joy before I burst her bubble.

"Okay, let me go and maybe stand over there," I told her, pushing her away gently.

"Why?" Cass took a few steps back but was watching me worriedly.

"He isn't sure, but I may have to miss the Luna Ball."

Her wail caused me to wince, and it also caused several pairs of feet to rush to her bedroom. Grant pushed the door open and looked at me with concern.

"She's being dramatic," I assured him. "I haven't hurt her."

Grant gave me a flat look. "As if, Kez," he admonished me. "Cassandra? Are you well? Will I need to get your father?"

Cassandra's nose wrinkled as she thought about it.

"Cass!" I warned her. "No, Grant, she does *not* need the Pack Leader. She's overreacting."

When Cass gave a noncommittal shrug, he pulled the door closed behind him as he left, but I noticed he left it off the latch. His *"as if"* didn't sound so reassuring when he left the door open.

"Are you okay?" I asked my friend dryly. "It's not my fault, Cass," I tried to placate my best friend. "If my heat is coming, you know it's out of the question for me to be in a crowded environment. I'm unmatched and a virgin...it's considered too dangerous."

Cass's eyes narrowed as she listened, even as her bottom lip pouted out fuller. "*If?* You told me it was definite."

"When?" I protested. "I said *he wasn't sure*, but it could be anytime. If the shaman says my heat's coming, he would know. The poor guy licks my blood every single time I leave and return to this town."

"Ugh, that's just disgusting," Cass said as her face screwed up in displeasure. "I mean, is it like a fetish?"

Blinking rapidly, I stared at her. "What? Ew, no! The shaman tests my blood each time I return. You *know* this. Why are you making this weird?"

Cass grinned at me as she played with her hair. "Because watching you squirm is funny."

"You're twisted."

"I know. It's why you love me."

Huh, that's what her brother said to me too. I sometimes wondered if I was merely a source of amusement for the pack leader's children.

Cass went to speak again, but her sudden huff of annoyance was quickly followed by an eye roll as she marched over to the bedroom door and opened it with a flourish. "Why are you such a creeper?" she demanded as Landon brushed past her and threw himself onto her bed.

"You had the door open. The door's never open, so, of *course*, I'm going to listen after you screamed like you were being murdered," he told her as he winked at me, and I turned my face away so Cass didn't see me laughing. I was glad it wasn't only *me* who was a source of amusement.

"We could have been discussing private things," she declared hotly.

"You were talking about Kezia's impending heat and the fact she'll miss the Luna Ball," Landon drawled. He gave me his full attention, and I felt a shiver of anticipation as he looked me over appraisingly. *Well, that was new.* "Do you need a bodyguard?"

"Landon!" Cass yelled at him. "You can't miss the ball too! I won't allow it."

I saw his pleading look before he returned his attention to his sister. "I think she needs me."

Cass stomped her foot as her hands fell to her hips in indignation. "*I* need you!" Cass, realizing what she sounded like, tried to pull back some dignity. "Anyway, you are male. Kris will never in a bazillion years allow any male within a yard of his sister during her first heat."

Which was true. My older brother was protective of me, which was understandable *sometimes*, if not a little overbearing. Okay, it was a lot overbearing, but as much as I resisted his urge to control my life, I was still incredibly grateful I had him. Losing our parents left us both with a hole in our lives, and I knew he did his best to fill it. I just wished he went about it differently occasionally because it seemed like his aim in life was to ruin mine.

"They will need *Kristoff* at the ball. He's the head of pack security. You think our dad is going to let other packs here and not have Kristoff on hand?" Landon said as he looked between us before his gaze settled on mine. "I'm just as good as your brother. I make sense to be his backup."

I could see his sister's eyebrows rising higher into her hairline the more he spoke, and I knew we were very close to Cass and Landon fighting. As a loyal friend in these situations, I did what I did best.

"Speaking of my brother," I said hastily as I got to my feet, "I need to get this pie home before he gets home for dinner."

"You're leaving me?" Landon asked as he shook his head. "With her? When she's about to screech?"

Patting him on the shoulder, I grinned at him as I passed. "You did it to yourself, my friend," I whispered.

"Screech? I do *not* screech!" Cass screeched, and I threw him a sympathetic shrug as I darted out the door.

I was a good friend, but after all these years, I knew the best thing to do when Cass and Landon started squabbling was to leave them to it. If I stayed, they would drag me into it, and since it was technically *about* me, I was more than happy to escape any uncomfortable situations.

CHAPTER 3

Kezia

As I quickly went down the elaborate staircase, I heard their voices rising and knew I had made my escape at the right time. The door opening to the pack leader's office had me slow my steps when the pack leader emerged and looked up past me to the room where his children were now in a heated argument.

"Kezia," he greeted as he continued to look past me, his head tilting slightly to the side as he listened.

"Pack Leader Bale," I murmured as I dipped my head in reverence as was befitting his station.

"What's the problem this time?" he asked me with amusement as his attention fixed on the upper level again.

"Landon is offering to..." I stalled. I did not want to tell the pack leader why I may not be attending the ball, especially in the hallway of his home, where every wolf in our pack could walk through. Grant was still hovering, and Landon knowing was bad enough.

"Offering what?" Kris asked as he opened the door wider, revealing himself standing behind Bale.

"I didn't know you were here," I said as I met his hard stare.

"What is Landon offering?" Bale asked me.

"To, um…guard me during…" I floundered and looked at my brother. "Well, you know."

Bale turned to Kris in confusion, but my brother was smirking in amusement.

"During the ball?" Kris asked me.

"Yes." I knew my cheeks were warming, and I wanted to leave or return upstairs, and if that were the case, I really was feeling out of my depth.

"Kezia's first heat is near," Kris explained to Bale. "It may fall during the festivities. It seems your son is offering to sacrifice his enjoyment of the ball to guard my sister's innocence."

It would have been so much more believable if he wasn't openly laughing at the idea, and as Bale turned back to me, his smile was wide.

"Good fortune on you, Kezia…adulthood awaits," he said with a dip of his head. "But I think my son will be better placed elsewhere that night."

"I couldn't agree more," I told him truthfully. I had no wish to be guarded by anyone. What if I were one of the unfortunate shifters who *cried* all night? Landon would never let me live it down. "Looks like it will just be me and Kris missing the ball." They both stared at me, and I faltered slightly at their hard looks. "If it happens then, I mean," I added hastily.

"Kris will do his duty as my security and as a brother," Bale told me smoothly.

He would? How? He couldn't be in two places at once, no matter how much skill he said he had. "Really?"

"We'll talk about this at home," Kris told me, and I knew I was being dismissed.

"Okay," I replied, knowing it was better not to argue with him in front of Bale. We could have our own sibling fight when he was home. "I'll see you later," I told him, and I saw the tightening around his eyes at my tone. "Pack Leader Bale." I bowed my head as I said farewell and left the house. I could feel my brother's attention on my back, landing right between my shoulder blades, like an itch I couldn't reach to scratch.

The walk home was quiet. When Kris sought refuge with this pack and they agreed we could join them, the elders had chosen a house on the outskirts of town.

We were coming into the pack as nomads, and it was obvious we liked our own space. They thought that because of my age and how we'd been living until we got here, our wildness needed to be kept from the more *civilized* of the pack, especially as I adapted to being in my human form all the time. The shaman and an older female in the pack had cared for us until I was more in control of my wolf.

We had tutors come to us, and then Bale had me taught alongside his children, choosing to introduce me to children my age and not overwhelm me with more than a handful of people at a time.

As we got older, Cass campaigned to get her father to agree to the three of us attending the communal school for the last two years of our education. It was something I could have done without, but we were wolves, and wolves thrived in a pack community.

I think I was living proof that this was a misconception, but as always, I did what I was told and kept most of my complaints to my brother's ears only. He would then remind me how lucky we were to be here.

I didn't feel lucky. Sometimes, I felt as lost and confused as I had on the very first day they required me to submit to the pack leader and had my shift forced on me.

Walking up the paved path to our cottage, I felt the knot in my chest loosen as it always did when I got closer to home. Our cottage was simple in its layout and design and suited us well. The small garden I had cultivated while being denied my chance to shift for so long bloomed with an abundance of flowers and hedgerows. The painted blue shutters gave the cottage a homey look, which I had done solely to piss off my brother, but to my annoyance, he had liked them and had refused to allow me to paint over them.

I put the pie in the refrigerator and wondered what to do with myself. Sometimes, we would eat in the communal hall, but since the shaman had told my brother about my heat, Kris had already told me he was keeping me close to home in case it came when I was with others.

Which made it all sound so much more elaborate and fanciful than it was. It wasn't my first bleed—I was a shifter—but I was still human. I'd had human periods for years, but a full heat was something else entirely. It's when a shifter's body, *my* body, sent the green light to every eligible male in the vicinity that I was ready to breed.

My body primed me for the breeding process by ramping up my hormones, and in return, every eligible male nearby would be driven to distraction, knowing an unmatched female needed to be bred.

It was animalistic, at best.

As we evolved in our society, we also evolved in our handling of our basic natures. A female would approach her heat and would be secluded as she fought her body's desires. Males knew to keep their distance. The days of ravaging each other in the wild with untamed lust were gone.

We were civilized.

Thank the Goddess Luna, that we were.

Actually, this was the Goddess's fault, so the Goddess could bite me.

It wasn't unknown for males to get excited, though, especially during a first heat, and a virgin's heat was allegedly more potent. Because why make it easy for us? Not only was I going to have to deal with my body changing and demanding things I'd never had demanded of me before, but I was also apparently the equivalent of catnip to every eligible male who was unfortunate to be near me during the heat.

However, the look in my brother's eyes from earlier lingered in my mind. He was up to something, and I suspected I wouldn't like it. So, I headed to my bedroom and shed my skirt and T-shirt. Wearing workout clothes, I went to the basement and spent the next hour with the punching bag and weights.

When Kris eventually came home, he greeted me as he usually did, with a half nod and told me he was going to change clothes and freshen up before dinner.

The shortness of his greeting didn't bother me. My brother was no wordsmith, and truthfully, we could go days without speaking.

As I pulled the casserole from the oven and served two bowls of stew, I heard him behind me in the kitchen while he got us both a drink and brought a loaf of bread to the table.

When we were seated, Kris ceremoniously broke the bread, and he thanked the Goddess for our meal. Handing me my half, he dug into his food.

"Too much salt," he commented as he lifted his fork for another taste.

Tasting my supper, I had to nod in agreement. "Lacks pepper," I confirmed.

"Still good," he told me as he dipped his bread into his stew.

"Thanks."

We ate in silence, and when he finished his second helping, he gave me his full attention. "Any change?"

"Not yet," I answered truthfully as I scooped up the last mouthful of my supper. "Well, I don't think so."

"You'll know."

"Oh." *How?* "Okay."

"I need to be by Bale's side. This Luna Ball is very important," my brother told me. "There's a new alpha in the Blackridge Peak Pack."

"Yeah, Grant said something about that," I told him, noticing his eyes tightening at my words. "I'll be fine," I assured him hastily, realizing I shouldn't have mentioned Grant, not wanting him to get into trouble.

He said nothing as he looked out the window to the backyard.

"So, you'll be at the ball?" I felt my stew sit heavy in my belly. I hadn't for one second thought my overbearing brother would leave me when I may actually need him. "I mean, it's fine. I under-stand. How bad can it be, right?"

Kris regarded me solemnly. "Terrible. Unbearable. And if not unbearable, really, really, fucking uncomfortable."

"Gee, thanks."

"I want to be near you," he started slowly. "I don't want you to be alone, but I have other duties to the pack."

"I understand," I said again, and meant it. "Your duty to the pack is important."

"My duty to *you* is no less important," he reminded me. "Which is why I have a solution."

"Really?" Was he going to knock me out? My brother was ruthless at times, but unconsciousness was not my preferred coping mechanism. "How?"

"You'll be where I am."

I didn't understand and understood it less when he wouldn't meet my eyes. "I don't know what you mean."

"I'll be at the hall for the ball, and you'll be there too."

My mouth dropped open. "You want me to attend the ball?" I asked incredulously. Was he crazy? My heat coming was my get-out-of-the-ball card, one which I had enthusiastically played. He couldn't take this away from me.

"No, that's insanity," he chided me.

Thank you, Goddess. "You said I would be in the hall."

"Yes, but"—he hesitated—"under the hall, really."

"Under?" I still didn't understand, and then I did. "The cells? You want to put me in *jail*?"

"I'll be the only one with the key," he said as he nodded. "Safest place you'll be, and I'll be right there should you need me."

"In the *cells*?" I asked again. "Like a *prisoner*?"

He rolled his eyes at me. "There's a cot. You can lie down."

"I'm not being locked up...*literally* locked up in the cells while you and our pack party above me!"

"Stop shouting, Kezia," he snapped at me as he frowned. "Are you sure your body isn't feeling any changes? You seem...shriller."

"*Shriller*? Do I?" I asked him as I angrily got to my feet, snatching the bowls off the table. "I wonder why? It's my first heat, I'm anxious, and instead of secluding and protecting me, my brother, the head of security, wants to put my virgin ass into a cell under a dance floor filled with *males*."

Kris snorted as he finished his water. "It may not even happen at the ball," he reminded me calmly. "And if it does, I'll be able to reach you. Trust me, this is the best option." He stood with grace, and as he looked down on my smaller stature, I had a startling moment of clarity.

"This was always your plan...to lock me up."

"It was."

"You know that's not rational behavior."

"It doesn't need to be rational. All I need to do is keep you safe," he told me gruffly. "And I will. Always."

"There has to be an alternative," I said quietly. "Can I try to find another solution?"

"I don't care if there is an alternative. The cells are my choice for you." He rinsed his plate and left me to go to his room, the discussion clearly over.

I stood stunned for a moment, and then I followed him. "All the males above me? When I'm in my first heat? Kris, my body is going to be demanding, you know *it*. Sex."

"I understand what your body will want," he said as he closed his bedroom window and turned to face me. "But you're strong, Kezia. You can endure the unbearable, and you will."

"That's the problem. I don't know if I can. This has never happened to me. I don't know how I will react, and neither do you!" He stared impassively back at me. "I could be a high-strung, sex-craved female! You want *that* under the hall? I could cause a riot!"

"Don't be ridiculous." His hard stare bore into me. "You will control this heat and resist the pull of the moon. You are strong."

"I *am* strong, but this? It's unknown. I've never done it before. I don't think I can fight nature, brother."

"I have faith that you can do this."

It was easy for him to say because I had no faith in myself.

In fact, I was pretty sure this was going to be a disaster.

CHAPTER 4

Kezia

"You mean...*in* jail?" Landon's head was cocked to the side as he questioned me for the *fourth* time.

We were in Bale's private training rooms. Cass was with her mother. They'd taken some of the pack to the nearest human city to get supplies and have a *girls'* day. I couldn't think of anything worse, so I hadn't hesitated when Landon suggested we sneak into his father's training room and train. Like my brother, Landon had no issue with me learning to be a better fighter.

"If I continue to say yes, will you suddenly believe me?" I snapped at him as I hit the punching bag in front of me with a sidekick as we trained.

"I don't even know, if you wrote it down and I could see it in black and white, that I would still believe it." He scratched his head as he looked me over. "Seriously?"

My second kick knocked him off his feet as he was holding the bag, and I watched with glee as he barely caught himself in time to land gracefully in a crouch.

"By the Goddess, Kez, there's no need to be violent," he

exclaimed as he straightened himself. "I get it. Your brother's a hairy ball sack." Landon approached the punching bag again, looking at me warily. "Kicks and punches to the bag only, okay? Leave a friend's body parts alone."

Scrunching my nose as I looked him up and down, I cocked my head to the side, mimicking his earlier pose. "Friends?"

"Mercy, you must definitely be close to your heat," he muttered as he took hold of the bag. The force of my combination punch and kick had him stepping back from me. "I'm done, I'm calling it. Go find someone else to bruise!"

"Chicken."

"I can kick your ass," he warned as he sized me up. "You know I'm bigger, better, and stronger. I'm not being a dick. It is what it is."

Maybe I *was* close to my heat because I knew what he said he believed to be true, but it didn't stop me from grinning as I took a step forward.

"Don't pull your punches, and I won't pull mine," I told him, eager for him to say yes to this. Normally, I would acknowledge he could beat me to a pulp without even trying, but today? Today, I could almost smell the spilled blood on the mat before it was even shed.

Landon looked at me, the speculative gleam in his eye letting me know he was considering it. He quickly glanced over his shoulder, checking we were alone in the training room. The pack was in a flurry of activity for the forthcoming visitors, and my brother may be a colossal ass, but he had let me off duties, citing it was unnecessarily cruel to let me pitch in and not be able to enjoy the festivities. The shaman had tested me again this morning and confirmed my heat would likely land at the same time as the ball.

Because he was *Landon*, he had somehow talked his father

into agreeing it was unwise to let me wallow in misery alone. I wasn't miserable. I was joyous. The pack was thrumming with activity, and here I was in the training rooms, alone and unhindered, allowing me time to sharpen my skills with no prying eyes or judgment from my peers.

Okay, I was with one of my best friends, but Landon didn't count. He never judged me for being who I was. He didn't care that I'd been wild and untamed when I joined the pack. He didn't care that I was a miserable hunter when human because he knew I more than made up for it when I was free with my wolf.

"You're thinking about it," I said with excitement as he turned to look back at the door again. The training rooms were below ground. Secluded. Passers-by wouldn't see us.

Landon gave me a mischievous wink as he crossed to the training room door. "You tell anyone, I'll deny it," he warned as he turned the simple lock.

He was really going to do it!

He was going to spar with me in human form as an *equal*. My nerves felt pulled too tight, and my heart fluttered too fast with adrenaline and fear, but the exhilaration was already wrapping itself around me. I was bouncing on my feet as he walked over to the center of the room, taking off his T-shirt and tossing it to the side.

His abs caught my attention, and I shook my head. When in the name of the Goddess had I ever been interested in Landon's abs? He was like Kris, a brother, only Landon was marginally more tolerable. But as the artificial light showed off his body, I watched as the light played off his shoulders, over the curve of his biceps, and across his pecs. When did my best friend grow into this man?

"You're having doubts?" Landon said to me in disappointment as he stopped himself from kicking off his sneakers. "I knew you'd bail."

Snapping my eyes off his six-pack, I wagged my head rapidly. "No!" I shouted and cursed myself when his eyes widened at my outburst. "No, I'm just wondering if we should strap our hands?" I held up my hands, and Landon laughed at me.

"Hell no, bare knuckles, girl. If you want to take on a man, then you fight like a man," he teased as he tossed his sneakers to the side. "Unless, of course, you want to stop?" Landon straightened, and once again, my attention caught on his physique.

Seriously, this was *Landon*. Why was I noticing the fine golden hair lightly scattered from his belly button to his shorts waistband?

"Kez, why are you looking at me like that?" he asked me hesitantly as he looked down at his chest. "What's wrong?"

"When did you get buff?" I asked as I finished taking my strappings off my hands.

Landon laughed hard. "*Buff*? What the hell?" He pulled his arms back as he stretched. "And who are *you* saying is buff? Have you seen the abs *you're* sporting? Or those biceps? I may feel these punches," he told me good-naturedly.

"Feel them?" I taunted, "I'm going to make you bleed."

Landon's eyebrows rose in surprise. "First one to bleed wins?"

As if. "Pfft. First one to tap out *loses*."

"Okay," he agreed with a final glance over his shoulder to the door. "You're going to have to be ready to shift to heal before your brother sees you," he warned.

"So confident you'll win," I jeered as my adrenaline picked up again, and my attention was no longer on his defined muscles.

"Kezia, you're my friend, and because of that, I'm giving you one final chance. We stop now. No blows need be exchanged, and we never talk about it again."

Shaking out my hair, I pulled it back into a tight bun, leaving no loose strands to be caught, giving my opponent an advantage. "I'm ready," I told him. "Ready to prove you wrong." I kicked off my sneakers and checked my clothing. Thinking about it, I pulled off my T-shirt, leaving me in yoga pants and a sports bra.

"Satisfied with your wardrobe?" he drawled with an eye roll.

"Shut up."

Landon gave an exaggerated sigh of acceptance, and then we circled each other on the training mat. He feinted left, and I held firm, and he bounced back lightly with a smirk.

"Playing?" I goaded him. "I thought we were fighting, *friend.*"

"I'm trying to make it to at least a minute before I beat you."

Ass. "You're giving me sixty seconds grace?"

"I'm a gentleman."

"You're a pile of coyote's dung," I growled.

Landon laughed as he continued to dance around me. "Your trash-talking game is weak, like you."

The blow caught me unaware, and my head spun as I staggered slightly to the side.

"See, if we were playing for first blood, I won." Landon's eyes were burning bright with excitement. "And it's not even been a minute."

Rolling my head on my shoulders, I felt the sting of the cut on my split lip. I watched him warily as we circled, and I saw the confidence in his movements.

My brother was the best fighter in the pack. They said that Bale was equally good, but Landon was a close second to them both. I saw it as I feinted a right punch and kicked with my left leg. Landon easily moved out of my reach, his smile at my attack irritating me irrationally.

He wasn't confident, he was *cocky*.

He needed to be taught a lesson.

Licking my lips as I prepared to strike, my world was suddenly spinning. The taste of the blood on my lips felt as if I had been electrocuted. Where I had been aware before, now it was like I was *awake*. Everything was heightened. I swear I could *see color*. I heard the snarl, but I didn't recognize it came from me until I saw Landon bring his fists up closer, his eyes narrowing as he appraised me.

"Kez? What's happening? Your eyes are changing."

I felt my top lip curl as I bared my teeth at him, forcing my wolf down.

"Kezia!" Landon said sharply. "Human only, don't change."

Darting forward, my speed surprised me. I punched him square in the jaw before I backed away on light feet. He spat blood on the mat as I watched his shoulders hunch in, his stance more boxer-like.

"Kezia, you're losing control. Hold it back," Landon admonished.

"I'm in complete control," I barked at him, my voice sounding harsh in my ears. "I thought you wanted to fight like a *man*?" I heckled him. "You bleed, and suddenly you're nothing but a *whining* little boy," I mocked him.

"I'm still in my human form," Landon protested. "You're barely holding on."

I forced myself back two steps and took a deep breath.

Down, girl. I got this. Stay down.

I felt her inside me before she slipped back and I was fully me again. "Okay, sorry, I've got it," I told him. "We still good?"

Landon watched me and then nodded. "I suppose you needed an advantage," he said smugly.

"I'm going to enjoy beating your ass," I warned him.

Landon sprang forward, his left hook landing squarely on my ribcage, causing me to grunt with pain. My left jab caught him on the jaw, and his head snapped back. Pressing the advantage, I followed with a high knee to his kidneys.

He stumbled.

"Feel that?" I taunted him as I advanced.

Landon dropped and swept his leg out, taking my feet from me, but I landed in a half roll and was on my feet instantly. Running at him, I half jumped and brought my fist down on his sternum, and both of us went down.

Landon twisted and had me on my back, trying to pin me. But my legs were free, and I used them to push me off the mat and buck him off me. Twisting, I sprang to my feet again.

"*Luna*, Kez, dial it back. I don't want to hurt you." He grunted as my roundhouse kick caught him in the kidneys.

Dial it back? I'd never felt so in tune with my body. There was no way I was dialing anything back.

"Have you been holding back?" I sneered. "Bring it, pretty boy, so I can say I beat you fair and square. Or are you scared of being beaten by a girl?"

"Pretty boy?" Landon's eyes narrowed. "You'll pay for that."

As I lashed out at him again, he was ready for me, and then neither of us talked as we sparred. I hit, and he hit back. I yelped in pain, and so did he. When he had me in a headlock, I bit him, and as he howled in pain, I punched him in the kidney, getting free.

With Landon in a leg lock, sure he would tap out as he struggled to breathe, I screamed in rage when he used his strength to flip me over onto my stomach and pressed my leg up and into my spine. I struck back wildly, and by sheer luck, I kicked him in the groin. As he rolled off me in agony, I was on him. Fists, feet, even using my teeth, I attacked, and he fought me off as he struggled to regain the upper hand. The blows were no longer felt. I was numb from pain or exhilaration. We went at each other, hissing and cursing, fists bloody and tempers high.

Large hands grabbed me, and I was hauled to my feet. I saw Landon being pulled away from me as I struggled against who held me from the fight.

"*No!*" I screamed. "I do *not* yield! I *do not yield!*"

"Bitch!" Landon shouted back. "You're damn right you'll yield to me!"

"*Enough!*" The roar filled the room, and we dropped to our knees as we recognized who was there. "What in the Goddess's name is the meaning of this?"

Firm hands still rested on my shoulders, and I recognized it was my brother who was behind me. How did he get into the room? I thought Landon had locked the door. With a quick glance, it startled me to see the door to the training room hanging off its hinges.

"Dad?" Landon looked up at his father, and I saw the glaze of fury fade from his eyes. He looked terrible. His right eye was almost swollen shut, and a cut was bleeding freely from above his eyes. Landon's nose was bleeding, and a large bruise was forming on his cheek. His body was covered in bruises, scratches, and bite marks. But as his eyes met mine, his widened in horror as he scrambled to his feet, ignoring his father's warning to stay down. "Oh Goddess, what have I done? Kezia?

Oh, holy moon, what have I done?" he asked as he fell beside me.

"You look like shit," I told him as I reached out to touch his face. Landon snorted as he lifted his hand but pulled back when he saw his torn and cut knuckles.

"One of you explain to me right *now*," Bale demanded from above us both.

I felt Kris's hand tighten on my shoulder, warning me to be quiet.

"I took it too far," Landon spoke hurriedly. "Kezia was training, and I told her I could beat her any day of the week, and she took the challenge. It was never supposed to be..." He looked at me once more and winced at whatever he saw. "This."

"Are you telling me that this was *your* idea?" Bale asked as he looked between the two of us.

"Yes, Father," Landon said clearly.

"You're telling me that *my* son, a renowned fighter in this pack, *willingly* struck a female in the fight circle as if she was his *equal*?" The scorn and disbelief of the pack leader's voice made Landon close his eyes in shame and me grit my teeth in temper.

"Yes, Father."

Kris's fingers were digging so hard into my shoulders. I tried to move out of his grip, but he simply tightened his hold.

"Look at her," Bale demanded as he watched his son's head dip in disgrace. "I said *look at her*."

Landon raised his head to meet my eyes, and I once again saw the guilt. "Kez..." he whispered, gazing over my face and body.

The fog of rage was clearing from my head, and I was suddenly acutely aware of the ache my body felt. But I also knew he was lying for me, and my brother's death grip on my shoulders told me he knew it too, and he was keen to keep it that way.

But that would be a lie.

"Bale." I stood and swayed slightly, and Kris steadied me. But I had heard the grunt of surprise at my use of the pack leader's name. "Sorry, I mean Pack Leader Bale."

"Shut up," Kris hissed in my ear as he loosely held me.

"It was me. I asked Landon to spar with me. I wanted to show him I was as good as any male in this form." It hurt to speak, and I wasn't entirely sure I still had all my teeth. "I goaded him, and then I went..." How did I explain it?

"Feral?" One of the pack security team spoke, and I turned to look at him, not realizing he had been in the room but recognizing the look of distrust in his eyes.

"Um, I don't..." I hesitated. "I don't know."

"It was *me*, not Kezia," Landon spoke loudly, and I saw he was also standing. "I used my superior strength and power after I tricked her into sparring with me."

"Landon—"

"I'm so sorry, Kezia," Landon spoke over me. "And I apologize, Father. I have disgraced you."

"It's her heat," Kris spoke for the first time to Bale. "It's coming, and her body will throw off pheromones, and he's reacted to it as any male would. He saw the challenge from a female, and he met it."

And now I felt nauseous.

Bale looked me over with a speculative look. "Of course. Your heat is coming. That explains a lot."

It really didn't. My heat coming meant that if it actually *meant* anything, Landon would have wanted to *protect* me, not fight with me. Had everyone forgotten basic wolf biology?

"She will need to shift," Bale spoke over my head to my

brother, avoiding looking at me. "The pack won't understand the delicacies of this. We keep this between us only."

When I went to ask what he meant, my brother once again tried to break my bones single-handedly as his grip remained punishing. I heard him agree, and then we stood silently, as Bale commanded Landon to shift.

I watched the dark brown wolf shake his head, then stretch, and Bale ordered everyone out of the room.

Leaving me with Kris.

Shaking out of his grip, I turned to demand what was happening, but my words died on my tongue as I was struck silent by the wrath in his eyes.

"I won't ask you what you were thinking. I won't ask you if you are trying to be cast out, and I won't ask *what the fuck you were thinking*?"

"You said that already," I mumbled.

"Do *not* push me, Kezia," Kris growled as he marched past me. "I may finish what Landon was failing at so badly."

"I thought I was to shift?" I called after my brother as he headed for the door.

"You'll be healed by the time we get outside," he snarled over his shoulder.

"I will?" When he cast an angry glare my way, I hurried to catch up with him. "Why will I heal so quickly without shifting?" I asked again. "I thought I looked worse than Landon?"

Kris stopped at the broken door and looked up the stairs, ensuring we were alone, before he looked at me, checking me over and shaking his head in anger. "No, you don't look worse. You look like you've been brawling, nothing worse."

"Huh?"

Kris sighed as he rubbed his forehead. "Your injuries are

minor. You always were quick at healing. Be grateful your friend is a quick thinker and an even better, more practiced liar."

"But I'm bleeding."

My brother's steely gaze stopped any more protests. "You're barely scratched, whereas the pack leader's son was getting his ass kicked by a girl, and we all saw it."

"I won?" I asked hopefully as I prodded the inside of my cheek. I don't care what my brother said. I *felt* like someone had hit me with a ton of bricks.

"You *won*?" Kris barked at me. "No, you idiot, you didn't *win*. You only highlighted to this pack how *different* you and I are. Will *always* be." Kris looked up the stairs for a long moment before he turned back to me. "We will never fit in," he told me quietly. "But we can try to blend. I *try* to get us to blend so we don't stand out."

Swallowing, I nodded. "I know." And I did. I just hated having to do so.

He gave a slow nod, and for the first time, I saw how tired he was. "Good, so make my job easier by *not* shouting to the pack that you can beat one of our best fighters, okay?"

Kris climbed the stairs, and I trailed after him as I felt feeling come back as my body healed itself.

"I still won," I mumbled as we headed home.

"Damn right you did," he said as he gave me a rare smile. "Just don't do it again."

"My life sucks hairy balls," I complained as we walked the trail to the cottage.

"Suck it up, sister," Kris said as we entered the cottage. "Once your heat passes, it won't get any easier."

"Why?"

"Why?" He started laughing as he walked to his bedroom, and

I headed to the freezer for an ice pack. "Because first comes your heat, and then comes marriage," he sang gleefully.

"Marriage?" I asked as I whipped around to look at his retreating back and heard him chuckling as he closed his door, leaving me hanging.

Who the hell said anything about marriage?

CHAPTER 5

Kezia

"I can't believe you beat Landon," Cass said as we sat under the shade of a tree, watching the flowers and garlands being taken into the hall.

"I think he let me win," I lied as I avoided her eyes.

"Goat droppings." Cass scoffed. "He's my brother. He told me you beat him and did it well." Cass nudged me with her shoulder. "And he said he knows why you did it. He understands, but he didn't think you would cheat."

Swiveling around to look at her, I took in my friend's expression as she pulled at the grass shoots beneath us. "Cheat?" I asked her. "What do you mean? I never cheated." Pushing myself onto my feet, I glared over at the training hall, my hands on my hips. "Is he telling people I cheated?"

"He can hardly tell people, Kezia…you'll both get in trouble."

Cass still gave the grass her full attention, almost like she avoided making eye contact. "Why won't you look at me?" Her shrug did little for my feeling of frustration. "Cass! What the heck is going on with you?" Crouching down, I grabbed her chin. "Look at me."

Her brown eyes met mine, and it surprised me at the anger in them. "I'm looking," Cass snapped.

"Whoa, what is going on?" I straightened as Cass jumped to her feet.

"You part shifted when fighting with my brother, *your* friend. What were you thinking, Kezia? You could have killed him!"

"I did not shift, part or even a bit. I felt my wolf, but I was in control. I would never hurt Landon."

"Hurt him? He had to shift three times before he was well again. My dad's not buying his shit, and yet Landon is still insisting it was him who wanted to fight when we all know it was *you*."

Shaking my head in confusion, I turned to the sound of approaching footsteps and saw my brother heading our way. The usual sinking feeling when I saw his tight-lipped expression was enough to let me know I was already hating this day.

"Kezia, you should be inside," Kris barked as he dipped his head in greeting to Cass.

"It's a nice day, and I'm out of everyone's way," I defended myself, my attention drawn to Cass when she gave a very unlady-like snort. "What is up with you? I told you I didn't do—" I stopped as I saw Kris move forward. "What you think I did," I added lamely.

"Your mother needs you," Kris spoke to Cass, and with a whispered thank you, she was practically running for the hall.

"What in darnation is going on?" I wondered out loud.

"So, you've heard then," Kris said, sighing as he turned and headed to the cottage. "Keep up, Kez, you're not a directionless pup."

Which would be embarrassing if this *pup* wasn't sticking her tongue out at her brother's back.

"Real mature, Kezia," Kris grumbled when he looked over his shoulder.

Snapping my mouth closed, I feigned nonchalance as we entered the cottage. Our cozy home was feeling more and more like a jail cell. Kris insisted I stay inside until either the ball or my heat passed, whichever came first.

"Why am I back in here again?" I complained as I flung myself on the couch. "And Landon is telling people I wolfed out on him? Seriously?"

"Quiet!" Kris hissed as he closed the kitchen window. "Do you want to broadcast it to everyone who hasn't heard?"

"Is he really saying that I shifted?" I asked Kris with more seriousness as I sat up straighter. "I didn't!" My brother's hard stare made me cringe internally. "Kris, I didn't. I know what it feels like to be part-shifted, but I wasn't. I did at the very beginning, but we waited until I was in control."

He scratched his jaw as he turned his head away from me. "Are you sure, Kez?"

He didn't believe me. My brother was a pain in the backside, but he usually was on my side when it came to things like this.

"Kris? I wouldn't lie, not about this." I walked toward him, and he finally stopped looking at the opposite wall to watch me as I approached.

"I know."

Frowning, I saw the hesitation as he drew himself up. "There's more?" Wrapping my arms around my middle, I held onto the soft cotton of my top as if the material could comfort me.

"Bale has asked for the shaman to test you," he told me gruffly.

"They don't believe me?" I said with disappointment, and I

saw the ridge in the frown on my brother's forehead tighten, and I suddenly understood. "Ah, they don't believe *you*." Closing the distance between us, I reached out to touch his arm. "I'm sorry."

And I meant it.

Kris had worked tirelessly in this pack to prove that we belonged, that he belonged. Bale accepted him, which is why Kris was head of security, but I felt the simmering anger in my brother as he covered my hand with his own.

"It's just another test," he said as he squeezed my fingers and dropped my hand. "Another fucking test," he added angrily as he glared out the window toward the rest of the village.

"Hey." I grabbed his hand again. "You trust me, don't you, big brother?" I asked him and was gratified when I saw him fight a smile.

"No." Kris danced out of reach of my playful swipe. He opened the refrigerator and offered me a bottle of Coke. When I shook my head, he twisted off the cap and sighed before he took a long drink. "I don't trust you not to cause me headaches, and I don't trust you to stay out of trouble," he added before he took another drink. "But I do trust you when it comes to this."

"So, when it matters, you mean?" I asked as I snatched the bottle out of his hand and finished the fizzy drink in one go.

"Kezia!"

"I know. I said I didn't want one, but then I saw yours, and I wanted one." I tossed the empty bottle back to him. "Come on, best get this over with." When I realized my brother wasn't beside me, I looked back and saw that he remained in the same spot. "Kris?"

"You can say no," he murmured. "You can tell them all to go get bit by snakes."

"Is that who you raised me to be?" I challenged him. "A coward?"

"If there's the slightest chance your wolf came through, even with you not realizing it, they...they can cast you out."

"She didn't." My tone was firm. "We lived in the wilds for over five years, and I know me being in my wolf form for that long worries people, but we have done everything they asked of us. I withheld my wolf for eight years at their request, at your request. Trust me, I know when she's present. I pushed her back, I swear."

Kris dipped his head slightly in acknowledgment as he reached out and tugged at my braid. "Okay."

Squinting, I stared at him. "Okay?"

With a low chuckle, he nudged me aside, opened the door, and went outside. "Yeah, let's get this over with."

We walked the short distance to the shaman's house when Kris broke the silence. "For the love of the Goddess, Kez, remember why we're here," he cautioned me as we approached the front door.

"I promise you have nothing to worry about." When I saw him frown again, I rolled my eyes with exasperation. "This time."

Pushing open the door, I entered the shaman's home, ignoring my brother's hiss of disapproval. My boldness fell flat when I saw that the pack leader was already there, along with Landon and the shaman. But it was the dark-haired stranger who sat on a wooden chair, long legs thrust out in front of him, his hands resting on his stomach as he lounged in front of Bale, that snagged and held my attention.

"Who the heck are you?" I asked him, resisting the urge to straighten when he looked me up and down and then looked away with disinterest.

"Kezia, Kris," Bale greeted, his glare reprimanding me silently for my rudeness. "This is Cannon. He's the new alpha of the Blackridge Peak Pack," Bale spoke to us both, but his attention was on Kris.

"Alpha Cannon," Kris greeted him coolly.

"New alpha?" I asked at the same time.

The new alpha ignored my brother and looked at me. "*New* alpha. I killed the old one."

"Wow, should you be boasting about being a murderer?"

"Kezia," Kris hissed angrily.

Cannon's dark green eyes looked me over, slower this time. "Yes, I should boast. Change was needed, and I am that change."

I felt my brother step closer to me, but the challenge in the alpha's eyes was not one I wanted to back down from, even though I knew I should.

"Kezia," Kris warned softly beside me. "Show the Alpha your respect."

With a sharp jerk of my head, I forced myself to look away from the man in front of me. "Shaman," I greeted the old shifter as I scrambled to calm the uneasiness inside me.

"Cannon, we have some business to attend to," Bale spoke with authority, but unlike the other members of this pack, when the pack leader spoke, Cannon looked unconcerned. "Perhaps we can finish this later?"

"What did you do?" Cannon asked me, ignoring Bale. He was still relaxed, still sitting as if he owned the room and was not the visitor that he was.

"Why do you think I did something?" I snapped at him. "There are four other people in this room."

"But only you smell frustrated." His dark green eyes glittered with amusement and something else as his head cocked slightly to the side as his eyes narrowed. "And you just look unruly...like trouble."

Unruly? *Trouble?*

I made to step forward, but the firm grip on my elbow stilled my movements. Glancing up at my brother automatically, I hesitated to voice my protest when I saw the warning in his eyes. Warning and fear? Looking back at Cannon, I puzzled over him as he watched me with a sly smile.

"So much testosterone," the shaman suddenly spoke.

"And that's just my sister," Kris joked lightly, but neither I nor the visiting alpha missed the slight emphasis on the word *sister*.

Landon chuckled at Kris's attempt to ease the tension, and as I forced a smile at my expense, I saw Bale's shoulders slightly relax. Cannon merely kept that half smile on his face, and I realized I really needed to smack it off.

Literally, *smack...it...off.*

"So, pup, what did you do?" Cannon asked as he shifted in his seat slightly.

"Nothing," Landon said as he stood gracefully. "I overstepped my rank," he carried on, ignoring my astonishment as he flung the word *rank* into the conversation so casually. "We were sparring, and I got carried away."

"You bedded her?" Cannon asked as he once again studied me. "Willing or by force?"

"Neither, asshole!" I snapped. "What the hell is wrong with you?"

"Kezia." Bale's sharp admonishment made me bite my tongue.

"I *harmed* her," Landon carried on as if no one had spoken. "I am male and superior to her when it comes to sparring. I used my strength to my advantage."

Cannon looked between the five of us, and then he threw back his head and laughed loudly.

"It is not a laughing matter," Bale said quietly, and I could see how tightly his hands were fisted at his sides, and if I could see that, I knew Cannon could as well.

"It *is* funny," Cannon said as he reached up and made a show of wiping his eyes. "You are male and *superior*?" he said with scorn. "You are male, and if a female cannot beat the shit out of you, then she shouldn't call herself a fighter."

"Our females do not fight in the pack," Bale corrected him.

Well, they should.

"Well, they should," Cannon growled as he stood, and I was pretty sure that had my jaw not been hanging open as he echoed my thoughts, it would have been as I assessed his sheer size.

He was huge.

If he were less than six five, then I'd eat my shoe. He was as wide as he was tall. His shirt pulled tight across the breadth of his shoulders, clinging snugly to his pecs and down to his trimmed waist. The buckle on his jeans was a snarling wolf's head, and as I took in his thick thighs and loose shit-kicker boots, my gaze returned to the buckle. It caught and held my attention.

"A pack that only allows half of it to fight is weak," Cannon said as he crossed his formidable arms across his chest. "And a weak pack"—he looked at me and smiled wide—"means easy prey."

When Bale went to protest, Cannon held his hand up for silence. "The girl's innocent," he said as he held my stare. He turned his attention to Landon. "She beat you because she's better, not because she shifted. You don't need to taste her blood, old man. Any shifter worth his salt knows that girl's been away from her wolf form for too long."

Even though he spoke in my favor, he still managed to insult me with his tone. Cannon winked at me, and I knew he was enjoying riling me up, and once again, I felt the need to hit him.

"Bale." Cannon's chin dipped fractionally, and I felt Kris tighten his grip on my arm. "My pack arrives tomorrow for the ball. You have any more of these delicate flowers in your pack..." he said as he jerked his thumb over his shoulder at Landon. "Because I'll tell my pack not to try in the games. We don't want anyone to get hurt."

He ignored Landon's scowl as he stepped closer to me. "You should enter, though. You, I'll enjoy wrestling with," he told me as he once more took in my body. Kris jerked me back toward him, and with a low laugh, Cannon left the shaman's house.

My head was spinning, but I still followed his form as he walked away from the village and toward the long grass.

"Shaman?" My brother's terse voice brought my attention back to the room's inhabitants.

"I would smell it too, this close to Kezia's heat. I would smell the wolf on her."

"Bale?" Kris demanded.

"Go," the pack leader was still looking out the window, his attention on the retreating alpha's back.

Kris's firm grip on my arm finally brought me out of my stupor when we were halfway home.

"What the heck is wrong with you?" I demanded as I wrenched my arm free.

"Cannon."

"Because he's a dick?" I asked eagerly as I rubbed my arm.

"No." Kris hurried me into our cottage, quickly locked the door behind him, and then checked that the windows were closed.

Bemused, I followed curiously after him to his bedroom, and my eyebrows rose in surprise as he pulled out a worn duffle travel bag.

"Kris?"

"Mm-hmm?"

"Where are you going?" I walked over to him and perched on the side of his perfectly made bed. "You're freaking out?"

"Pretty much," Kris said as he tugged open the bag and inhaled quickly. "Ugh, it stinks. Don't be fussy about what you put in here. That stink will stay."

"Me?" He was making no sense. "What's going on?"

Kris stopped and looked at me. "You might need to leave."

"Leave? Where?" I was on my feet, alarm racing through me.

"Cannon..." Kris closed his eyes as he tilted his head back. "The belt buckle. Did you see it?"

"The angry wolf? Yes."

"Recognize it?" Kris asked quietly as he watched me cautiously.

"No, should I?"

"I did." Kris gave me a sad smile. "It was our father's."

"Dad's?" Looking at my brother, I knew he could see I wasn't following. "What are you saying?"

"I'm saying that the new neighboring alpha could be part of the pack that killed our parents, and I will not let the bastard get my sister too." Kris thrust the duffle bag into my arms. "So, get your things and be ready to leave."

"You said our parents were killed in an accident," I shouted, pushing the duffle back at him. "Are you saying you lied?"

"There's a lot you don't know, Kez." Kris watched me. "Pack the bag. Essentials only."

"I'm not leaving," I told him stubbornly. "Not until you tell me all these things that I *don't* know."

"We don't have time for this," he scolded me. "Pack some stuff, Kez."

I knew not to push when he gave me that look. My brother was more stubborn than a mule.

"And then what?" I demanded as my shock wore off. "I pack, and then what? Run?"

Kris's dark blue eyes held mine with a calmness I wasn't sure he was feeling. "If you have to, yes."

CHAPTER 6

Kezia

"I am *not* running."

"Yes, you are." Kris marched past me to my bedroom and flung open my closet. "You think he wants either of us to recognize their crime?"

"So why aren't you running?" I demanded. "Why do I need to go? Surely, you're the threat here?" Tugging my brother's arm, I finally pulled him around to face me. "Kris, this is insanity. Talk to me."

"They attacked us. Mom hid us in the long grass. I was in human form, and I held you tight," Kris told me, and I watched as his eyes narrowed in remembrance and his jaw clenched. "You struggled, but Mom told me to keep you quiet." He ran a hand through his hair. "They came at night...five of them. They thought we were rogues, wild. They killed Mom first." He gulped as he told me the truth for the first time. "I can still hear her screaming to run."

Kris walked to his bed and sat down heavily. "I remember them laughing and taunting Dad, saying he had nowhere to run."

"She was talking to you," I whispered, feeling tears spill over.

He nodded. "I didn't know what to do."

"How could you? We were children."

"You're still a child," he teased me gruffly.

"And Dad?" I asked, although I wasn't sure I wanted the answer.

"Fought them, but there were five of them and…" Standing, Kris looked at me. "The buckle was Dad's, Kez. I know it was his. I dented it when I was five, bit it as my wolf, and got no supper. And the dent on that buckle was exactly the same."

"You're sure?"

"Kezia…" His look told me all I needed to know.

"Confront him," I said as the anger surged within me. "Demand answers."

"And what? Challenge him?" Kris paced. "I can't do that. I know nothing about him. I need to be smarter. I need to be patient."

"Then we'll be smart," I assured him, brushing the spilled tears away. "If he or his pack have answers, we'll get them."

Kris stopped pacing and looked at me. "You're being impulsive," he scolded. "It's not a five-minute fix. I need to talk to Bale."

"Fine, we'll talk to Bale."

Kris gave me a flat look. "*I'll* talk to Bale. You're just a child."

"A child? My heat is what? Days away?" I snapped, pulling my braid off my neck. It was so hot in here.

"Fuck!" Kris rubbed his hand over his face. "Your heat," he muttered as he resumed pacing. "I can't let you go."

"Okay, first, you don't let me do anything, second—"

"You need to stay in the house," Kris spoke over me, but when he saw my frustration, he sighed. "Promise me you'll stay out of his pack's way. Stay out of his way. We'll get you past the first heat," he said, almost to himself. "I can talk to Bale, form a plan, keep you safe."

"And who keeps you out of *his* way?" I asked him scathingly. "Or am I the only delicate one in this cottage?" I added with a sneer.

"Why are you fighting me on this?" Kris demanded suddenly. "Everything that I do is to protect you. Why must you make it harder?"

I was stunned for a moment, and then I was furious. "I don't ask you to do that! I can keep *myself* safe. No matter what you think or how you treat me, I am not the child you think I am!"

"Then stop acting like one!" he shouted.

His anger silenced me. My brother was often annoyed with me, as I was with him, but he rarely raised his voice to me.

Kris tilted his head back and looked at the ceiling. "I'm sorry. I've got a lot to think about, but I shouldn't shout at you." Lowering his head, he looked at me. "This time, it isn't your fault."

A small laugh escaped me, and I saw his relieved smile. "If you let me, I can help," I told him.

"Help me by staying out of trouble," Kris said seriously. "Please?"

It was the *please* that got me. For all his faults, my brother rarely asked me for anything. Other than trying to fit into the pack, he expected nothing from me.

"I'll stay in the area around the meadow," I told him reluctantly. "I won't go into town."

His shoulders loosened with relief. "If you feel any change..."

"I'll find you."

"Come home and send for me. Or go to the shaman's. Don't

come into town. Promise me." Kris looked at the duffle that lay discarded on the floor. "Kez?" he glanced at me quickly.

"I promise."

"Okay." Stooping, he picked up the bag. "I'll source a better one of these," he told me. "Just in case."

I chose not to comment. What else was there to say? There was plenty, but I also knew my brother. He had dug his heels in, and I knew better than to talk to him when he was in this mood.

It would be better to wait. Let him think on it, remind him I was perfectly capable, and in time, he would see what I already knew. I could help him. He wasn't in this alone, just like I knew I wasn't.

"Have you made supper?" Kris asked me, jolting me out of my thoughts.

"No."

He gave me a level look, then with a heavy sigh, he walked past me to the kitchen, grumbling the whole way.

"It's not that big a deal," I protested, following him. "It's the middle of the day, for Luna's sake. Go back to work. I'll find something for you to eat for later."

"Most females of the pack have supper already prepared," Kris reminded me as he stood in the kitchen, looking as lost in it as I usually felt.

"Well, go see if you can eat with them," I sassed at him. "It's ridiculous to expect me to cook a full meal every night. Can't you just eat a salad and shut up?"

"Salad?"

His face twisted in disgust, and I groaned in despair. "Yes, it's healthy. Lots of people eat salad."

"Are they shifters?" My silence was his answer. "Shifters eat meat."

"I'm aware," I muttered. "I might need to go to the market to buy food."

"Kezia!"

Throwing my hands in the air in protest at his scowl, I scowled right back. "You eat a lot. And I can't plan out dinners for a week when I don't know what you're in the mood for! We usually eat in the common room. Is it my fault you went all caveman protector and decided to eat my cooking regularly? No."

Kris held my stare for a long moment. "The market and back. Talk to no one."

"Because I'm such a regular chatterbox," I snarked at him, ignoring his huff of irritation.

"You're right. I'll come with you."

Watching my brother stride to the door in disbelief, I jumped in surprise when he barked my name over his shoulder. Biting my tongue, I followed like a dutiful sister, repeating like a mantra that he was under a lot of stress in my head.

The walk to town was uneventful. The few pack we saw called hello to Kris, and some gave me a smile, but most did not.

It was pretty much how I went through life in this pack. Some days, I was more popular than others. Today was not that day.

I knew my brother noticed it, but he said nothing. The one time I caught his eye, I saw his anger, and that was enough to quell my own. Kris often stayed silent about the pack's behavior toward me, but I was positive he knew and had a list of the members who treated me poorly.

I hoped I was there the day he kicked their ass. Or more likely, he was there the day I did, because I'd need him to bail me out of trouble.

When we got to the store, I heard someone call for my brother. Together, we turned, and Grant was hurrying toward us.

"Pack Leader Bale is looking for you," Grant said as he approached.

Kris glanced at me and then at Grant. "Right now?"

"Yeah, he's been waiting for you." Grant looked between the two of us. "You okay?"

"Of course," I spoke quickly. "My brother was giving me his list of demands for his supper tonight," I added with a good-natured eye roll, placing my hand on the small of my brother's back. "You know how he gets about his meat."

Grant laughed, and I gave Kris a slight push.

"Kezia..."

"I've got the list," I told him with a firm nod. "I won't make any detours off of it."

He hesitated, but with a sharp jerk of his head, he turned away. I watched them as they left to go to the pack leader's house.

As they rounded the corner out of sight, I felt my chest loosen for the first time since I had been in the shaman's house today. Taking a deep breath, I headed into the store.

With a basket in hand, I went straight to the refrigerated section and considered the selection in front of me. Steak? Boring. Lamb? We had it last night. I looked at the ground beef—I could make meatballs. They were easy.

"No matter how hard you glare at it, it needs a flame to cook."

Turning to the unfamiliar voice, I came face to face with a handsome male. With light brown hair cut short at the sides but long and wavy on top, it gave his masculine features a more boyish look. Green eyes twinkled with laughter, and his smile was wide as he watched me.

"Who are you?"

"Nikan." He held his hand out in greeting. "At your service."

My eyebrow rose. "I've never had someone at my service before. What does it entail?"

His laugh was easy and free, a fact I liked about him. "I don't know," he said with a shrug. "Maybe it's like a servant or something?"

I wrinkled my nose in distaste. "I definitely don't need one of those."

"What do you need...um..." His expectant look reminded me I hadn't introduced myself.

"Kezia," I told him, holding my hand out. "Are you new to the pack?"

Nikan's hand was smooth and warm as he gripped mine in a brief shake. "No, visiting pack."

Shit. Kris was going to kill me. He hadn't even been gone five minutes, and here I was talking to the enemy.

"Oh, right." I didn't know what to do. To walk away was rude. If I continued to talk to him, my brother would pack my bag in seconds.

Nikan lost his easy smile. "Disappointed?"

He looked sad, and I felt a twinge of sympathy. "No, I just wasn't expecting to meet a neighboring pack member in the store," I answered truthfully.

"Wolf's gotta eat," Nikan said, smiling once more, but I noticed it was less warm than before.

"That we do," I agreed, turning back to the packaged meat. Deciding, I reached for the ground beef. "Meatballs it is."

"How are you cooking them?" Nikan asked as he picked up two large venison steaks.

"Rosemary, garlic, and cayenne pepper for a little kick."

"Nice," he said in appreciation.

We walked to the vegetable aisle, him seemingly comfortable, me not entirely sure how I felt about that. Picking up two large potatoes, I watched Nikan select two onions. He looked at me as I waited.

"What?" he asked.

"That's it? Onions? For two venison steaks?"

Nikan looked down at his basket and back up at me. "Yeah?"

"Seriously?"

"You have two potatoes," he argued, pointing at my basket.

"Because I'm making fries. What are you making with two onions?"

"A red wine jus."

"A what now?"

"A red wine sauce," he explained, fighting a smile.

"So venison, a fancy-named gravy, and..."

"Good company?"

I burst out laughing, and he joined me. We headed to the checkout, and I ignored the disapproving look the store clerk gave me.

Outside, Nikan looked over his shoulder to the store. "She should not work in customer service. Did she even smile?"

Self-conscious, I looked away. I knew why she wasn't friendly, and it was all about her dislike of me. "It's pretty late in the afternoon. She's probably all smiled out."

"Maybe," he said quietly. We looked at each other for a long moment. "So..."

"Yeah, I better go," I told him hurriedly. "Dinner doesn't cook itself."

"Nikan!"

We both turned to the gruff voice, and I once more found myself face-to-face with the new alpha. He looked even bigger than before, and I wasn't sure how that was possible.

"Here we go," Nikan muttered under his breath. "Alpha?"

Cannon gave him a flat stare before he turned his attention to me. "I see they let you out, pup."

"I wasn't in jail," I snapped at him.

"But you were in trouble," he taunted me, and that half smile was back on his insufferable-looking face.

"I was cleared," I grumbled, shifting on my feet uncomfortably.

"What'd you do?" Nikan asked curiously.

"Won a fight," Cannon spoke for me.

Looking around, I quickly shushed him. "Keep your voice down!"

He said nothing, but I saw his agitation, his eyes narrowing further when I stepped back.

"I need to go," I spoke to Nikan. "It was nice to meet you. Enjoy your meal." Turning to Cannon, I looked him up and down. "I...yeah, I got nothing. Bye."

Quickly, I walked away from them, Cannon's rumbling laughter burning my ears red. I just disrespected an alpha. I would be in so much trouble if Bale found out. Even more trouble if Kris learned I had spoken to him.

"You run away more than you should."

My startled yelp caused him to laugh again. Glancing to my left, I looked at him in disbelief. I hadn't heard him approach me. I hadn't even been aware he was beside me until he spoke.

How did he do that?

"How did you do that?" I demanded, looking back to where Nikan was still standing.

"I'm a hunter." Cannon looked down at me, and I felt my mouth go dry at the look in his eyes.

"We're all hunters," I retorted sharply. "Doesn't mean I can go into Batman mode and jump out of the shadows."

"What the fuck is Batman mode?" he asked me curiously, that stupid smirk back. "And it's bright sunshine this afternoon. I don't hide in shadows, pup."

"With your looks, maybe you should." *Oh my Luna, what was I saying?*

Cannon laughed. Loudly. Drawing attention to us. Again.

"Will you stop?" I hissed at him. "Do you want my entire pack to judge me?"

Cannon stopped laughing. Reaching out, he pulled me to a stop. Nervously, I stood in front of him. "What?"

Coolly, he looked me over, taking his time, making me even more uncomfortable for an entirely different reason. "Let them see you, pup," he told me.

"They see me just fine," I told him, my gaze flicking back to the pack members who watched us.

"I don't think they see you at all."

As I looked at him in surprise, he gave me that half smile again. "You don't know me," I told him, my voice croaky and dry. "Or my pack."

Cannon tilted his head to the side slightly. "Don't I?" He dipped his head in a brief nod and walked back toward the store. Leaving me completely confused about our entire exchange or how the heck I was going to explain this to Kris.

My brother didn't disappoint.

I was rolling meatballs when he came charging through the door. "It wasn't my fault!" It was embarrassing how many times we started a conversation like this.

Kris threw his jacket on the sofa as he glared at me. "What did I say?" he demanded.

"You said make you dinner. How was I to know he'd be at the store?"

"And you were flirting with his brother?"

"I was what?" Shaking my head, I picked up another handful of beef. "Who's his brother...oh." Realization dawned on me. "Nikan?"

Kris's unamused stare said it all.

"He introduced himself to me. You taught me to be polite."

"Not to them!" Kris said with exasperation. "Why are you so difficult?"

As I went to defend myself, a wave of dizziness hit me. Staggering, I dropped the meatballs. "Shit."

"Kezia?" Kris sprang forward. "Are you okay?"

CHAPTER 7

Kezia

A SURGE OF WARMTH ERUPTED IN MY BELLY, MY stomach muscles clenching so unexpectedly and tightly that they caused me to double over in pain. "Oh, shit." Gasping, I clutched at my sides. "That's one hell of a stitch," I told my brother through gritted teeth as I straightened.

"Kezia?"

"Mm-hmm?" Another sharp stab in my gut had me bending over again. "What the hell is this?"

"Your heat." I heard his growl, and then I was being lifted off my feet. "I need to get you to the hall."

"I can walk!" I protested as my brother ignored me, and with a hurried step, he opened the front door. As we neared town, I felt it. The sudden stillness of those nearby. Of the *males* nearby. "Kris?"

"Shh, Kez, don't speak and hold everything in," he warned me. Another stab in my gut had me clutching his shirt as I bit into my fist, keeping the groan of pain at bay. "I know, sis. I know it hurts. Hold it in for me," Kris ordered soothingly as he stroked my back.

It *did* hurt. It hurt like a thousand venomous snakes all biting at once. But even through the pain, I knew what my brother was telling me. Any sound of pain or need from me, in my heat, would cause the men to react. I was an unbred wolf in her first heat and potent to the surrounding wolves. *Their* wolves were riding their senses now, not the men.

"I'm fighting," I whispered to my brother as he cradled me closer, his long strides eating up the distance between our cottage and the hall.

"You're so strong, Kez. Hold it a little longer," he whispered.

My head burrowed into his neck as another wave of heat and pain crashed over me. All I could feel was my heat exploding, but I also heard my brother's warning growls to others as he hurried through our village.

Not able to hold back the tears any longer, I let them fall free as my back tried to arch in pain, made more intolerable as I forced my body to stay still. Through the agony coursing through my body, I realized we had stopped.

"You need to move," Kris's voice was low, guttural, almost intelligible through the growl, his wolf riding close to the surface —a brother protecting his family.

"I want her."

I dimly recognized the voice, but the crashes of pain washing over me kept me distracted enough.

"Step away before I make you," Kris warned.

"She's mine." It sounded like a roar. A distorted roar that felt so close but sounded so far away.

"Get back!" An unfamiliar voice barked, authority dripping from its tone.

I felt my brother press me closer, tighter, in his arms. Strong.

Safe. My body pushed closer to him as I warred internally with the foreignness of my heat.

"Do not let her go," the new voice ordered, and I felt Kris nod.

"I have her," he assured the newcomer.

"Where to?"

"The cells."

I heard the snort of amusement. "Savage."

Part of me wanted to agree, but I was so hot I needed air. "Kris"—I moaned as I tried to put space between us—"it's so hot."

"No, Kez. Fight it." Impossibly, his hold got tighter, squeezing me and making it difficult to breathe.

"I need air." Pushing against his chest, I tried to break free.

"We need to hurry, or she's going to snap." He pressed my head into his shoulder, and I was roughly jostled before I realized he was running.

Metal clanged, and a foul odor overwhelmed me, causing me to gag in my brother's hold.

Dimly, I was aware that I was on my feet, and then I was alone in a *cell*. Metal banged against metal, and I heard the ear-piercing turn of the lock.

"This may not hold her," I heard the voice from before murmur.

"It'll hold," Kris answered grimly. "She's strong...but she won't fight this. I know her."

Standing in the cell with my eyes closed, I heard everything. I heard their low voices and Pack Leader Bale above me, telling the others who had been called to my heat to back off. I felt the surrounding air—thick, heavy, and cloying on my skin. A strong smell of urine overpowered everything, making my stomach roll, and then the familiar scent of cedarwood and pine drifted to me.

My brother.

My protector.

My *jailer*.

Growling, my lips curled back over my fangs, which I could feel growing from my gums. I opened my eyes and stared at my brother.

"You'll be okay," Kris assured me as he stepped forward. "The first heat is the worst. You have this...you can do it."

Lunging forward, I grabbed for him, a small rational part of my brain registering that my hands had shifted to claws.

"Kezia!" Kris barked at me, his stare hard and unyielding. "Control it."

"Fuck you." I reached through the bars, straining to get to him. I needed to maim him. *Hurt* him. He did this to me. He caged me. "Let me out."

"No." Kris stepped into my reach. "Hurt me if you need to, little sister. I'm here."

He hardly finished the words before my claws raked down his bare arm, drawing blood and making my mouth water.

Wildly, I licked at my claws, savoring the taste. It was so good, but I needed more. "More."

"Bale," Kris ordered, and even my wolf stilled at the authority in my brother's voice. I forgot as soon as we smelled the blood. "In the corner, Kez," Kris ordered me.

My answer was a low, warning growl.

"Kezia, *now*. Get in the corner of the cell." Kris held up a deer. Its blood was warm, and I could hear its heart slowly dying. The slow rhythm called to me, and dutifully, I stepped back at the promise of what he held in his hands. "Slowly..." Kris warned Bale beside him. "She's fast."

I knew he meant me, and any other time, I would have felt pride at his praise, but my eyes were riveted on the deer's neck— the pulse of a promise of what was to come.

Carefully, the deer was dragged into the cell. Shoving past my brother, I fell on it, my teeth sinking into the neck and ripping at the flesh. Warm blood filled my mouth, and I felt a jolt of euphoria as I chewed on the meat. With my claws, I tore into the carcass, the blood running down my chin as I gorged on the flesh.

Tearing into its haunches, I felt my heat burning through my veins, and absentmindedly, I shrugged out of my shirt, kicking off my pants, my clawed feet holding the deer close as I went back to feed.

A while later, satisfied with a full belly, the heat within me had dimmed. Rolling onto my back, I stared at my cell's ceiling. Awareness slowly returned to me, and I knew I still wasn't alone.

Sitting up, I looked beyond the bars and saw my brother and Bale still standing, watching me. Kris looked pale but gave me an encouraging smile. Bale looked worried.

"Wha—" my voice was raw and wrong. With a tentative probing of my fingers, I realized my teeth were still fangs. Pushing at them, my awareness recognized that I couldn't force them to recede with just my fingers. Closing my eyes, I sought my inner calm.

Instead, I found my wolf.

White-furred and beautiful, she looked back at me with deep amber eyes and a need so raw she took my breath away.

I know. I know you need out. I know the deer wasn't enough. You need to hunt. We will. But not yet.

Steady eyes held mine, and I refused to look away.

We need to get through this. Show them we can.

Irritation flickered in her eyes, and I felt it in my soul. She didn't need to show anyone *anything*.

I understood her need.

I understood her desire.

I understood her anger.

I know.

I watched her dip her head in acknowledgment, and I saw her take a step back. As she moved backward, retreating, I felt my fangs retract. My claws shrank back into my fingers.

"Would you look at that." A low whistle of appreciation sounded throughout the room, echoing in the emptiness.

His voice jarred me. My wolf hesitated and looked beyond me. Searching. Another roll of heat erupted from my core, and I felt us both struggle to contain it.

My eyes flew open, and I met his dark green stare.

"You," I snarled as I scrambled to my feet. "Monster."

Cannon stared at me. "Pup, you have *no* idea."

Kris stepped in front of him. "I appreciate your help," he told him, and I saw the tension across my brother's shoulders. "I can take it from here."

Cannon didn't look away from me. "Yeah? Well, I have five of my pack upstairs guarding this door to keep your townsfolk away from her. So, I don't think you can."

"Five?" Bale asked him as he looked toward the stairs that led out of the cells.

"Already restrained three." Cannon flicked his attention to the pack leader. "Your boy needed to be knocked out twice."

Kris grunted in displeasure but never moved from guarding me from Cannon.

"Go," Kris told Bale. "I'll stay with her until she sleeps."

"I'm right here," I reminded them as Bale looked between my brother and Cannon.

"Yes, you are," Cannon spoke softly, stepping around my brother as he moved closer to the cell. "You're a wild one, aren't you, pup?"

His eyes glittered with wickedness and something else as he approached me. Unsure, I stepped back, stumbling over the deer's leg. Looking down, I saw the remains of the carcass.

Limbs were torn, the belly ripped open, and the throat was shredded. This was me? It looked like a pack had descended on it, not one wolf. Not one girl.

"Kris?" My frightened whisper brought my brother closer.

"It's okay. It's your first time and natural to go..." He hesitated, searching for the right word.

"Wild," Cannon said with a wicked grin.

"Feral," Bale grunted at the same time, and I saw my brother wince at the pack leader's choice of words.

"It won't happen again," I tried to assure the pack leader. "I'm okay now." It was a lie. I wasn't. I could feel the need building again, the hunger growling in my stomach, the heat in my core pulsing.

We all heard the shout, the sounds of fighting above us. Bale cursed and ran for the stairs, and Kris watched him go, torn between duty to the pack and to protect me.

"Kris, I need you *now!*" Bale ordered, and my brother still hesitated.

"Cannon," Kris spoke sharply. "Help with your men up there would be welcomed."

Cannon nodded as he kept his eyes on me. "In a moment."

My brother went to speak, but Bale had reached the door and opened it. We heard the shouts and fighting getting louder.

The sound and pheromones crashed down toward me, and my feet took me closer to the bars. A whimper in my throat.

"Kezia," Kris warned.

"Kristoff!" Bale shouted for him again, his pack leader tone forcing my brother to turn from me and run up the stairs to stop the brawling.

Brawling to get to me.

I should have been repulsed. I wasn't. Instead, I was agitated. I wanted out.

"You're stunning," Cannon said as he watched me. "If I could take a picture of you like this, without your brother taking my balls, I would."

Frowning, I looked down at myself. I was almost naked. My panties and sports bra were my only covering. Blood streaked all over me, painting me in gore. My hands were stained red with the deer's blood as were my feet. Licking my lips, I tasted the dead dried blood on my tongue. My white hair hung around me, tinged with red.

"You fear my brother?" I asked him.

"No, pup, I respect his place as your protector."

"Respect?" I looked over the mountain of a man in front of me. Strong. Solid. *Sexy.*

What the hell?

I saw his amusement as I looked him over, appreciating his build and physique, which made me angry.

"I'm surprised you know the word," I taunted him. Rolling my head on my shoulders, I stretched my arms over my head, satisfaction running over me as I watched the alpha in front of me dip his gaze to take in *my* body.

"I don't think you know it much either," he answered as his gaze traveled appreciatively back up to mine.

"You haven't earned my respect," I jeered.

"Good." Cannon moved closer. "I don't want it. *Yet.*"

My mouth became dry as his stony gaze stayed fixed on mine. Fascinated, I watched as he unrolled his shirt sleeves, his muscles bulging with his movements. Long fingers opened his shirt more, and I stepped back as he shirked it off, revealing shoulders I wanted to dig my nails into.

"What are you doing?" I asked when he pulled at his belt buckle, dragging the tails of his shirt free.

In silence, he tossed the shirt through the bars to me, which landed at my feet as I failed to catch it, too entranced with the sculpted perfection in front of me.

"Hold it close to you when it comes tonight. It's not perfect, but an alpha scent should help."

I did not know what he was saying to me, a fact that Cannon realized quickly.

"Your first heat comes in three stages. First, you need to gorge fresh blood to satisfy the hunger. Second, you need to fight. Your wolf needs to show she isn't prey."

I knew this. Kris had taught me all the things I needed to fight them. "And this is for the third?" Now that I knew what he meant, I was skeptical. "Your scent will stop me from wanting..." I may be in heat, but I wasn't blurting it out. Not to *this* male.

"To fuck?" Cannon's smirk was as dickish as he was. "Yeah."

Walking up to the bars, I looked up at the arrogant alpha, his shirt in my hands. Reaching through the bars, I stroked my fingers boldly over his pecs, stroking down his abs, resting lightly on the wolf's head buckle, pushing aside what it meant as I reveled in the sudden hunger in his stare.

"Take this," I showed him the shirt, pulling him closer by my father's buckle. "And go fuck yourself, *Alpha*." Dropping the shirt at his feet, I turned my back on him. "I need nothing from you."

I heard his low chuckle as he walked to the stairs. When he was gone, I turned back and saw the shirt draped through the bars, taunting me.

And it *was* taunting me because I could feel the need building within me. Hearing the fighting above me, I knew my brother was just as miserable as I was. Drawing in a deep breath, my core clenched as I inhaled Cannon's scent.

Wood, smoke, *danger*.

With a disgusted growl, I snatched his shirt from the bars, inhaling deeply one more time.

This sucked worse than anything. I needed to be stronger. That arrogant alpha whose pack killed our parents was *not* the reason I would get through my first heat. Bringing his shirt to my nose again, I inhaled, and then, in a fury, I threw it to the far side of the room.

Miserably, I picked my way over the dead deer and lay on the small cot. Emotions raced over me—anger, rage, need, hunger, and *want*.

Closing my eyes, I willed myself to sleep. I would get through this. Goddess help me, I would.

CHAPTER 8
Kezia

THE SOUNDS ABOVE KEPT ME FROM SLEEPING. THUDS and shuffled steps across wooden floorboards, followed by the occasional crash, kept me awake. Each time I tried to find my inner calm, a noise from above jerked my awareness back to those who moved above me.

My hands wouldn't stop shaking, so I sat on my cot, my back to the wall, with my knees drawn up to my chest and my arms wrapped around them—anything to stop the shaking. With my chin resting lightly on my knees, I watched the stairs. Waiting.

I could smell *him*. Cannon.

At first, I thought it was his stupid shirt which lay across the room in a heap where I threw it. But the more *still* my wolf became inside me, the more *his* stench surrounded me, and I knew it couldn't be the shirt. I inhaled deeply again, my eyes closing as I drank him in.

The ache from clenching my stomach muscles would linger for days. I was a healthy pack member—I trained religiously, and I fought with no fear. My body was one of a hunter. My wolf was ready to hunt, and her patience was running thin. With his added presence suffocating me, it wound me as tight as a coiled spring, and I knew my muscles would protest when I finally unclenched them.

"He's not worth it," I whispered to her, appalled that it was a very *distinct* thing she thirsted for from him. I didn't need to speak out loud. My wolf wasn't separate from me. We were one.

But I needed the noise and distraction because, my Goddess, what the *hell* was he doing up there? Was he lying against the door with a fan behind him or something, purposefully sending his scent into the cells? Was he deliberately taunting me? Didn't he have better things to do? Was he such a complete and total asshole to make a mockery of me like this? Knowing this was my first heat, did he think it was a game to test me this way? Groaning, I pressed my forehead into my knees.

His scent was driving me crazy.

I wasn't in the right frame of mind to be tested right now.

Snarling, I got to my feet, stalking to the bars of the cell. "Cannon!" I screamed, the high pitch of my voice actually making me jump at the loudness. "Cannon, you bastard, get away from the door!"

Hearing a shuffle from above, I stood poised, waiting. Slowly, my shoulders relaxed. He heard me and was moving away. Maybe I was being unreasonable, or he hadn't realized what he was doing. Satisfied I had everything under control, I stepped back when, once again, his scent drifted down to me.

Teasing me.

With rage, I threw myself at the bars.

I was going to rip his throat out.

These bars wouldn't stop me.

I was going to kill him.

My body was lithe and strong, but I needed more power.

With a roar, she came forth. My beautiful, fierce wolf burst forward, her howl of anger reverberating off the cells as she charged repeatedly at the bars. I could feel the walls of my prison shaking. In my back seat of her awareness, I saw the dust falling from above as she crashed against the iron bars.

Everywhere was pain and need.

She needed out of this cell.

She needed to hunt.

She needed—

"*Kezia!*"

The male in front of her was not who she sought. She moved back from the bars, fangs bared, and a low warning growl rumbled in her chest.

It's Kris, I told her. *He means you no harm.*

She growled at him in warning.

No! It's our brother. He will not hurt you.

The growl became deeper.

"Kez, pull her back," Kris cautioned, moving closer to the bars.

My wolf leaped at the bars, jaws snapping as she pushed her muzzle through, desperate to bite.

"For fuck's sake, Kezia!" Kris yelled. "Get your wolf under control! *Now!*"

Control? There was no control. I could feel myself shaking as hysteria overwhelmed me. There was *no* control, only the hunt.

We needed *out*.

She threw herself again at the bars, her body strong, the iron stronger, but even so, she fought.

She would not be contained.

"Kez," Kris pleaded. He looked scared. I'd never seen that look from my brother before, not that I remembered.

My wolf didn't care. I felt her rib crack as she charged against the cell again, the pain insignificant in a body already strung too tight.

"Let her out."

Kris whirled to the voice of him. "Are you insane?" he demanded. "Look at her!"

"I am," Cannon told him as he walked to the cell, the dim light illuminating his bare chest. "If you don't let her out, I'm going in." Hard green eyes watched my wolf, and her growl echoed loudly. "You don't want me to go in," he murmured softly.

"If she's free, I can't protect her like this," Kris whispered desperately.

Cannon laughed. "Look at her! She doesn't need protection. Let her out. She needs to hunt."

"We gave her the deer. It was fresh."

"The *wolf* needs the kill." He turned to my brother. "If you don't open the door, I'll knock it down myself."

Kris hesitated before elbowing him out of the way. "She doesn't like you," he grumbled. "The other cell is open. I suggest you stand in it to avoid her claws."

"What about you?" He cocked his head to the side in question. "You put her in here. I don't think she's a fan of you either."

"But I'm the one letting her out," Kris snapped.

"You're going to run with her?" Cannon said in understanding. "I thought your duty was here."

"My duty is my sister." Kris pulled off his T-shirt, tossed it behind him, and shoved his jeans down. Standing in his boxers, he crouched to meet my wolf's eyes. "You bite me, we're going to have a problem." She growled. "You try to outrun me? Remember, I know where you run to, and when I catch you, we're going to have a problem." She snapped her jaws. "You run, you hunt, and you let my sister surface. Anything else, and we're going to have a problem." She shook her head. "*Kezia!* I know you hear me. You make her know she stays with *me*, or she stays inside."

Please, listen. He's letting us out. Please. We need to be away from here. From him.

I could feel her frenzy. The wildness wanted freedom. We had too much itching in our skin, but one thing, one *feeling*, was still overpowering everything else.

The need to run. To hunt.

She dropped her head. I heard the lock turn and then the quick crack of bones. Raising her head, she saw the large brown wolf step back. Eyes bright with anger watched her as she nudged her head against the bars, gently pushing the cell gate open.

His scent caught her attention, and she jerked forward, but the brown wolf banged into her side. With his head lowered into her shoulder, he herded her to the stairs. Stopping at the foot of the stairs, she looked back. *He* was at the cell door, not in it as he had been told.

Calm. Watching. Unafraid.

The door at the top of the stairs opened, and she smelled fresh air. She wanted to bite *him*, but she also wanted to run. Cannon gave a curt nod, giving his permission, and she spun from him.

With a howl, she barged past the brown wolf who sought to shield her from the other, ignoring the yells of surprise as she burst through the door at the top of the stairs, and then she was out, the stars bright in the night sky.

SUNLIGHT STABBED AT MY EYELIDS, and with my hand raised to shield them from the bright intruding rays, I carefully opened my eyes. Slowly, I lowered my hand as I turned my head from the blue sky and tried to figure out where I was.

Trees were to my right, an open glade to my left, and in front of me was my very naked brother.

"I will never unsee your huge hairy butt," I complained as I pulled myself up into a sitting position. Every part of me hurt. Even my ears hurt. Why the hell did my ears hurt? "Did I fight a bear?"

Kris snorted, turning his head to look at me over his shoulder. "No. You fought me."

I fought him? *Shit.* "Oh." Looking down at my body, I noticed I still had all my limbs. "Did I win?" I asked in disbelief.

"You knocked your head very hard," he told me. "Probably have a concussion...explains the kind of thinking you're experiencing."

"So you won. Fine." Rolling my eyes, I looked around again. "Where the heck are we? Is my heat over? I can't believe you let me out."

"Slow down, Kez." Kris chuckled as he sat on the grass. "I had no choice. She was going to get out anyway or hurt you trying."

"I remember little," I admitted. "How badly did I fuck up?" I braced myself for the lecture, so when my brother grinned at me widely, I was completely perplexed.

"It's perfect."

"Huh?"

"No one followed. We're far from the pack," he told me, but his smile disappeared. "We're far from them."

"Them? You mean Cannon and his pack?"

"You can run." He looked pleased about it. "They won't

follow, and if you're careful, they won't find you, Kez. Your wolf is so smart. Think about it, Kezia...you can be free."

I was shaking my head in denial before he even finished speaking. "What? No! Why would I leave you?" I scrambled to my feet, ignoring the fact my body swayed or that I was naked. Wolf shifters didn't really care about nudity. It was a fact of pack life, but I tended to avoid giving my brother a full frontal, and he paid me the same courtesy.

"His belt buckle was Dad's. Which meant that he got it from the wolf that killed our parents, or *he* killed them. He's stopped aging, but I don't know how old he is. I need to know more, but I *know* you're not going back there. You aren't his."

"His? What? No! How do you know he's guilty? Shouldn't you ask? Make inquiries?" Flapping my hands wildly as I spoke, my thought process was fried. "What do you mean, his?"

It was Kris's turn to shake his head. "You were pretty out of it, but he can calm you down. Or rile you up. Your emotions were extreme, your reactions were...exaggerated."

"You think he's...my *mate*?" I sat down with a thump. Stunned.

"No," Kris corrected. "Maybe," he conceded with a shrug. "*No*. But he's a powerful alpha and *can* control you."

"He's not my alpha," I snapped.

"Exactly my point," Kris snapped back. "Which is why he should have no power over you."

"I'm not a coward. I'm not afraid of him."

It was my brother's turn to roll his eyes. "Who said you were?" With a deep sigh, I watched as he rubbed his forehead. "You hate living in that pack. You resent hiding who you are. *What* you are. A better hunter and fighter. This is the best opportunity I can give you to go."

With my eyes closed, I listened to him. The man who'd raised me, who knew how much I had to fight to fit into a pack that didn't want me. A pack that would always look at me as an outsider. "It's not an opportunity," I whispered as I felt the tears slip free. "It's a punishment."

"Kezia, no." Kris rose and moved closer to me, hunching down beside me in the grass. "It's what you wanted."

"It's nothing if I'm alone." Looking up at him, I saw his despair. "Come with me. They only barely tolerate you more than me, and only because you've had to prove to them you're worthy of them." I felt my anger rising. "You *owe* them nothing."

Kris shook his head as he turned away from me. "It's not that simple."

"Of course it is!" I cried out. "Leave them. Let's both run, and together we can find out more about Cannon and his pack and find the bastards who killed our parents." I grabbed his hand as he stood and turned away from me. "Kris, you took me there when I was a pup. We needed them then. They protected us when we were weak. I'm not weak anymore. We don't need them now."

"Cassandra is my mate."

It felt like someone had doused me in freezing cold water. "What?" my voice was barely a whisper. "That's...that's...no."

My brother gave a long sigh. "Yeah, she is."

"Does she know?"

"No. Suspects, I think. But on her first heat, she'll know."

"How?" I mean, it wasn't unheard of, but it was improbable all the same. "How will she know?"

"Because I spend nearly every day in her space. Her wolf knows me. Her scent is my scent. When she goes into heat, the woman will know as much as the wolf."

"You think she's spoiled," I blurted. "You think she's pampered."

The slight smile on his face was alien. "I do."

"Kris, this is Cass! She *annoys* you."

He gave me a long-suffering look. "Well, my sister taught her best friend a lot of bad habits."

"I don't believe this." Standing, I paced. "That's why you take all Bale's shit. He knows."

"He does."

"Why the fuck didn't you tell me?"

"Maybe because I thought you may overreact. I can't imagine what I was thinking," he added dryly.

Glaring at him, I continued to pace. "I hate your stupid, secretive ways."

"I know."

Coming to a stop, I gave him the full force of my anger. "This is bullshit."

"I'm sorry. I can't leave her." My brother looked truly torn. "And I can't let this opportunity to keep you safe slip past us, Kez." Running his hand over his hair in frustration, he met my narrow-eyed glare. "Tell me how to choose?"

Well, that wasn't fair. It was an impossible choice—leave his mate behind to run with his sister and find out who killed their parents or leave his sister behind to keep his mate.

"Why do you think Cannon will move against me?" I asked him quietly.

"Because he's fascinated with you." Kris frowned in anger. "I can blend, mostly, but you? Few teenage girls have white-blonde hair, Kez. Your hair was this color as a pup. If it wasn't him, whoever's in his pack will remember you."

"*If* it was them."

Angry blue eyes snapped to mine. "It was them."

"So, we're back to where I was before my heat." Rolling my head on my shoulders, I tried to loosen the tension in my neck. "I run. I hide. I become the coward you tell me I'm not."

"No. You *survive*."

"Do I? How?" Looking down at my naked body, I gestured to myself. "I'm naked. I have nothing."

"You have your wolf," he corrected me.

True. She was clever, more than me which was kind of weird. "Do you think he'll look for me?" I asked, but my gut told me he would.

"Possibly."

"Will Bale?"

"No."

One of my brother's finer qualities was that he didn't pull punches. "Wow, that hurt more than I thought it would."

"Sorry."

"Are you?" I challenged him. "I go, and your life becomes easier in the pack."

"I'm going to pretend you didn't say that," he growled as he crossed his arms over his chest.

"This is bullshit," I mumbled angrily. But my wolf was ready. I could feel her sitting there in the back of my awareness. Waiting. Tears slipped down my cheeks. "I can't believe this is really happening."

"You're ready, little sister," Kris whispered. "I wouldn't let you go if you weren't."

"I think this is terrible parenting on your part."

Kris laughed loudly in the glade's quiet. "I will send out a daily apology to the universe to ask for forgiveness for letting you loose upon it, completely unsupervised."

Sniffling, I grinned. "What if I never shift back?" I asked the question I'd always been too scared to voice before.

I watched as he swallowed hard, his unspoken fear confirmed in that one action. "We have to hope that you will." Kris looked away briefly, breaking eye contact. "I *know* you will."

I groaned loudly, tugging at my hair. "This is a horrible idea."

"Trust your instincts and trust your wolf."

Nodding, I looked to the south. Seeing the wide-open grasslands, I wet my bottom lip in anticipation. "I do trust her."

"Then go." I heard the snap, and his brown wolf stood in front of me. I knew why he did it. I would have too—neither of us was good at showing emotion.

With a cry, I threw my arms around his neck and squeezed him tight. "It serves you right, you get Cass," I told him as I cried into his fur. "She's ten times worse than me. She'll make you miserable and probably ridiculously happy."

The wolf huffed, and I grinned despite my tears.

Rubbing my hands over my face, I scrubbed away the wetness from my cheeks. "Don't let them treat you like shit," I warned him. "And I guess, um..." I swallowed hard. "I love you." I was going to start bawling like a baby. I needed to shift.

Closing my eyes, I let her come forward. As my body shifted and my paws sank into the soft earth, I looked through her eyes at the wolf that was my brother. His cold nose grazed my ear in affection, and with a whimper, my wolf turned away from him and ran.

The grass tickled as we ran. The sky seemed brighter. The birdsong lighter.

We ran faster. The open beckoned us. We could smell deer to the west of us.

We would hunt.

A whisper of a presence caressed our mind.

Moonstar.

The forlorn howl behind us didn't stop us. How could we stop now? The horizon was calling.

Unbroken.

Undisturbed.

Uncontrolled.

Free.

CHAPTER 9

Kezia

Four Months Later

THE SMELL WAS WORSE THAN NORMAL. THE PLACE looked like a dump, but really, the smell was the problem. My nose was too sensitive, and the aroma of my surroundings was making my eyes water. Standing in the corner of the large barn with sawdust covering the floor, I looked around at a large steel frame with wood-slatted and cracked and broken walls.

Wind and watertight, this place was not. Looking up at a high skylight in the corrugated metal roof covering, I saw the sliver of the moon shining down on me.

Are you watching me, Luna? Are you frowning at me like Kris used to tell me you were?

The dull ache in my abdomen at the thought of my brother pulled my attention away from my musings to the heavenly goddess. It had been four *long* months, but I was surviving. I had a place to lay my head at night and a job, but most of all, I had my freedom.

I'd gone through a huge change, and while I may not have

achieved happiness yet, I was managing. Plus, I was human. I'd come out of my shift. The temptation to stay wolf had been there, but I'd turned on my own.

Kris was right not to doubt me. Knowing my brother had risked a lot on my ability to shift gave me a sense of calm, and I'd proven him right.

The ringing of the bell signaled the end of the match. I rose on tiptoes to see who had won. The victor surprised some of the standing crowd, but it was not a surprise to me. The skinny man won the fight and celebrated while the heavyset opponent lay unconscious. It had nothing to do with their weight. But when you were as bulky as the loser of the match was, what he had in muscle and bulk, the opponent had in speed and agility.

"You're next."

Turning, I looked at the man beside me. Vance owned the warehouse and most of the guys in it. He'd slicked his dark hair back with too much gel or grease—I couldn't tell without looking too closely. With blue eyes, a scruffy jaw, and a wide smile, he'd surely be considered handsome to some females.

But I'd seen the hardness he didn't mask. The indifference with which he watched the fights and his complete lack of empathy when opponents were carried out of the ring told me he had little humanity left in him.

"What's it tonight?" I asked him casually. "Rounds or knock-out?" I could feel his assessing gaze on the side of my face, but I refused to look at him.

"You took a few hits earlier this week," he drawled.

"It's a fighting ring." Bouncing on my toes, I was eager to start. "If I don't get hit, my opponents are not doing their best."

"Zia..."

It was his tone that made me turn to look at him. Was that

concern? "What's wrong with you?" When his eyes shifted to my side, I barked out an incredulous laugh. "Are you *worried* about me?" I could hear my shock, and so could he.

His eyes narrowed defensively. "Not worried, but you seem to be eager to fight more and more."

"So?" I moved to face him head-on, turning my back on the crowd. "You keep betting on me, I'll keep making you money, and everyone's happy, right?" When he chewed the inside of his cheek and said nothing, I stepped toward him. "Right?"

Finally, he met my gaze. "Get in the ring...try to let this one walk out."

Glancing over my shoulder, I eyed the winner of the last fight. Turning back to Vance, I grinned. "Give me five percent more on my win, and I'll make sure he can still walk."

Vance tilted his head to the side as he considered me. "You're too young to be such a fucking savage."

Walking backward to the ring, I held his stare, my eyebrow lifting in a challenge.

"Two and a half," Vance growled low enough not to be heard by everyone else. He saw I heard him and shook his head at my mock pout. "Zia!" he called out, and I could hear the warning in his tone.

I pretended I didn't hear him, turning to face the ring. I jumped onto the skirt of the ring and rolled under the ropes. Leaping to my feet gracefully, I grinned at my opponent as I kicked off my boots. In bare feet, tight black jeans, and a black tank that molded to my body, I jumped on the spot, shaking my arms out and loosening them up.

My eyes never left my opponent. He'd won his last fight, and in this ring, you kept going until you couldn't. He'd beat his last opponent easily enough, so he wouldn't be too fatigued.

When Vance met me the first night, he'd laughed in my face when I laid down my five hundred dollars to enter. He'd then asked me where I stole the money from, and when I said nothing, he threatened to kick my ass.

I told him it was none of his business. He didn't need to know that the money came from another fight in another town.

I'd been alone for two months when I knew odd jobs would not keep me going in rent and food. I was a shifter. I had a healthy appetite, and my wolf was always hungry.

I'd stumbled across the first fight ring by accident. I'd watched from the shadows, and when I had studied all their fighters, a week later, I was in the ring myself.

I wasn't stupid. I was careful, and I never brought my wolf forward. The simple truth was I was genuinely a better fighter than these stupid hulks of men who thought muscles and tattoos made them fighters.

They were brawlers, nothing more.

They were missing the two vital components I had—agility and years of my brother's training.

This "mere slip of a girl" as Vance had called me, beat their asses fair and square every night I fought. Because I fought with my brain as much as my fists and feet, I reserved my strength for the finishing blows. I didn't hammer into them the minute I got in the ring.

I waited.

I took the punches.

I let them wear themselves out by using all their energy, and then I fought back.

Cranking my neck from side to side, I looked at Bullet in the middle of the ring. He was the emcee, and he was already frowning at me. Bullet and I weren't on friendly terms.

The first night I was here, I accidentally broke his nose on purpose. He'd made a comment about my ass and what he'd like to do to it under his breath, and my elbow had flung too wide and smashed into his face when I stumbled.

My bad.

I'd apologized. He hadn't accepted. It may have been my wide grin as I said sorry that made him not believe me.

"Why are you back in this ring, Zia?" he asked, coming toward me. "You fought two nights ago."

"And I fight tonight," I told him. "Vance let me in. Let's get to it. Start the fight."

Bullet looked to the back of the room where I left Vance. I didn't look, knowing he was checking to see the fight terms.

"Rounds," Bullet said with a grunt. "I hope he kicks your ass," he added with an insincere smile.

"I bet you do," I told him with a wide, sweet smile. "Now fuck off, and get out of my face."

When I heard the bell ring, I was prepared for the attack. My opponent surely hadn't been to the ring in a few weeks because he'd just made his first mistake. A fact several in the crowd knew because I laughed at the collective groan that ran around the barn.

He lunged forward, and with my fist already raised at my jaw, I let it fly. My fist jabbed out with my whole body weight behind it, and my knuckles connected with his throat in a solid punch, which I followed up with an elbow right to the Adam's apple.

He stumbled backward, his body trying to bend in half as he coughed reflexively against my assault. I didn't give him time to recover. As he straightened, I executed a perfect roundhouse kick and got him square in his gut.

As his body bent over, I jumped onto the ropes, and from the second rope, I pushed off and came down hard, my elbow hitting him square between his shoulder blades. As he crashed onto the mat, I grabbed his left leg and brought it up to his back, and then I pressed all my weight into it.

I heard his scream.

I didn't care.

He was clawing at the mat and screaming as I stretched his leg back at an unnatural angle and no doubt tore his ligaments.

With the force of the pain, he kicked me away from him, and I danced back, barely avoiding a kick to the gut. When he tried to rise, I grabbed his hair and bounced his face off my upraised knee. I felt his nose burst, and I heard the crowd go wild at the spilled blood.

Tossing him away from me as he fell backward, I raised my foot, and with my heel pointed at the right angle, as Kris taught me, I smashed my foot into his face.

He fell onto the mat, unconscious.

Looking up, I shrugged when I saw Vance at the back of the barn glaring at me.

"Winner! Zia!" Bullet said from behind me, his voice tinged with frustration.

As the crowd spoke excitedly or went to make another bet, Bullet came closer to me. "Smug little bitch, aren't you?" he hissed.

"You wanna go?" I asked him as I watched my opponent come to, and one of the bouncers helped him to his feet. When he hobbled out of the ring, I looked back at Vance and pointed at the retreating figure of my defeated foe.

I saw the eye roll and grinned in triumph.

Ha! I got my two and a half percent.

"You think because you're fucking the boss, you can cheat?" Bullet demanded furiously.

My punch hit him square in the jaw.

I knew he'd been waiting for me to lose my temper. Bullet didn't even need a second to recover. His fist flew out and caught me on my cheek. His follow-up punch connected with my right eyebrow, and I felt the flesh burst.

I ignored the screams of surprised excitement from the crowd as we circled each other.

"I'm going to make you bleed, you little bitch."

"Yeah," I snarled as I watched his fists and feet. "I'm going to make you a bitch when I cut your dick off."

"What the fuck are you doing?" Vance yelled as he got into the ring. "This is not happening!"

"It's happening," Bullet spat to the side. "I'm teaching her a lesson."

I said nothing as I watched him. A *lesson*? I'd teach *him* a lesson. The arrogant prick was going to bleed tonight, and not just his nose.

"A hundred on Bullet!" someone in the crowd roared.

"Two hundred on Zia!"

More bets were called, and I heard Bullet chuckle darkly. "Better take the bets, boss. This is the fight they want." We both heard Vance hesitate. "Or are you scared I'll mess her up too much to suck your dick tonight?"

Vance looked right at me as I wiped the blood from my eye. "Knockout," he bellowed. "Kick his ass, girl," he murmured under his breath.

The crowd went wild, and I heard Vance leave the ring, which left Bullet and me.

I'd never seen Bullet fight, but he'd been watching me for weeks. He knew my tells and my moves. For the first time, I was at a disadvantage.

My wolf prowled closer, but I pushed her back. Bullet was a pig, but he was still human, and I would beat him as a human.

The bell sounded, and he came at me surprisingly fast. His fist knocked my head back, and I staggered back. My counter-jab missed him as he danced backward, a smirk on his face.

I went on the offensive and hit out at him with quick jabs and strikes and tried to control my frustration when only half of them met their mark. He was so fast on his feet, I would have suspected wolf if I hadn't known better, but his scent was definitely human.

Bullet kicked out and caught my upper thigh, and I stumbled once more. Unlike me, he had kept his boots on. Bastard. As I lost my footing, his other boot crashed into my knee, and I knew that would hurt later.

Moving back a few steps, I watched him waiting for me. He wasn't following me to attack. He was watching. Waiting.

That was my trick.

My head lowered, and I raised my fists in front of me. I studied him as we slowly circled each other.

He was fast.

He was assessing.

He was clever.

Running my eyes over him, looking for any tells, I saw once more the smirk. He was *cocky*. He thought I was just an unruly girl who needed a lesson taught to her.

Smugness, I could fight. Arrogance, I could beat.

Squaring my shoulders, I matched his smirk. *Come at me, fucker. I'm ready.*

It was as if Bullet read my mind—he darted forward and rammed his fist into my belly. The wind rushed out of me, and I doubled over. He didn't wait, and the next punch landed hard against the side of my head, bringing me to my knees.

Shaking my head to clear it from the fog, I rolled out of the way of his boot just in time. With a backflip, I landed back on my feet, my landing not as steady as I would like, but I was on my feet, and that's all that mattered.

Bullet was watching me, his eyes narrowed. Calculating.

When he came at me again, I stood my ground. I was usually on the offense, but I could defend as well as anyone. I had every kind of fighting training that Kris knew. I dodged the next two punches, spun from the next, and blocked the fourth. But Bullet grabbed my wrist and spun me, his hold viselike on my arm as he twisted it up my back.

"You look better bleeding," Bullet grunted in my ear.

Bracing my neck, I threw my head back and heard something crunch when my head connected with his. He let me go as he was moved backward from my headbutt.

Turning quickly, I saw his nose gushing. "Funny, you look better when you bleed too, dick."

Jumping up, I half spun and landed a kick to his jaw, sending him sprawling backward. As he fell, I leaped after him, the force of my follow-up kick in his side, lifting him off the mat.

Bullet reached out and grabbed my leg, pulling me off my feet, and I landed on my back on the mat. Quickly, I rolled to the side as his leg flung out in an effort to pin me.

Back on my feet, I took another running jump at him, but this time he was ready for me and caught me midair, and with my momentum, he threw me against the ropes, knocking the air out of me.

His fist on my side made something crack, and I yelled out.

It was time to finish this. I went on the offense again, fists flying, elbows jabbing, and feet raised in punishing kicks. Bullet took a lot of the punches, even hitting me back.

When he jabbed out, I managed to grab his arm, and using his weight against him, I flung him over my shoulder. He landed on his back, and I wasted no time in bringing my full weight down in one hard kick to his chest. I ignored his yell and brought my knee down on his throat.

He grabbed my hair and pulled my head back until I released the pressure on his neck. I still felt my foot connect with his jaw as he dragged me back. Turning, I was upside down on his body, the bitch in me unleashed, and I punched the asshole in his dick.

Back on my feet, I saw him curled in a ball as he cradled his crown jewels. "You want to fight dirty?" I sneered at him. "Pulling my hair?" I kicked him in the stomach. Bending over, I grabbed *his* hair, dragging him up. I looked into his hate-filled eyes. "Here's your lesson, *bitch*." I kneed him in the jaw, and with a last punch to his face, I knocked him out.

Standing over him, I heard the silence of the barn. Looking up, I watched Vance roll into the ring. Getting to his feet gracefully, he watched me warily as he approached. He was lean but not scrawny. I knew the man had muscle under his denim shirt, but I'd never seen him fight.

Licking my lips, I waited, unsure if I was ready for a fresh fight.

"Winner, Zia!" Vance shouted loudly and grinned. I didn't miss the kick to Bullet as he stepped over him.

The crowd was cheering when Vance leaned into me. "You look like shit...get to the back. Let me get ice on that."

"No more fights tonight?" I asked, knowing it was still early.

"No, you crazy girl. You won. Your money's in the back. Walk out while you still can." Vance looked me over one more time. "If you won't wait until I'm back there, I'm telling you now. You don't come back here for a week." When I went to protest, he stepped closer. "A *week*. I mean it, Zia. You're no good to my bets if you come back weak. Heal first."

"Fine." I wouldn't hurt tomorrow because as soon as I was in my apartment tonight, I would fully shift, and my wolf would heal me, but he didn't need to know that. "A week?" I scrubbed the blood from my eye again, and then wiped it from my nose with the back of my hand, grimacing at the mess and wiping it on my jeans.

"Girl, I see you anywhere near here, I'll fucking shoot you. Understand?"

That made me snort a laugh. "Fine." Pushing my hair off my face, I looked down at Bullet. "He pulled my hair."

"And you punched him in the balls," Vance gave me a disapproving look. "That's just plain nasty."

"I'm not sorry."

"Get your money and go. Make sure one of my guys sees you to your car."

Rolling my eyes, I looked at Vance. "You're freaking me out with this nice shit. Stop it. *Your* balls are safe."

Grabbing my boots, I rolled out of the ring. I accepted the slaps on the back and *well done*s as I headed to the back of the barn. One of Vance's guys led me inside Vance's office and wordlessly handed me a brown bag of money.

"Thanks." Stretching out my arms, I winced. "This is going to hurt tomorrow," I said lightly.

He said nothing but waited for me to put on my jacket. When he went to escort me out, I waved my hand.

"No need, friend." I pointed to a car at the very back of the open area the barn used as a parking lot. "My friend's waiting." With a pat on his shoulder, I hurried away before he could look too closely and see that the car I'd pointed at was empty.

When I got there, I looked over my shoulder and saw the barn entrance vacant. With a sigh, I slipped off the track road and into the trees. Clutching my bag of money, I knew I would have to move towns soon. I winced in pain as my knee protested at the walk.

Looking up through the tree cover, I looked for the moon. I liked it here. Maybe I just needed to find a new fighting circle and leave Vance's fights alone. Tonight, he was different. *Nice.* I didn't go to earn money so he could be nice. Or friendly. I shivered. I definitely didn't need his friendship or anything else he was offering.

Letting out a heavy sigh, I groaned as my ribs protested. Under the cover of night, letting my wolf come forward, I felt the magic slowly start to heal me as I walked back into town, my wolf sight navigating the darkness.

CHAPTER 10

Kezia

I WORKED IN A BAR AT THE EDGE OF TOWN.

With lots of cheap makeup on, I passed for twenty-one. Just. I had no ID for myself—pack life didn't need it. But thankfully, the owner didn't look too closely at the picture of the driver's license I stole three towns back.

He also kept me in the kitchen. I washed dishes, kept my head down, and never drew attention to myself. I was pretty sure some of my coworkers knew I fought at Vance's barn, and for that, they stayed away from me.

However, it meant I had to learn to get creative with makeup. I created bruises on my face that looked realistic but also like I had tried to cover them up. I was pretty sure I was fooling the people who only looked once, but the ones who may stand too close would see the lie I was trying to sell.

As a stranger to this town with an unknown past, I kept the curious busybodies averted with my naturally unfriendly personality. Kris would wince if he heard the way I spoke to some of them.

My already healthy use of curse words in the pack had become my defense mechanism against probing questions. I'd even learned new swear words. My brother would blush if he heard me these days.

Rinsing greasy plates before I scrubbed them properly, I wondered if Cass had come into her heat yet and if my brother now had his mate. How would the pack feel that the rogue beta was mated to the pack leader's daughter?

They would probably be happy. They reluctantly accepted Kris in our pack, more so when he became the packs security leader. It had been me they were wary of. I'm sure fighting for money in dirty barns with ruthless, desperate humans wouldn't surprise any of them.

Not even my brother.

Sy, the cook, came in through the back door, fresh from his smoke break. I grimaced as he bypassed the sink and went straight back to the grill without washing his hands. I could smell the stale scent of smoke on him, and I didn't want to think about the hygiene issues of his cooking after smoking.

I had nothing against smoking. If that's what you wanted to do, then that was up to you. But if you were a cook, simple decency dictated you washed your hands first. Didn't it?

As the door closed slowly behind him, I caught a strange scent in the air. The double sinks I spent my days in front of had two large windows that faced the woods and surrounded this small town at the base of the mountains.

I'd left my pack, but I hadn't left the mountains I was born in. The Rockies covered a vast range, and I knew my pack and their footprint of the mountain well. I was several hours from them, confident that our paths would never cross again. Kris had said it himself—Bale wouldn't come looking for me.

None of the Anterrio Pack would.

Yet, as I stood frozen in front of the sinks, I searched the woods in front of me. Pushing away from the sink, I crossed the kitchen to the back door.

"Zia?" Sy asked gruffly. "You okay?"

Nodding, I reached for the handle. "Yeah. Just need some fresh air."

"Left the faucet on," Sy grumbled, reached over and flicked it off. "Using all the hot water."

I ignored his grumbling, pulled open the door, and took a deep breath as I stepped outside. Turning slowly, I scented the air, jumping slightly when the door banged closed behind me, knowing it was Sy being a dick.

I could smell the kitchen and the chargrilled, overcooked meat Sy served in the bar. The smell of the fryers, the grease always making me feel nauseous for the first thirty minutes or so of my shift, hung in the air. I could also smell the car fumes from the trucks, bikes, and other vehicles in the parking lot.

In the distance I could hear the passing traffic on the freeway that bypassed this town. Another reason why I picked this one—no one rarely came here. The freeway whisked drivers past this small town, leading them to bigger and better places.

I inhaled again. My wolf came forward curiously.

Do you smell it? I asked her. *There's something in the air.*

We inhaled again as I once more turned in a circle. I felt her huff as she retreated. The scents of the small town's pollution were enough to dissuade her.

Once more, I took a deep breath, but whatever I thought I'd smelled was gone.

With one more look over my shoulder, I returned to the kitchen. Back at the sinks, I reached over, and with no word of protest from Sy, I pulled the thin netting across the window, hiding the view outside and *me* from it.

When I first started working here, Sy and I had a two-week fight about it. He liked them closed for the glare. I preferred them open. I eventually won the argument because Sy didn't have the energy to push for what he wanted about anything unless it was the bar menu.

Then he became more stubborn than a mule.

As I predicted, he said nothing, and I resumed my dishes, my eyes on the windows and my senses alerted every time Sy went out for a smoke break.

Closing time came, and as was my custom, I took my pay and declined the offer to sit and have a drink. All employees were paid for their work that day and allowed one staff drink.

Cash in hand suited me. I never knew if I was coming back for the next shift, and it was perhaps the only thing I had in common with my coworkers.

On my way out, one guy who worked the bar was still cleaning tables. "Surprised to see you walking," he said quietly.

His words caused me to slow, looking over my shoulder in case anyone else heard. "Why's that?"

I should've kept walking.

"Took quite the beating," he said. Stacking up his tray of glasses, he looked me over. "Not even a limp," he added, gesturing to my knee.

"Looked worse than it was," I told him coolly.

"No amount of makeup can hide the shiner," he told me, straightening. "No stitches though, not even a mark." His eyes searched my face, coming back to my eyebrow that Bullet had burst open last night.

Careless, Kezia, I chastised myself.

Walking over to him, I took in his weight and height—trim, not lean, toned forearms and biceps—he was no stranger to keeping in shape. I couldn't for the life of me remember his name, although he often worked the same days as me.

With his dark, chin-length blond hair, short and trimmed blond beard, and cornflower blue eyes, he was pretty in a kind of shady dick way.

"You have something you want to say to me?" I asked him boldly.

"I lost two hundred last night," he said simply, putting the cloth he was holding on the tray. He folded his arms across his chest, and I saw the biceps bulge. His loose T-shirt hid his physique well.

"You shouldn't have bet against me," I replied with a smirk. He was pissed he lost. Well, he'd seen me fight before, so how was it my fault he bet wrong? Turning away from him, I headed back to the door.

"Didn't know Vance was rigging the bets."

The accusation stopped me dead. Slowly, I turned back around to face him, my eyebrow raised. "What did you say?"

"You took a beating. Bullet got you good. Yet you're walking around here like you hardly stubbed your toe. I call bullshit."

"I *won* the fight," I hissed at him, stepping into his space. "Or did you forget?"

"You *won*? Or Vance *staged* it?" His tone and his look told me he thought it was the latter.

Running my eyes over him again, I quickly glanced at the others in the bar—some were openly watching while some were trying to be more subtle. I was confident that they couldn't hear us over the low-playing jukebox.

"Look, I can't remember your name"—I told him honestly,

noticing his surprise at my admission—"but I won, fair and square. Next time, bet smarter."

"How are you walking?" he demanded. "How are you even standing?"

"Natural ability." I spat at him. "Bullet hits like a girl."

"You *are* a girl." He scoffed, unimpressed.

Shit. I *was* a girl, but shifting into my wolf had healed me. I should have played it smarter.

Fuck. I needed to think fast.

"So...you worried about me?" I tried for coy. My rapid shift in attitude caused the opposite effect I was hoping for. Instead of being flirtatious, his eyes narrowed, and he looked me over once more.

"No. You deserved to lose, but you didn't. You took a beating, or you looked like you did. But looking at you now, seeing you work all day without a complaint, tells me one thing."

"That you have staring issues?"

"That it was staged. Vance rigged it. I was cheated, and I don't like being cheated."

I gaped at him. He held my stare steadfastly. Angrily. He was sure he was right, and I did not know how to persuade him otherwise. So, I played the only hand I had.

"You're a sore loser. You have a problem with your bet? Go tell Vance." I saw him flinch. "He's very open to talking about money. I'm sure he'd love to hear your theory that he cheated you."

Finally, making it to the door, I pushed it open and stepped out into the night. My anger fueled my feet to walk quickly, but two or three times, I slowed as I caught the unknown scent from earlier.

Was it a wolf? No. I knew wolf.

Didn't I?

Halfway back to the small attic apartment I rented over a garage, I heard the sound of engines, guttural and loud. I hastily looked behind me as I jogged home. The lights in the distance were getting closer.

Motorbikes?

My walk home was along a dark track that no one else used. It suited me. Tonight, it may be another reckless mistake on my part.

The bikes were getting closer. Quickly, I left the track and ran to the trees. Entering the woods, I took cover as the bikes raced along the track. When I heard them coming through the trees, I spun in alarm.

Dirt bikes.

This wasn't an innocent ride through the woods in the dark. Were they looking for me? Had I been foolish to come off the path? *Shit.*

I couldn't shift entirely because they'd find my clothes. Plus, I couldn't have rumors of a white wolf running free near towns —that would bring too much attention. But I could run, and I did.

I heard a shrill whistle in the air, and I took off as fast as I could. Running through the woods with the bikes closing in on me, the headlights weaved in and out of the trees. Which did two things at once—they lit my way, and it also let them see me.

I knew I couldn't go to the apartment, and they probably knew where I lived, so leading them there would be folly. I wasn't safe there. I had nowhere else to go, and I needed people. I had one place, so I corrected myself.

It wasn't exactly safe, but it had the numbers.

Cursing myself for not thinking of it sooner, I swerved and double-backed on myself. They weren't prepared for me to run toward them, and I took advantage of being on foot as I ran deeper into the woods.

I stumbled once and was furious at myself for doing so because it happened when the headlights had once again found me, and it let them know I was failing and where I was. I'd thought that the more uneven the terrain, the more difficult it would have been for them to follow me.

It became obvious that this was not their first drive through the woods, and I belatedly realized that my pursuers knew these woods better than I did.

My wolf surged forward when a dirt bike suddenly cut in front of me, and with her strength and skill, I dodged out of the way. Pushing her into me as much as I could, I let her pick up our speed.

Vance's barn couldn't be too far now—I just hoped he was hosting fights tonight. When the barn suddenly appeared, I saw the almost deserted parking area. I needed more people. Witnesses.

Or I could shift.

Too many lights kept finding me in the darkness.

Humans didn't know about shifters, and for all my faults and recklessness, it wouldn't be because of my desperation that they found out from me.

Gritting my teeth against the burning in my thighs and the shin splints in my legs, I decided to abandon Vance's barn. Breathing heavily, I started running deeper into the woods.

A dip in the ground caused me to tumble forward, and I face-planted into the vegetation. My wolf had me on my feet, even though I could feel the blood running down my face.

The dip meant I had lost the lights for the moment, and she played the advantage. With an inhuman leap, I jumped into the cover of the nearest tree. Climbing quickly, my hands morphed into claws to help me scale the tree.

On a high branch above the ground, I pressed against the tree trunk and hoped whoever was following me didn't look up when they realized they had lost me. When I was free of my pack, I'd had the foresight to dye my hair black, and I'd never been so glad that I had. Tugging my hoodie up and over my head, I settled in to wait for either morning or their hunt to be over.

One thing for certain? I was leaving town as soon as possible. Vance's fight may have earned me good money, but it wasn't worth this.

Trying to school my breathing so I didn't give away my position, I pressed my hand over my racing heart. This was not what I was used to. Had I been sure who my pursuers were, I would have turned the tables on them.

Instead, I would wait it out, then collect my money from where I'd stashed it—thankfully, not at the apartment—and split.

It was time to move on. I'd brought too much attention to myself here. I'd be more careful in the next town.

I just needed to get out of this tree first.

CHAPTER 11

Kezia

DAWN BROKE LOW OVER THE MOUNTAINS, AND IT TOOK a long time for the sun to illuminate the woodland I'd spent the night in. The dirt bikes had stopped their search about an hour ago. I heard them grumbling beneath me about what a waste of time their night had been. No one was more pissed off about their tenacity than I was.

Several times, one or more of them would get off their bikes and look around the woodland floor. Flashlights swept the canopy of the trees but not high enough to penetrate the branches I hid in.

If my brother had been in front of me when one flashlight almost illuminated the branch below me, I would have hugged him and thanked him for the rigorous training he put me through. I had no doubt his harsh insistence that I be better and stronger had saved me from a gruesome attack tonight.

Even when the sound of their dirt bikes had faded, I stayed high in the trees. When I heard more movement from the town and more cars on the streets, signaling the town was awake, I cautiously climbed down the trunk and then jumped to the ground below.

I landed clumsily, falling to my knees, wincing in pain as something else cut into me. Pushing myself up on tired legs, I wearily started the walk back to my apartment.

My legs were tired. I'd run a lot last night and then spent several hours crouched on a high branch. I ached for a hot shower and food. I knew I would get neither. I needed to grab what I could, get my cash, and leave this town behind me.

I didn't realize a vehicle was behind me until it drew up beside me.

"Zia?"

I jumped in surprise, and when I saw the black truck alongside me, I wondered how I'd zoned out. "Vance?"

He was looking me over with concern. "What the fuck happened to you? You sleep outside?"

Looking down at my torn and filthy jeans, I shrugged. My sneakers were covered in mud, and my hoodie had a ripped pocket. "Um...kind of."

"Get in."

Looking at the truck and the occupier, I took a step back. Why was he on the road? Was it a coincidence?

"I'm okay walking."

Vance gave me that flat stare of his. "You look like shit. You're going to scare someone. You've got blood all over you, for fuck's sake. Get in the truck."

If he tried anything, I could always beat the shit out of him— one-on-one, I could handle. Slowly, I made my way around the front of the truck. Pulling open the door, I hesitated when I saw him laying a rug over his seats.

Vance looked up at me. "You're filthy," he said defensively.

"Asshole." Gingerly, I got into the truck and closed the door behind me.

Vance looked in the rearview and pulled out. "Want to tell me what happened?"

I shook my head. "Not much to tell."

"You fight last night?" he asked shrewdly. "Somewhere else?"

"No."

"Then why do you look like you're about to drop dead?"

Turning to look at him, I raised an eyebrow. "It's not that bad."

Vance snorted and looked back at the road. "You need a doctor?"

"No."

"I know a female doc I can take you to."

Leaning my head against the passenger window, I stared out at the passing scenery. "I don't need a doctor, Vance."

"Cops?"

That got my attention. I looked over at him. "*You* want to take me to the cops?"

Vance ran his right hand through his hair. "Girl, you look like you got mauled by a pack of dogs. You're bleeding, you're disoriented, and you look completely checked out. Did..." He hesitated, and I heard him grind his teeth. "Did they get to you?"

"No. I fell when I was running. I may have hit my head harder than I thought. Then I hid." Shame washed over me to admit I hadn't stood and fought.

"Why were you running in the first place?"

"Some fuckers were chasing me," I told him honestly. I noticed we were at the garage. "How did you know where I lived?"

"There are few secrets in a town this size when you ask the right questions," he said dryly. "Who chased you?"

Shaking my head again, I sighed. "I dunno. Hey, do you know the blond guy who works the bar at Joe's?"

"Should I?"

"He accused me of cheating on the fight with Bullet...says he thinks you staged it. I think it was him."

Vance's eyes narrowed in anger. "Has he seen the fucking state you're in?"

I didn't tell him I looked better yesterday. The night in the woods had helped mess me up, and I wasn't planning on healing myself until I was long gone from here.

"I had a lot of makeup on yesterday," I admitted. I had to give him something.

"What's his name?"

"I honestly don't remember," I admitted truthfully. "Is Bullet still pissed?"

Vance looked me over. "Spitting nails last time I saw him. You think this guy chased you?" he asked carefully. "This guy from the bar?"

Rubbing my forehead, I winced in pain. Looking at my hand, I saw dried blood and fresh blood. "Shit."

"I'm taking you to the doctor," Vance said firmly, putting the truck into drive.

"No. I just need to sleep." Reaching for the door handle, I looked back at him. "Thanks for the ride. Not sure my feet would have made it."

Vance was watching me, then let out a long sigh, his head tipping backward. "Do not make me regret this," he said with a growl. "Put your belt on. I'm taking you to my cabin."

My eyes opened wide with alarm. "I don't need—"

"Shut up, Zia. You're bleeding"—he looked me over again—"everywhere, I think. You've probably got a concussion, and you're telling me some dicks chased you last night. You're coming with me."

"I can look after myself," I told him, pulling the door handle. "Thanks." Stiffly, I got out of the truck, ignoring my aches and pains. I was five steps away from his truck when he picked me up and carried me back to it. "Vance!"

"Shut up, Zia."

I went to protest again, but my strength was gone. I was so tired. This was the first time I genuinely felt human, and it sucked.

Docilely, I let him put me in his truck. I said nothing when he glared at me, and he walked back to the driver's side.

Fifteen minutes later, we were heading up a dirt track, the trees thick around us.

The cabin was small with an open plan. There was one door in the far corner, which was obviously the bathroom. I hoped.

"This it?" I asked cautiously as I looked around.

"Yup," Vance opened a small closet and pulled out two towels. "Bathroom," he said, pointing to the corner, then held the towels out to me. "Shower. When you're done, come out, and I'll stitch you up."

I hesitated. It was only him and me. I'd never been alone with someone before, except my brother. Vance didn't give me brotherly vibes. In fact, Vance gave me don't-mess-with-me- or-I'll-kill-you vibes.

"You bleed on my floor, I'll be pissed." He looked me over and thrust the towels at me again. "Let me make this simple. I don't want to fuck you, I'm not going to fuck you, and if you ask me to fuck you, I'll say no."

"So...you're just being a good guy?" I asked dubiously, taking the towels off him.

Vance snorted. "Fuck no. But I'm not leaving you alone until I know who the fuckers are that chased you."

Twisting the towels in my hands, I squinted at him. "That sounds like a good-guy thing to do."

"Shower before I change my mind."

The bathroom door didn't lock, but it didn't stop me from stripping out of my clothes and turning on the water. The shower was over the bathtub, so I waited for it to heat and then cautiously climbed into the tub.

I needed to stay fragile so he would buy my story, but even human, the shifter in me would heal quickly and draw attention to myself. However, my concerns melted away as the first spray hit me.

The water stung my cuts and scrapes as it cascaded down on me. Twigs and leaves fell at my feet when I wet and washed my hair, and I wondered what the hell I'd looked like when he saw me. No wonder I'd forced him to be nice.

Finally clean but definitely bleeding again, I tentatively dried myself. With toilet paper pressed to my head, I exited the bathroom wrapped in a towel. The thought of putting my dirty clothes on made me feel icky.

"There." Vance pointed to the bed, where a pair of sweatpants and a T-shirt were lying. "Can't help you with underwear," he added with a carefree shrug. "I gave you socks."

"Thanks." Picking up the items, I headed back to the bathroom.

"Nope, here first."

I stilled, but there was something in his gaze that made me cross the room to him.

"Up," he directed, tapping the table, and I moved onto it with a barely repressed groan. "Fucking knew they did a number on you," Vance said with a scowl.

I didn't correct him. I never mentioned it was because my muscles had seized and were aching from hugging a tree most of the night.

Vance stepped closer, and I unconsciously tightened my hold on the towel. To his credit, he didn't even look down. He didn't possess a gentle touch, and I flinched a few times as he cleaned the cut on my forehead and the other ones he found with his no-nonsense approach.

Cuts that weren't too deep got large Band-Aids. He cleaned the scratches but left them alone after that.

There was no warning when he pressed the rubbing alcohol-soaked cloth to my forehead, and his grin when I cursed him out was the first time I relaxed with him. He opened a packet of strange fabric-looking strips.

"What are they?" I asked curiously.

"Steri-Strips," he answered gruffly, picking up another bottle.

"What are they for? What's that?"

"Glue."

When I automatically jerked back as Vance went to apply *glue* to my head, his hand whipped out so fast that I flinched. Grabbing a handful of hair, his forceful grip held me steady. Bringing the glue to my face, he met my gaze.

"It's medical glue. It seals the wound, doesn't scar, and is quick," he told me. "It also means I don't have to stitch you up. Needlework isn't my thing."

"You have quick reflexes."

He grunted but said nothing, and I held still as he applied the glue to my head. Carefully, he applied the Steri-Strips afterward, and I sat immobile throughout.

"You're done." Vance stood back and picked up his first-aid kit, shoving things back in the box. "Get dressed."

Wordlessly, I got off the table, using the edge to steady myself. Picking up the clothes he gave me, I dressed quickly in the bathroom and collected my stuff.

Vance was on his cell when I came out. "I don't give a fuck who has a day off, find them. Find the dick from the bar and whoever was with him and bring them to the barn." I watched him as he listened to whoever was on the other end of the call. "I said I *don't* give a fuck. Get it done."

He'd changed into a black T-shirt and had put on a gun holster. I tried not to look at the gun he had placed inside it.

He tucked the cell in his back pocket and looked over at me. "You need to eat?"

He looked pissed, but I was hungry, so I nodded. "What are you going to do?"

"Not your business," he told me. Vance pulled out bread and cheese and made me a simple grilled cheese sandwich. When he saw how quickly I ate it, he made me another one.

Finally finished, I watched him as he tidied his space. "Thank you."

"Don't mention it." Wiping his hands on a towel, he looked around his cabin. "You good to go?" I watched him pull on a denim jacket, and I was happy not to see the gun he wore.

Standing, I nodded. "I am."

We left his cabin, and I was once more in his truck. Only this time I was clean, not as disoriented, and healing.

"You leaving town?"

The simple question caught me off guard. "Yes." I opted for honesty.

Vance sniffed loudly. "Smart move. Where's your cash?"

"Safe." He gave me an indecipherable look, and unease stirred in my belly. "Unless you know something different."

"Do you know what CCTV is?"

Blinking in confusion, I nodded slowly. "Surveillance cameras."

"You think my barn doesn't have them?" he asked quietly.

"I think you'd be stupid to have them since you run illegal fights."

Vance grunted out a laugh. "I have them, Zia. I also watch them." Looking down at my hands, I tried not to react. "So when I see a shady-looking fuck skirting around my property and digging, I investigate."

Lifting my head, I looked over at him. "Did you take it all?"

He shook his head. "What the hell were you thinking? To bury it at the barn?"

"Obviously, I wasn't thinking at all." I'd thought it was safe there. After all, no one stayed later than they had to. The place was deserted most of the day, and I thought I was clever, putting it in a place where no one would think to look for it. So much for clever.

Pulling up at the barn, he jumped out of the truck. "Come on."

I had no choice but to follow him inside. He'd watched me bury my winnings in a hole on his property, and he'd gone and dug it up. My feet slowed when I saw Bullet hanging from a beam, his arms over his head, tied with rope, as he dangled above the ring, beaten and bleeding. He looked like he'd passed out.

"Zia!" Vance barked at me and motioned for me to follow. In

Vance's office, he opened a safe and handed me a brown bag, heavy with cash. "You need to count it?" he asked, closing the safe door.

"No."

Vance gave me a look of approval. "There's a bus that passes this barn in twenty minutes. Flag it down."

"Okay."

He assessed me as I stood unsure in front of him. "You're not going to do something stupid like go back to that apartment?"

Opening the bag, I took out a handful of dollars and shoved them in my pocket. I rolled up some more and put them in each sock. Vance watched me as I placed the money around my body. It didn't take long, and without a bra or panties, I had limited opinions, but I managed. When I was finished, I met his watchful gaze.

"There's nothing I need there."

"Smart girl." Vance turned at the sound of the barn door opening. "Walk out of here, don't interfere, and forget what you saw or might hear."

My mouth was dry, and I could almost taste the change in the air. The danger.

"Why?" I asked him and saw his confusion. "Why help me?" I clarified.

Vance gave me his usual smirk. Taking out his gun, he tucked it in the back of his jeans waistband.

"This has nothing to do with you. That stupid fucker out there disrespected me. The people who chased you think I cheated them out of cash." Vance shook his head in disbelief. "If I don't stop that shit from escalating, people will think I'm weak."

"I..." The look he gave me stilled my tongue. "Thanks for the clothes."

"Look after yourself," Vance said when he heard voices in the barn. "I have work to do...go out the back door."

"There's a back door?" I asked in surprise, and when he grinned at me, it almost made me forget all the shady shit that was happening right now.

"There's always a back door, Zia. Know your exits." He gave me one more once-over look and held the office door open for me. "Eyes left," he ordered quietly when I turned my head toward the raised voices.

The back door was almost invisible. It was a glorified hatch that didn't even swing open. It must have been for some farming use when this place used to be an actual barn for farming and not a fighting ring.

The hatch made me wonder what else had been hiding in plain sight. Vance opened it halfway, and I ducked through the opening. When I straightened, he was blocking the view, his face hidden.

"See you, Vance." I'd be lying if I didn't say my voice was shaky.

"Not if you're lucky, kid."

Ten minutes later, I saw the bus approach. I'd had a nervous wait, but as the bus pulled up, I heard the gunshot from inside the barn. I hesitated, but I took the advice from my unlikely ally this overcast morning.

I pushed aside what I'd seen and heard and got on the bus. Settling in a seat at the back, away from curious stares, I closed my eyes and put the town and the night's events behind me.

In the next place, I'd be more careful.

CHAPTER 12

Kezia

BAYWATER CREEK WAS MUCH LIKE THE TOWN I LEFT behind. And the one before that. And the one before that. In fact, when I first got off the bus, I'd trudged out to the town sign to make sure I hadn't been asleep on the bus for so long that I'd circled back on myself.

I wasn't mistaken, though. The town—population of two thousand four hundred and three, plus me—was indeed a different town from the one I had left.

But everything was the same.

The only difference was that this town had a high school, and as far as I could tell, there was no bay or creek anywhere.

As I walked through the town, I felt the familiar sense of uncertainty as I tried to blend in and not bring attention to myself —a lot easier to do with dark hair than my natural white-blonde. Wearing Vance's T-shirt, sweatpants, and my own torn hoodie, I was actually surprised by how much attention I *wasn't* getting.

First things first, I needed a place to stay, a place to work if there was any, and then somewhere to earn real money. Working was fine, but I needed to make quick cash so I could split at the last moment if needed.

It wasn't ideal, but a night being chased by dirt bikes and hunted had reaffirmed that I needed money to be flexible. I also needed that money to be accessible, but the idea of walking around with a few thousand dollars on me at a time wasn't sitting easy with me either.

If I got mugged, I would lose everything.

My go-to places for simple work with few questions asked were bars. I'm not saying bars were shady, but they had a higher staff turnover, especially the menial tasks, than other places. They also didn't mind if you preferred lurking in the kitchen washing dishes rather than being out hunting for tips in the front of the bar.

Once I had the job and a place to stay set up, then I'd see what Baywater Creek offered for night-time entertainment of the illegal sort.

Before I did any of that, I knew I had to change clothes. I'd gotten rid of my bruises and scars soon after arriving here. A rather uncomfortable shift behind a shed to my wolf form had me healed and energized quickly.

Passing a few stores, I found a general store that offered hiking supplies and a wide range of outdoor clothing. I liked the hiking boots these stores sold. They also had a good variety of hoodies, and if I was truly lucky, they sold basic T-shirts in packs.

Twenty minutes later, I had new boots, jeans, a pair of heavy-duty hiking pants, a new black hoodie, and two thermal T-shirts, all carried in my new backpack.

I found another clothing shop three stores down, past the gun store and bookstore. Two bras and a pack of underwear later, I pushed my new purchases into my backpack, along with a face cleanser, disposable toothbrush, and toothpaste.

Now, I looked less like a runaway and more like a hiker following the trails through the Rockies.

"You find everything, sugar?" the woman who rang up my stuff asked me with a wide smile.

"Yeah, I did. Thanks." I returned her smile with a more hesitant one of my own.

"You visiting?"

"Maybe," I told her reluctantly. "I'll see how my luck goes. Thank you." I gave her a small wave as I left and avoided any more questions.

I'd figured this out in the second town I came across. Give them a story that was believable but not alarming. Initially, I'd foolishly implied that I was running *from someone*, and more people than I wanted paid attention.

Now, I knew to make it sound like I was merely a girl with a free spirit exploring her independence at her own leisure. If they concluded I was on a gap year from college, then let them. I never said I was, and that also avoided the questions of where I was attending and what I was majoring in—two questions I didn't know the answers to.

Both gap year and majors were things I needed to google one night, but now I knew how to use the terms in sentences. I also knew how to use a computer—well, more a smartphone than a computer. Living with the Anterrio Pack didn't have the freedom of things like this. We were a pack and didn't need that kind of technology.

However, the more I used it, thanks to a kind coworker who was careless with their mobile phone, I did a quick crash course in all things web-related. Not that the pack was ignorant or kept in the dark, we just didn't need to know half the things humans wanted to know.

But we also didn't live in the dark ages. We knew what technology was and enjoyed movies and music as much as the next person. But the incessant need to sit with a phone in your face almost every moment of the day was something we didn't do. Or need.

Only Bale and his betas had cell phones in our pack. As I stood on the wooden promenade of the storefronts, I looked around for the bars. A larger structure in the center of the main street kept catching my attention, so I slowly made my way over to it.

On tiptoes, I peered through the high windows and saw many tables with chairs on top of them, a bar at the very end, and several large-screen televisions dotted around the room.

"You lost?"

Turning to the voice, I met the guarded look of a blonde, middle-aged woman who was eyeing me with amusement and wariness. "When does it open?" I asked her casually, shoving my hands into the pockets of my hoodie.

"Ten minutes if you move your butt out of the door," she said, gesturing to the door behind me.

Stepping aside, I watched as she unlocked the door and pushed it open. "You work here or you the owner?" I asked her with what I hoped was a friendly smile.

She didn't turn again as she answered, letting the door close behind her, "You need work?"

Grabbing the door and following her inside, I spoke quickly, "Yes, I've worked in bars before. Not up front." I hastily added, "Kitchen, glass washer, dishwasher, that kind of thing."

Dumping the keys on the bartop, she reached behind her and

flicked on the lights. "I have three dishwashers, and we only serve food on the weekend."

Looking around, I took in the tables, counting twenty-two and five booths along the back. The floor was wooden, and I'd already heard the stickiness of it as I followed her to the bar area.

"Cleaner?" I asked.

Her bark of surprised laughter stunned me. "I have one. She's lazy, though."

"Fire her," I answered, seeing my opportunity. "Hire me."

"She's me," the woman said with a grin. "Maggie Dreaver, I own the place."

Humans liked to shake hands, I learned. Holding out my hand, I introduced myself. "Zia Hopkins. You hiring?"

I winced as soon as I used Zia. I'd dropped the *Ke* from my name in the second town, but after the run-in yesterday, I was going to change it again. Habit had made me use Zia, and now I was stuck with it.

"Pretty name," Maggie said as she took in my appearance. "You running from something, Zia?"

"No, ma'am." Pretending to look around the bar again, I told her my well-executed lie. "Got the wanderlust bug. Doing a tour of the Rockies while I can." Looking back at her, I gave a half shrug. "I won't be here for long, so even if you just need a few weeks' break from cleaning, I can help."

Maggie studied me. "College in the fall?"

Again, I shrugged. "Maybe. My feet haven't decided yet."

Her smile widened. "My grandfather had the wanderlust bug. Grams said he walked the entire length of America and up and down too before he finally settled."

I gave a nod of pretend understanding. "What stilled his feet?"

Maggie took her light jacket off and placed it on the bartop.

"My dad," she told me with a laugh. "Gramps went out on one of his walks," she told me with air quotes over walks, "and when he came back, my dad was waiting to meet him for the first time."

"I hear your first kid does that to you," I lied easily.

"Dad was baby number three," Maggie said with a wink. "We're open six days a week and serve food Friday to Sunday. The pay is shit, the hours are shit, and I have a bad temper."

Nodding as she spoke, I returned her earlier look of appraisal. "I talk little," I told her. "I'll stick to the back and do whatever you want me to. I'll take over the cleaning at the end of the night. I bet it's tough at the end of a long day of bar work to tidy and clean."

"You twenty-one?"

"Not yet," I told her truthfully, knowing it would keep me out of the public's way.

"Pity," Maggie said as she indicated I follow her. "You're pretty and new. Some of my regulars would like to see an unfamiliar face."

Maggie opened the door to the kitchen, and I spotted the double sink immediately. "We get pretty busy on Saturdays. The town kids like to use this place as their backwater hangout. No mall here," she deadpanned. "Then we have the few families who still think my husband's cooking is better than theirs." Maggie leaned over to me and whispered, "It isn't, but don't tell him I said that."

"So...it's a family place?" I guessed.

"Nope." Maggie popped her *p* as she spoke. "We stop food at eight thirty, and then the die-hards come in and drink till one."

"Every night? Or just weekends?" I wasn't sure if I was to work weekends or the week.

"Comes and goes," Maggie told me. "You got ID?"

The question took me by surprise, and I pulled out my worn wallet.

"Jesus, what happened to this?" Maggie asked as I handed her a water-damaged fake ID.

"My wallet got stolen in the last town, and they dumped this in a puddle. I need the post office to get some stuff sent to me." I did not know if that was a thing, but my lie did not put Maggie off at all.

"Free-living is all well and good until you need the essentials. Am I right?"

I had no idea what that meant, so I simply agreed and hoped it was the proper reaction as I watched her look at my ID before she handed it back to me.

"That tells me nothing," she said with a grim smile. "But I think I saw your name, so that'll do until your replacement comes through."

Taking it back, I hurriedly put it away before she wanted a second look.

"You drink?"

"No, ma'am."

"Drugs?"

I shook my head. "Never."

Maggie's eyes narrowed. "You sleep around?"

"I…" I flushed bright red when I realized what she meant. "No, ma'am," I told her gruffly.

"My husband could cook eggs on your face," she said with a huge grin. "Gotta ask, honey…can't have you bringing drama to the place."

"Honestly, hardly any of your customers will know I'm here," I reassured her.

"Where's the longest you've stayed before moving on?"

"Four weeks."

Maggie nodded, her eyes observing me. "It'll do for me. You start tonight."

"Now?"

"No, you good to come back in two hours, and one of the guys will show you the ropes?"

"Of course," I told her. She walked out of the kitchen, and I hurried after her. "Do you know of any places that are renting rooms?"

Maggie was back behind the bar, filling a glass with soda. She took a big drink before she answered, "In this town, you'll only get in at the B&B. Tell Lottie you're passing through, that you're working here for a few weeks and won't need breakfast." Maggie took another drink. "Trust me, you'll thank me for missing the breakfast," she added conspiratorially. "Lottie will drop your rate."

Worried the rate was unaffordable, and knowing how much money I had, I pretended to look anxious. "Is the rate...high?"

"It depends how she's feeling. When you come back later, tell me what she charged you, and I'll tell you if it's reasonable."

After getting instructions on how to get to Lottie's, I left Maggie with the promise I'd see her later.

Lottie's B&B was called Evergreen Shades. It sounded more like a retirement home, and as I walked down the slowly steeping driveway to the wooden cabin, I decided it looked like a retirement home too.

Huge, thick trunks of wood made up the cabin's walls, and as I got closer, I saw the rusted tin roof covering. Window frames that needed a good clean, with decaying timber frames, ensured me the rate would be affordable.

The door opened outward, which surprised me after I tried to push it open at least twice. Inside, every soft furnishing was woolen or knitted. There was a large leather sofa that took up the floor, an open burning fireplace, and a small desk I assumed was for reception. I saw no sign of the owner.

"Hello?" I called out, seeing one other room tucked behind the main area and a staircase. When no one answered, I walked deeper into the building. "Hello?"

Turning the corner, it surprised me to see the room opened up farther than I first thought. The cabin was built in an L-shape, and another reception room waited for me with more stairs.

An older woman wearing a shawl and armed with a feather duster looked back at me through huge tortoiseshell glasses. "You lost?"

"No?" I looked around. "Are you Lottie?"

"Who wants to know?"

"I'm Zia, Maggie sent me. I start working with her tonight and need a place to stay for a while. She said Lottie may have a room for me."

"Maggie said that, eh?" She lowered her feather duster. "You got money?"

Blinking at the abrupt question, I nodded. "I can pay my way."

Lottie tipped her head. "How tall are you?"

"Um...I don't know..."

She sniffed. "You're taller than me," she told me.

"No offense, ma'am, but I've seen squirrels taller than you."

Lottie laughed out loud. "Maggie said you could clean?" She held out her duster. "I can't reach."

Crossing the room, I took the offered duster, dropping my backpack on the floor. Maggie had spoken to her already, and I wasn't sure if I was grateful or not. "What can I help with?"

Lottie looked around the room. "All of it?"

Following her stare around the room, I eventually looked back at her. "Do you have a room for me?"

"I do." Lottie jerked her thumb over her shoulder. "Back cabin, pretty basic...you need fancy?"

"Nope." I popped my *p* like Maggie had done.

"Good. Dust first, talk later."

Lottie shuffled off, and I was left standing in the middle of the reception area, a feather duster in my hand and silently wondering if the two women I had met in the last few hours were related. They were definitely unusual.

Lottie came back when I was almost finished dusting. Running her finger over a bookshelf, she sniffed when it came up clean.

"Come on," she instructed.

Hastily, I picked up my backpack and followed her out the back. Seven cabins were placed in a semi-circle in the back area— the main house completely obscured them from the road. Woods lay beyond the boundary of Lottie's land. I paid more attention to the area and the cabins as we passed, and I realized some of them were occupied.

Until we got to the last one. Smaller than the others, it sat in darkness. Lottie fiddled with a key and turned the light on when she stepped inside. It was narrow, with room for a single bed and a chest of drawers. The only other door opened to a small bath-room, not the closet I was expecting.

"It's small," Lottie said unnecessarily.

"How much?" I asked, knowing it would be reasonable.

"Twenty dollars."

"A night?"

"A week."

I gaped at her. "Huh?"

"You help me clean the lodge and the cabins, and you only pay twenty dollars for your room."

"Okay."

Lottie scowled at me. "Okay? You don't want paying more?"

"You're paying me with the room, right?" I asked, putting my backpack on the bed.

"Right…"

"Then okay. Can I start tomorrow? I start at the bar soon."

Lottie's hand rested on the door handle. "You can start tomorrow," she told me with a frown. "You better come back to the main house. You'll need towels and a shower before you work tonight."

Looking down at myself, I looked back up. "Did you just tell me I smell?"

"You one of them sensitive people?"

"Nope."

"Good, 'cause you stink." The wide, toothy grin she gave me made me laugh out loud.

Baywater Creek may not have a bay or a creek, but I could already tell it had good people. Maybe I wouldn't need to find anything illegal to do to make money while I was here.

Maybe in this town, I could stay.

CHAPTER 13

Kezia

Three Weeks Later

"I swear to all that's holy, that damn man is trying to piss me off," Maggie mumbled as we both looked over the kitchen and the mess it was in.

Her husband, Dean, was the chef for the bar on the weekends, and while I couldn't deny the man could cook, he was the messiest cook I'd ever seen. Every pot, pan, and griddle had been used. There wasn't a spare space on either counter, and one of my sinks was piled high with dishes.

I'd been in Baywater Creek for two weeks, and I slipped into a rhythm between the bar and Lottie's cabins easily enough. I still hadn't mastered the chaos of Dean's cooking yet, but I kept up with him while he was cooking, dish-wise. However, when the kitchen closed, he simply downed his tools and left, leaving his mess behind for Maggie and me to clean up.

When I first met her, I was sure she was simply kindhearted. After spending one weekend with Dean in the kitchen, I knew why she was willing to pay a stranger cash in hand to work in her kitchen. It had nothing to do with a big heart and more to do with the fact that most people would have insisted Dean do his own cleaning.

"Tell me again why you don't make him stay and clean this up?" I grumbled as I started emptying one of my sinks of the dishes he had piled high.

"There are some fights I win with my husband," Maggie told me seriously. "This isn't one worth having. Again."

One of the servers walked through the doors and stopped dead at the sight. "Holy shit," Brian murmured. "He gone?"

"Yup," Maggie confirmed. She looked Brian over. "What's happening out there?"

"Thursday night football?" Brian answered with a shrug. "I'm pretending to ask if the kitchen's still open," he added with an eye roll. The whole town knew that the kitchen closed at eight thirty, and it was ten to nine now.

"The kitchen is closed forever," I mumbled, returning to my sink.

"You got this, honey?" Maggie asked me, and I could almost feel her inching to the door.

"Mm-hmm." There was no point arguing or protesting. Dean was a dick for leaving me with this shit, but Maggie was a sweetheart, and I was still grateful I had a place here.

It had been a few weeks since moving to town, and no one had bothered me. There were no fights that I knew of, but between the bar and Lottie's, the two women kept me busy. The woods at the back of Lottie's B&B weren't deep, but they gave a girl enough cover to run free undetected in her wolf form.

"I'll talk to him," she promised, and I heard the door swishing behind her as she left the kitchen to serve the customers.

When I first tidied up after Dean, I had taken more care and asked Maggie a hundred questions about what could be kept and what couldn't. Now, after he pulled this crap for the seventh night, I just emptied everything into the trash.

If he wanted to keep it for tomorrow, then he should have put it away. That was my thinking, and when I told Maggie that later after closing while I mopped the floor, she'd laughed and mimed a high five.

"When does Brad get home?" I idly asked as I moved the bucket along the floor. Maggie was wiping down the bartop, and I had learned early on that not only did she love to talk, but she loved to talk about her son, Brad, the most.

"His school gets the whole Thanksgiving week off," she told me happily. "He comes home the Saturday before."

"Nice."

My pack didn't pay attention to human traditions—we held festivals and celebrations to the lunar cycle. I was enjoying the pumpkin spice flavoring of everything though, so I had decided I liked this human holiday.

I always enjoyed autumn colors. The turning season was more noticeable lower on the mountain, or maybe I was just growing more accustomed to orange and brown decorations everywhere I looked.

"Zia, honey, you want me to drive you home tonight?" Maggie asked me when I was putting the mop and bucket away. "The nights are getting so dark," she added as she frowned at my head shake.

"I like the walk home," I told her with a confident smile. Reaching for my hoodie, I pulled it on. "The night walk is peaceful."

Which was true. Baywater Creek had a small police station with three police officers. The most troublesome event they'd encountered so far since I'd been here was a cat stuck up a tree and dealing with its hysterical owner.

Had I been passing when it happened, I could have saved them all the drama. Cats weren't friendly with wolves. I could have let my wolf surface, and that cat would have been down on the ground in the blink of an eye.

"Have you bought a cell phone yet?" Maggie demanded while we checked the place over before locking up.

I'd told her I had lost my phone when I got mugged. Sometimes, she would remember I didn't have one, but most times, she never mentioned it. Maggie was good at giving you space unless she was fretting over you.

She was currently in "mom" mode.

"No, I want to make sure I have enough cash in case I need it for an emergency. I told you," I added with a calm smile, "no one is looking for me."

"Even though you say you're alone, there must be someone who misses you," she said with sympathy in her eyes.

"You don't need to worry about me," I assured her as she set the alarm, and we dashed outside before it set. After locking the door, she turned to me, and I held steady under her scrutiny.

"You're still young, Zia. Let me worry."

We said our goodnights, and the irony wasn't lost on me that I made sure she got in her car safely and watched her drive away.

Walking back to Lottie's took around twenty minutes. I hadn't lied—it was a nice walk. I enjoyed the stretch of my legs, knowing that when I got back to the cabin, I'd be able to slip out under the cover of darkness and run through the woods undisturbed.

The sound of an engine approaching made me tense—a flashback to the night dirt bikes chased me making me almost stumble.

Looking over my shoulder, I searched the road behind me for the source. Seeing nothing, I made the decision and slipped off the road and into the nearby woods.

Knowing I was probably overreacting didn't slow my step, and instead, I hurried toward Lottie's, eager to be home.

When the low lights of the B&B and the cabins lit up the darkness, I made my way back onto the track. An engine back-firing made me jump and look over my shoulder again, but the road behind me remained empty.

Opening my cabin door and slipping inside, I locked it and stood in the small space, my heart racing. For the first time since coming to Baywater Creek, I didn't shift that night. Instead, I took a long shower, washed my hair, and went to bed, hoping my sleep would be deep enough to forget the fact I'd been jumping at shadows.

MORNING CAME TOO SOON with mixed emotions.

My wolf wasn't content that she'd been kept from running last night. She was used to being free nightly now, a far cry from living with the pack, and her restlessness had meant my sleep had been broken.

On the other hand, I *did* sleep, and despite my disgruntled wolf, I felt quite rested. Getting dressed in my usual jeans and T-shirt, I noticed my hair color was fading, and my blonde roots were threatening to show.

Lottie was making eggs when I entered the main cabin. Maggie's warning that very first day had proven to be accurate. I'd thanked her for telling me not to try Lottie's cooking. I don't know how her guests swallowed down what she served them.

"Are they supposed to be brown?" I teased Lottie, taking a seat near the breakfast bar.

"Wretched girl, they are *golden*," she corrected, waving her spatula at me.

"There's golden, and then there's that," I said with a grin. Resting my elbow on the counter, I propped up my chin. "I think that may be more burnt orange than the *golden* you're aiming for."

A bagel narrowly missed my head. Hopping off the stool, I bent and picked it up off the floor. Tearing a piece off, I popped it in my mouth.

"That was on the floor," Lottie said with disgust.

"Five-second rule." I chewed quickly. "Plus, I clean these floors...you *can* eat your dinner off them." *And I'm a wolf, we don't care about these things*, I added silently.

"Just because you can eat your dinner off the floor doesn't mean you should." Lottie tapped the box from the bakery the bagels were from. "Take another."

I retook my seat, eating another piece of the dropped bagel. "Best leave these for the guests. I know the eggs aren't supposed to be *that color*."

"Hush," she scolded, lifting the pan off the heat. "Fetch the bacon," she added.

Wide eyes and with a mournful soul, I pulled the pan of bacon from the oven. What was once brittle and crisp was now stale and leathery. What Lottie could do to bacon was a sin against stomachs everywhere.

"Biscuits too."

Biting my lip, I pulled the hard bricks from the warming drawer.

"Are you having breakfast?" Lottie asked, transferring the eggs into a large serving dish.

"Never."

"What was that?"

"I can't," I said hastily. "I need to get to the drug store."

Lottie sniffed dramatically at the rejection. Armed with my half a bagel, I left her to poison her guests with breakfast as I headed into town.

I left my pack four and a half months ago during my first heat when my brother had set me free. Alone and free, my heat had faded as quickly as it came. It hadn't been fun, but I had controlled it. My human body had kept a regular cycle, but I knew from the uncomfortable scratchiness that seemed to be under my skin that my heat was returning.

Unsure of how this would play out in a town of humans, I was eager to take precautions. As I walked down the track, I kept looking at the trees. My wolf was restless that she hadn't run last night, but I kept a tight hold on her as we walked.

I didn't need her shifting right now. I knew why she was restless.

Something dark and spicy teased at my nostrils, and I hadn't realized I had stopped walking until I turned a full circle.

Was that cinnamon? Inhaling, I sensed the scent again. Cedar? Licking my lips, I took a step toward the trees.

A car driving past broke my trance-like state, and I realized I had been zoned out in the middle of the road. Blushing at my foolishness, I hurried to the drug store, trying to push the enticing scent away.

As I waited in line, three girls not much younger than me came in, each carrying a pumpkin spice-flavored coffee. I'd smelled cinnamon earlier and a woody smell—nutmeg? Of course, I was scenting everything pumpkin spice. Laughing to myself, I got what I needed and went to the town library.

The library had two computers, and each townsperson could book use of the computer for an hour every week. It didn't matter the whole town, except me and I think Lottie, had a computer, I was still only allowed one hour of usage. But it was more than I had ever had, and in the almost three weeks I'd been here, I'd been trying to teach myself to be more computer-literate.

I didn't understand the human trend of social media. People seemed to put a lot of their personal information on these platforms. Having learned about cyber security and how to keep your information safe, I didn't understand why people then answered questions on social media posts that were the answers to most humans' passwords.

The more time I spent with humans, the more I knew I would never understand their ways. Learning how to use the computer was fun, though. I hated I was restricted to one hour, but the woman who ran the library looked at me with suspicion every time I came in. She also hovered nearby, and I did my best to ignore her, although sometimes I would ask what something meant, and she reluctantly helped me.

The town librarian was like many of my pack back on the mountains, and I handled her the same way I did with them. Polite and reserved. Just like at home, it didn't make her thaw toward me. I was used to dealing with those who would rather not deal with me, so I took her standoffish nature in my stride.

After my hour was done, I made my way back to the cabins, pumpkin spice latte in hand. This time, when I thought I caught a scent in the wind, I convinced myself it was just the spices in my coffee.

I spent the rest of the morning cleaning the cabins and the

main lodge and doing the laundry. Lottie couldn't cook, but the woman ran a clean house. Tucked behind the other side of the house was where the clothesline was kept, and in the afternoon, I hung the sheets up to dry while the weather allowed it. The smell of fresh linen and the pine trees nearby made me smile.

After I did my chores around the cabins, I colored my hair, ensuring my black locks remained intact.

Late afternoon, I returned to town to start work at the bar. The routine was simple and well-known to me. For the first time in a long time, I felt comfortable. Lottie and Maggie may not have known it, but a small part of me was beginning to think of them as pack. Both women had accepted me and my quiet ways easily—a thing the pack I left behind had never done.

In the few short weeks I'd been here, I could see a future for myself in this town. Maggie wasn't as scary as she thought she was, and Lottie was blunt but fair. Both women were good company, and the work, although menial, was fun.

In this town, I had something I didn't have on the mountain. I had a future that was mine to dictate. If that wasn't freedom, what was?

The shift at the bar flew by fast. Friday night, even in a small town, was a busy one. Dean had not been happy about me tossing most of his food out, and when I countered his yelling with my own reasonable argument that he should have tidied his shit, we had a tense stare-down.

I'd been glared at by my brother for years and on the receiving end of Pack Leader Bale's disappointment more than once—a hard stare from a disgruntled man-child would never bother me. Dean realized that quickly, and although he kept his silence the entire night, he *did* leave the kitchen tidier than usual.

I didn't gloat when Maggie commented on it, but neither of us hid our smiles.

On my walk home that night, I had more than a spring in my step, and I will forever blame my small victory over Dean as to why I missed the bat swinging through the air and connecting with my head until it was too late.

CHAPTER 14
Kezia

My awareness came back slowly. Smells surrounded me long before I realized I was conscious. Keeping my eyes closed, I tried to figure out why I couldn't move. My arms were bound behind my back, and I was sitting on something.

Something hard.

A chair?

Straining to listen, I searched for any sound that wasn't my pounding heart. Was I alone? Opening my eyes slightly, I peered into the darkness, my wolf sight sharper than any human's.

I was in a shed—a tool shed, by the looks of it. Lifting my head, I winced at the throbbing pain in my skull.

Stupid and careless, that's what I'd been. How had I not heard them approach? How had I missed the scent of a wolf pack?

Pulling at my wrists, I paused. Wolves wouldn't tie my arms. I was a shifter. These ropes wouldn't hold me, which led me to a more worrying reality.

A human had done this.

Flexing my arms, I called on my wolf's strength and ignored

the burn of the ropes as I wrenched my arms free. Rubbing my wrists, I stood, and on silent feet, I explored the small shed.

Where the hell was I? Inching closer to the door, I stilled, listening for voices. When I was sure there was no one waiting for me, I tried the handle. The door creaked open slowly, causing me to wince.

They hadn't locked me in? Whoever had assaulted me was either very confident or a complete idiot.

Right now, I wasn't going to stop to figure it out. I had a good idea of what men did to captive women, and I wasn't hanging around to find out if that was my assailant's intent.

The shed was against a high wire fence. Looking around, I saw I was in an industrial yard of some sort with a big warehouse to the front. I didn't recognize this as part of Baywater Creek, and I didn't like not knowing where I was. Reaching back into the shed, I picked up a wrench and kept tight hold of it as I quickly made my way to the main gate.

The gate was chained but loosely, with a heavy-looking padlock securing it. I was sure I could squeeze through, and crouching down, I shuffled sideways through the gap. The gate rattled, but I was almost free. Through the gate, I straightened and once more looked around.

This was too easy. Was it a trap, or had I truly been jumped by someone who severely underestimated me?

Either way, I wasn't hanging around to ask. Setting off in a slow jog, I made my way to the large warehouse and came to a sudden stop. Pressing closer to the building, I heard them then— voices.

Carefully, I moved around the building, stopping when I heard the voices getting louder, but still, I couldn't hear what was being said. There was definitely more than one person inside the warehouse, and I wasn't sure of my chances against more than one attacker.

Biting my lip, I froze as a wave of dizziness swept over me. Breathing slowly, I waited for it to pass, using the wall for support. While I struggled to stay upright, I became aware of the sound of feet on gravel.

I didn't want to be caught again, so pushing off the wall, I ran back the way I'd come and around the other side, hoping to make it to the front entrance before they knew I was out of the shed.

Edging around the front side, I saw the open gates to the yard. Stealing a glance to the front of the warehouse, I saw a side access door, slightly open, where light and voices spilled out into the night. Looking between the door and the yard, I considered my options.

Don't do it, Kezia.

One small peek wouldn't hurt.

Moving swiftly, I ran across the concrete to the door and peeked inside. My jaw dropped at what I saw. A group of men were gathered around a central area, and inside...was that a ring? Yes, I could see two men fighting in the ring.

What the fuck?

Backing away, my mind raced to make sense of everything. A yell from the back of the warehouse sounded and spurred me into action. Spinning away from the door, I bolted across the yard.

My wolf rushed forward, and I used her strength to run faster —I wasn't looking to be caught again. I'd figure out who attacked me, but I'd do it on my terms, not theirs. I didn't know where I was, but I could smell pine. There were woods nearby. I needed to get to them and then I could shift.

A loud crack split the night, followed by another crack, and pain ricocheted into me.

My feet tripped over themselves, and I was falling forward, losing the wrench as I fell. My shoulder was burning, and I was aware of wetness. The smell of blood surrounded me.

Landing face down, I yelled out in pain at the impact as my shoulder jarred against the hard ground. Rolling onto my back, I clutched my shoulder, struggling to stand. Three figures were running toward me.

Moving quickly, despite the pain, I ran again. I heard the crack again, and I ducked, knowing now it was gunfire. Ducking did no good. The shot hit my left calf.

Screaming in pain, I fell again.

Quicker than I would have liked, three men stood above me. Looking up, I looked at the strangers' faces, and then I watched the third one step forward, fear coiling in my belly.

"Bullet."

"Hey, bitch...miss me?" he snarled right before his boot came down heavily on my face, knocking me out cold.

I AWOKE in the back of a truck.

My hands were tied again, the pull on my shoulder excruciating around the area where I'd been shot. My feet were tied too, my left leg numb from the blood loss and the cramped position I was in.

"She's bleeding a lot," the man in the back with me said to the two in front.

"Good," Bullet grunted, and I realized he was driving. "I want her alive for the next bit, but if she dies, well...I won't shed a tear for the bitch."

I felt a hand run over my hip, lingering there, and I forced myself to remain still. "She's too pretty to die," the man said quietly, his hand moving closer to my jeans button.

Bullet heard him, though. "She's a stuck-up bitch who deserves what's coming to her," Bullet growled out.

I heard shuffling, like someone was moving in their seat, and the third one spoke, "You said we could play with her before she dies... Have you changed your mind?" he grumbled, and I knew with absolute certainty what "play" meant.

The truck came to an abrupt stop, and it knocked me forward, the air in my lungs whooshing out of me. My shoulder struck the seat in front, and I inhaled sharply at the pain.

"She's awake," the guy in the back with me said.

Giving up the pretense, I looked up and met Bullet's hate-filled glare. "Good. The next part's not as much fun when they're unconscious."

Panic swirled in my belly. I felt faint from the blood loss, but I could heal. They planned to kill me and much more than that before they took my life.

Pack laws forbade any wolf to shift in front of humans, but I was dying.

And I was no longer *pack*.

She came forward. I felt my eyes shift to the low, icy glow of my wolf, and I saw Bullet's fear right before I shifted, and my jaws snapped around his friend's neck as my human awareness was pushed back.

Pushing the hair out of our eyes, we ignored the stickiness of blood that coated her hands and arms. Naked, we walked up to the man face down on the ground.

We felt vacant. Disoriented. Strange.

Looking down at him, we watched as he pulled himself along on his belly, whimpering with pain as he tried to crawl away from the horror behind him.

His two companions were dead. Their body parts were strewn around the area beside their truck.

We had left this one until last.

"Where are you going?" we taunted the man as we crouched at his side. "I thought you wanted to play?"

He was weeping. We watched him as he pressed his forehead to the wet ground and started mumbling. Leaning into him, we listened.

"You're...praying?" Standing, we laughed, raising our arms out to the sides. "Are you listening to him?" We shouted at the sky. Then looking back down at the man, we shook our head. "We don't think your God is listening," we mocked him.

Kicking the man's side, the force of our kick knocked him onto his side. We crouched again. "Would you have listened to her?" we asked him. Our naked body was covered in blood. Not ours, though. "Tell me, Bullet, would she have been given the mercy you now beg for?"

"Please."

"Please?" We tilted our head as we looked at him. We saw his fear, but under it all, we saw his hate. "No, Bullet, she wouldn't have been given mercy," we told him bitterly. "And we give none."

Daylight woke me.

Pushing myself up into a sitting position, the smell of rotting flesh assaulted my nostrils first. With my arm across my face, covering my nose and mouth, I stood, not noticing the dried blood until I stepped forward.

Horrified at what lay in front of me, I stumbled back a step.

"Luna, help me..." With wide eyes, I tried to take it all in. The black truck was covered in blood. Inside and out. Dismembered body parts lay around it. "Goddess, no," I whispered as I forced my legs to move.

With tentative steps, I inched closer. A glance at what was left of Bullet made my stomach churn. Tears flooded my eyes as I looked at the carnage I'd created.

My body stilled as I heard traffic in the distance. Panic forced me into action. Running to the bodies, I searched them until I found a lighter, fighting back sobs as I did. Trying not to look too closely at what I'd done, I pulled the dead to the truck until they were in a pile.

Uncovering the back of the truck, I grabbed two overnight bags. Finding rope, handcuffs, and weapons of torture in the first one, I tossed it aside in disgust. The second bag had clothing. With gritted teeth, I pulled out a pair of sweats and a T-shirt. I needed something to wear, but the thought of wearing anything of *theirs* turned my stomach, so I dropped the clothing on the ground. I'd rather be naked.

Standing back, I searched for the gas tank. Urging my wolf forward, I bit back the pain as I forced her claws to come out of my human hand. One swipe and I punctured the tank, the sharp-smelling liquid burning my nose. When it touched the first of the dead, I dropped the lighter and ran back to the safety of the woods.

The fire caught their clothes quicker than I thought, and then the explosion shattered the morning air.

I watched it burn the truck and the dead, and then when the sirens pierced the air, I shifted as I turned to the woods and ran.

Ran from the death and the knowledge I'd killed three humans.

～

MY WOLF RELEASED her hold on me when deep snow covered the ground. For weeks, I'd been in my wolf form, and the horror of that autumn morning was still fresh in my mind. Over the weeks I'd been under her control, we'd traveled high into the Rockies, and waking up in a semi-sheltered cave high in the mountains, naked and freezing, was enough to bring anyone's awareness into focus.

Looking around the den she had made, I took in the sight of animal bones and tufts of fur scattered about, causing me to frown. I felt like an unimpressed parent as they surveyed their child's room after telling them to tidy it. My wolf was messy, and it kind of pissed me off.

Slowly, carefully, I checked my body—a faint silver line on my shoulder, a similar one on my right thigh. Reliving the feel of the bullets as they tore into my skin, I turned my leg and looked at my left calf. A silver scar looked back at me.

It fit that they marked me on the surface as well as under my skin for the events that happened the night Bullet came for me. I remembered little, but I'd seen the evidence of her rage when I woke, and I knew the sight would haunt me for a long time.

Swallowing hard, I pushed my hair back, noticing it was white-blonde once more. Approaching the mouth of her den, I looked out into the white world beyond. The snow wasn't as deep as I thought, but it *was* cold, and my human body wouldn't survive for long. I needed clothes, and for clothes, I needed humans.

Will you behave? I asked her, feeling her come forward. She gave me a look of indifference, and I felt her lack of interest at my ire.

I need to shift, you've stuck me up a damn mountain, and I'm naked.

Had I not known better, I could've sworn she shrugged at me.

I shifted, but I kept tight control of my awareness and her. We left the den, and once I was more aware of *where* I was in the Rockies, I turned tail and headed south. We traveled for three days when we finally came across the first scattering of cabins.

Stealing clothes in summer is a lot easier. People put washing outside to dry, but in the winter, everything is indoors. Naked, blonde-haired teenage girls stand out in stark weather.

A flannel shirt in the back of a truck was the first thing we took. Old combat boots that were too big were next, and on the edge of a familiar town, light fingers snatched a forgotten pair of work jeans in a garage with a broken window that I wiggled through in the rain and stayed dry until morning.

In my borrowed clothes, I skirted the town, keeping to the woods for a few days before I felt I was familiar with the patterns of the townsfolk once more.

Under the cover of the night, I slipped up the small path, hesitating before my knock on the wooden door finally connected.

Apprehension coursed through me as I waited, finally hearing the fall of footsteps.

The problem was they weren't coming toward me from inside.

They were behind me.

I heard the telltale click of a gun. Turning slowly, I came face to face with familiar blue eyes, which widened in surprise as he lowered the gun.

"Zia?"

"Hey, Vance," I greeted him with a tight smile, shoving my hands into my jeans. "Guess I wasn't lucky."

Kezia

"WHAT THE FUCK HAPPENED?" VANCE DEMANDED, shoving the gun into his jeans. "And why the fuck are you here?"

His anger took me by surprise, but with Vance, his temper was as unstable as his morals. Pushing past me, he opened the cabin door, and I followed him inside.

"What do you mean, what happened?"

In three strides, he was across the floor at his kitchen counter, and I watched him as he poured an unhealthy amount of liquor into a glass. He drank it in one swallow. Pouring himself another one, I waited as he downed that one too.

"Why did you come to me?" he asked me while he ran his eyes critically over me.

"I need money," I told him honestly. "You got a fight for me?"

He was already shaking his head. "No," he bit out. Suddenly, his glass slammed on the counter. "Actually not no, it's *fuck* no."

"What's wrong with you?" I demanded, my temper rising.

"What's *wrong* with me?" He looked both bewildered and furious. It was a strange expression to see. "Do you know you're presumed dead?" He gave a bitter laugh at my shock. "You're either dead or a murderer. Or a dead murderer."

"Stop saying murder!"

"Why are you not asking who you murdered?" Vance shouted at me. "Or do you already know?"

Looking away from his angry glare, I gave a half shrug. "My guess? Bullet?"

"You really killed him?" Vance asked me in a stunned whisper.

"Don't judge me," I scoffed as I looked him over. "Last time I saw you with him, he was hanging from the rafters in the warehouse, and someone had beat the shit out of him."

"He got his ass beat, yes. I didn't fucking kill him!"

"And you think I did?"

Vance pushed both hands through his hair, his hands stilling on top of his head as he stared at me. "You don't know, do you?"

His question unsettled me. How did he know I had no clear recollection of what my wolf had done? For the first time since deciding on this plan, I felt uncertain. "No idea about what?" I asked him as I took a step back.

"Your face has been on every news channel in the country. You're either missing or dead."

What?

"What?" I gave a fake laugh. "That's impossible. No one is *missing* me."

Vance poured himself another drink. "Yeah, you want to tell the old woman who keeps pleading for her Zia to come home?"

"What old wo—"

Shit. Lottie?

"Yeah, that would be her." Vance drank his liquor and put the glass down. "So...Zia, tell me why the fuck you're here, what you did to Bullet, and did you tell anyone you were coming here?"

"I…" I swallowed. Dammit, how did I get out of this? "Am I missing or wanted for murder?" I asked instead.

"Missing." Vance looked at the bottle, and then after a brief hesitation, he poured another drink. "And wanted for questioning regarding the murder of John Quib, Samuel Tenant, and Wayne Lovie."

"Who are they?"

"Bullet, SamT, and Lovie the Loser."

My hands were fists in my pockets, a fact that Vance noticed, his eyes narrowing as he looked me over. "You were stealing clothes again?"

"Kind of."

"Why are you here, kid? I've finally paid off the cops to stop sniffing up my ass, asking questions about you."

"I need money. I thought I could do a couple of rounds in the ring." Rocking back on my heel, I gave him a wry smile. "I've been lying low. Bullet shot me," I told him. "Three times." Vance's jaw clenched, but he said nothing. "I got away. They were going to do a lot more than shoot me," I added quietly.

"Did you kill him?"

"No. Maybe. I don't know."

Vance shook his head. "You got to get better at lying," he muttered. He watched me for a long time. "I can't put you in a ring, kid. Even with your hair colored like that, you're recognizable."

"I get it," I told him as I walked to the door. "I didn't know about all the…stuff. I wouldn't have come."

"You eaten?"

Pausing at his door, I shook my head.

"Pizza?"

"Why?" I asked cautiously. "You don't need me here."

"Maybe I feel guilty," Vance told me as he stared at the countertop. "Maybe if I hadn't let Bullet walk, he wouldn't have come after you."

"Maybe is a game people like us should never play," I told him quietly. "I'll skip pizza," I said. When he looked up, I lifted a foot. "You got any sneakers? These boots are killing my feet."

"Does this place look like a retail unit?" Vance asked with a small smile.

"No, I guess not." Pulling the door open, I lifted my hand in a wave. "See you, Vance."

I didn't hear his reply. I had already turned in fear, my eyes searching the darkness. Slowly, I stepped out of the cabin. Lifting my chin to sniff the air, I felt my wolf prowl closer.

He walked up the path, the gloominess of night parting for him as he stepped into the dim light. Shadows accentuated his sharp features in the darkness, but his deep green eyes met mine and held as he approached.

Fear ran down my spine as I met the hard, unyielding glare of an alpha.

"Pup."

"*Cannon.*" Looking behind him, I saw two more shifters. Vance was saying something behind me, but I couldn't hear him over the thumping of my heart as I looked at the alpha.

"Kezia," Cannon warned softly. "Don't."

I darted out the door, and at the side of the house, I shifted midrun. My wolf ran straight for the trees, and as I ran from Cannon and his pack, I heard the howls of pursuit behind me, urging me to run faster.

I knew these woods, and I ran through them swiftly as I headed to the mountains beyond.

A black wolf barreled into me, knocking me flying. My wolf

landed with a thump, but I was already urging her to her feet. We ran again, but the second wolf hit me, and I was knocked down again, landing on my back.

Twisting to get up, his shadow fell over me.

Stop!

The power of the alpha had my wolf whimpering in submission. Her head lowered, and I knew I was caught.

Shift.

Naked and panting in the snow, I raised my head in defiance as I looked up at Cannon's wolf. He was magnificent, taller than any wolf I'd seen. His coat was a deep black. His shift to man was seamless, and I averted my eyes as he stood naked before me.

"Nikan," Cannon ordered, and I looked up as his brother handed him a thick flannel shirt. "Not me, her."

Startled, I accepted the offered shirt from the alpha's brother. Quickly, I pulled it on and was instantly hit with the familiar smell—cedarwood and nutmeg.

"How long have you been following me?" I asked as I buttoned the shirt.

"How long have you been running?" Cannon asked with a smirk, pulling on a pair of basketball shorts.

I ignored him. "What now?" I refused to meet his eyes, the numbness I felt not only because of my bare feet in the snow.

"Back to the pack," Cannon told me. "Come." He turned away from me.

"If I refuse?"

He looked at me over his shoulder. "You misunderstand, pup. I'm not asking."

I refused to move, and with a huff of displeasure, the alpha walked the short distance back to me, picked me up, and uncere- moniously tossed me over his shoulder. His arm clamped over the back of my legs like a solid band as he walked and ignored my protests and struggles.

I heard an engine approach, and trying to twist to see what was happening, I gave up when the hold on my lower body remained unmoving.

"Open it," Cannon ordered someone.

I heard a creak and someone asking him if he was sure, and then I was shoved into a cage.

A *cage*.

"Are you out of your mind?" I shouted at him as I shook the bars of the cage.

"Quiet." The force of the alpha command silenced me. The alpha couldn't stop my glare, though, and the bastard smiled at me. "Glare at me all you want, pup." With a low laugh, he got in the truck and then we were driving up the mountains. "Take us home, brother."

Home? Shit. This was worse than I thought.

I rattled the cage again and was about to shift when the one-word command stilled my movements.

Sleep.

WHEN I WOKE, I quickly realized my cage's bars had changed. Springing to my feet, I realized I was no longer in the cage Cannon had put me in when he caught me. I was in a much larger cage in the middle of a barn.

A cell.

The cell's roof was also bars like the four walls currently holding me in. The cage was high, the square floor enough for six to eight paces. Turning slowly, I took in my surroundings. The cell was elevated from the floor, and I wasn't sure why.

A large spotlight shone on the cage, making it hard to look too far into the corners, but I sensed something was there.

From what I could tell, they had stripped the barn of everything except this cage.

I eyed the small cot I'd been lying on. How long had I been here? Looking down, I saw I was in the same flannel shirt, but a pair of sweatpants and underwear were in the corner of the cell.

"You look confused, pup."

My head snapped up at hearing his voice.

"Call me pup one more time..." I half growled at Cannon as he stepped out of the shadows.

"You don't like being called a pup, *pup*?"

My instinct was to throw myself at the bars, but I refused to let him see how much he pissed me off. "I'm not a child," I said instead. With my head held high, I returned to the cot and sat. "Why am I in a cell?"

"Alpha."

I looked at him with what I hoped was disdain, and I saw his top lip curl slightly in a semblance of a smirk. "I wasn't aware that I was, but if you think I am..."

Cannon's head tilted to the side as he gave me a full mocking once-over. "You're definitely not an alpha," he said with a head shake. "But you *will* address me as one."

"As one? One what? Bastard?" I sneered. "Easy. Why am I in a cell, bastard?"

Cannon stepped closer, his eyes narrowing slightly. "Be very careful, Kezia. You're on thin ice, and I'm the only thing keeping you from falling through."

Standing, I approached the bars. "Let me fall...I can swim just fine."

Cannon held my defiant stare for a long moment. I felt my mouth go dry as his green eyes bore into mine. The hairs on the back of my neck raised, and I felt a single bead of sweat trickle down my back. More than anything, I wanted to look away and break his heavy stare, but I refused to show him such weakness.

"You killed three humans, pup."

Swallowing hard, I shook my head, finally able to look elsewhere. "It was self-defense."

"You're a shifter." Cannon folded his arms across his chest, the biceps bulging. "Your strength is already superior to theirs. Tell me what happened."

How did I tell him I didn't know? How did I admit that weakness to an alpha who was part of the pack who killed our parents?

Looking at the canvas floor covering my cell, I refused to meet his enquiring stare. "They attacked me. I fought back."

"Did you shift?" When I refused to answer, he stepped closer. "Kezia."

The commanding tone had my head snapping up in answer. "Stop trying to force me," I snapped angrily. "I told you what happened. They attacked *me*, and I defended myself as is my right."

"You *killed* three men," Cannon snarled. "That is *not* your right. Your *right* as a shifter is to bring the *least* attention to yourself amongst humans." Cannon shook his head as he looked away. "It is not to be on every national news channel. It is not to be in their newspapers. It is *not* to be a fugitive being hunted by their law enforcement!"

"Hunted?" Rubbing the back of my neck, I refused to let him see my fear. "I thought I was just missing?"

"So you know they are looking for you?"

"No, Vance told me."

"And who the fuck is Vance?"

I wasn't prepared for his tone. The *possessiveness* of it. "A..." I hesitated again, and Cannon noticed. *Who was Vance? A friend? Was he? Kind of.* "It's complicated. Let's just call him a friend."

Cannon's eyes glowed briefly, and I almost stepped back. "A friend? Define *friend*."

Blinking rapidly, I looked at him in confusion. "Dude, if you don't know what a friend is at your age, then that tells me a helluva lot about you."

In an instant, he was in front of the cage, and this time, I stepped back from him, from his anger. "Do not push me, pup. I am *this* close"—he held up his thumb and finger barely with any space between them—"to coming in there and knocking some sense into you. Do *not* push me."

The fact I really wanted to push him said more about me than I wanted to admit. Instead, I moved closer to the bars and opted to change the subject. "How long am I to be held prisoner?"

"Until I let you out."

"That isn't an answer, Cannon."

"Not Cannon," he growled. "From now on, you'll call me *Alpha*." His eyes ran over me before he looked back at me with firm resolution in his eyes. "It's the only answer you're going to get."

I was so stumped by the finality of his statement that Cannon had left me before I had a retort. Instead, the barn door closing jarred me out of my shock. He'd left me alone in this cell, and his pack wouldn't go against him. He was their alpha.

If he thought I was calling him *Alpha,* he could think again. But whatever I called him wasn't my problem. My problem was how I got out of this. How did I fix the fact humans were hunting for me?

Sitting on the cot with a thump, I dropped my head into my hands as I tried desperately to find a solution. I was in an enemy pack, wanted by the human police for killing three men, and I had nowhere to run. Rubbing my temples, I couldn't help but think of what my brother was going to do when he found out how badly I'd messed up.

But first? First, I needed to get out of this cage.

CHAPTER 16

Kezia

I couldn't sleep.

They locked me in a cage, and my wolf wanted out. I refused to shift in here, though. The last time I shifted, I took months to come back. I didn't trust her to relinquish control anymore.

I didn't trust myself not to hide behind her either.

Instead, I sat on the small cot and watched the shadows for Cannon. They never dimmed the spotlight, whether I was supposed to be intimidated by being under the *literal* spotlight or it was supposed to be a punishment, I wasn't sure. If anything, I was grateful it was keeping me awake. I'd pulled the underwear and sweatpants on earlier. It was cold in here, and I was grateful for the warmth the pants offered.

I wasn't sure how much time had passed when I heard movement, but I didn't bother reacting. I kept my back to the bars, one leg pulled up to my chest as I waited for whoever it was to appear. I wasn't sure if it was *him*, but I couldn't afford to react to him.

I felt my shoulders release a small fraction of tension as Nikan approached with a tray in his hands. Cannon's brother looked at me warily as he approached.

"Hey," I greeted, my throat dry and croaky from being silent too long and having nothing to drink. "Been a while." I tried to be lighthearted, but Nikan's expression remained blank. "Oh, are you not allowed to talk to me?" I dropped my leg and leaned forward, my elbows resting on my thighs. "I get it."

Nikan approached the bars—the tray had a covered plate and a bottle of water.

"For me?" I asked hopefully. I moved forward, but the look in his eyes stopped me.

"Stay there," Nikan ordered quietly. "There are people behind me, so don't try anything when I open the door."

Swallowing back my protests, I nodded, resuming the position I'd been sitting in before I realized it was him. "I won't move...you're safe." I heard the bitterness in my voice, and when he looked at me, I averted my gaze so he couldn't see my disappointment.

The cell door opened, and I willed myself to stay where I was, although I felt her surge forward at the thought of freedom. I pushed back my wolf, whispering to her that she had to let me handle this.

Nikan slipped the tray onto the floor. He didn't hurry to close the cell door, and I didn't take it for a slight but more a reassurance that he didn't think I was the monster his brother thought I was. He met my gaze as he closed the door, and I saw the faint glimmer of the man I had met in my packlands.

"Thank you," I whispered. "Unless it's fish, then I'll know I'm definitely being tortured."

He wasn't quick enough to hide his amusement, and I felt the tension lessen even more.

"Nikan!" The command was from the rear of the barn. It wasn't Cannon, but I saw Nikan jerk as if it was.

With the door closed and locked, I got off the cot and uncovered the tray. A simple beef sandwich looked back at me. I was already sitting on the cell floor, eating it when I heard the door to the barn close again, leaving me alone once more.

Opening the water bottle, I drank it in a few gulps. When I was done, I looked at the plate and empty bottle in remorse. I should have probably savored that more. With a sigh, I got back to my feet. The water and food energized me, and I carried out a few stretches to stop me from seizing up when I felt him.

How long had he been there?

Why hadn't I sensed him before this?

Slowly, I let my arms drop, turning to the side to search the darkness for him. I couldn't see him, and he knew it.

"Lurking in the dark your favorite pastime?" I challenged the darkness. "You like sitting in the shadows and watching girls who you keep in cages?"

Silence was my answer.

"You look the kind of man who would like to watch," I said, turning my back to him. "No talk, no action. Is that what your bedmates say about you?"

I knew my insolence was bound to get me in trouble one day, but either Cannon didn't care or my words didn't matter. I heard the door open as I sat back on the cot, and as the door closed, the light went out, plunging me into darkness. The sudden lack of light was disorienting, but I started to laugh at what I had just thought.

Get me in trouble *someday*? This was hardly my ideal surroundings. Still, the dark was welcome, and I lay on the cot, looking up into the darkness. It was the faint clicking on the floor that had me sitting up and swinging my legs over the side of the cot.

"Who's there?" Slowly, I turned in a circle, my wolf sight allowing me to see in a darkness my human eyes wouldn't penetrate.

The clicking happened again, and I turned to the sound, my claws punching out as I prepared to defend myself. I jumped back when blue eyes appeared in the dark, a faint glow emanated from them.

Alpha eyes.

He was in his wolf form as he circled the cell. My brain registered how tall he was—the wolf's head level with the floor of my cell. The wolf sniffed, and I wished for the spotlight to be on now so I could see him. My glimpse of his wolf when they caught me was too short.

The wolf stopped moving, and we stared at each other in the dark.

Was I supposed to speak? It didn't feel right to talk to him when he was like this. Cannon wasn't my alpha, so the only way he could communicate with me was if he put his Will on me. He'd done it when they captured me, but I got the sense his wolf didn't want that now.

The wolf sniffed. It sniffed one more time, and my cheeks burned with embarrassment as it took a long, deep inhale. A low whine sounded, and I'd never felt more self-conscious than I did right now, as I knew it had been weeks since I'd bathed like a normal person.

Did I stink? Of course, I did. I'd been running the mountains in my wolf form, and then I'd taken clothes from various people and not cared about the hygiene level of those people or their clothes because I'd been running.

Always running these days, it seemed. A huff from the wolf in front of my cell brought me out of my head.

"Cannon?" I whispered in the darkness.

The wolf stepped closer to the bars of my cell, and even though I was standing looking down at it, it felt like I was the one being judged.

My wolf prowled in the back of my consciousness. She wanted me to release the hold and let her come forward, but I refused her. After a long stare-off, the wolf melted back into the shadows.

Sleep.

~

THEY MOVED me while I slept. I didn't like it, and I didn't hide the fact. But they had moved me anyway. I now had a toilet in the corner of my cell. The cell had changed too. I was off my elevated perch and instead in a normal rectangular cell with the same cot and basic toilet facilities and a hose. The hose was to wash with, I guessed.

I resented everything about the hose.

I had a bar of soap, toothbrush, and toothpaste. That was it.

I resented everything about it *all*.

Even human prisoners got a shower. Didn't they?

I'd been in this cell for an additional three days. Once a day, Nikan would come with a tray, with guards I never saw at his back, and he would deliver a tray with food through a slot at the bottom of the cell door.

The first day, it was a simple sandwich and a bottle of water. The second day, I got soup and a sandwich. I said nothing, eating my food faster than being polite.

Today, they had moved away from sandwiches, and I could smell the chicken as Nikan walked toward me. Eagerly, I stayed on the cot, but I was salivating already at the rich aroma wafting toward me.

"Stay where you are," Nikan warned me, but the coldness had gone from his face, and I almost glimpsed the playful man I'd met in the store all those months ago.

"Not moving," I assured him, my eyes trained on the tray. "What is it? Chicken and…"

"It's chicken with—"

"Nikan!"

He grimaced as it cut him off. The reprimand was heavy in the air. They may have moved me, but the spotlight and the darkness concealing watchful eyes hadn't changed.

"I'll find out myself," I whispered as he slid the tray inside. The tray was barely through, and I was on the floor, removing the metal plate covering it. A simple chicken breast looked back at me. Nothing else. Just a plain, *tiny* chicken breast.

Looking up at him, he looked apologetic as he stepped back.

"What? This is it?" I asked in frustration. "I'm a wolf," I reminded them all, my voice rising. "Why keep me here if all you want to do is starve me?"

"I—"

"Nikan!"

"Oh, for fuck's sake, let him speak!" I snapped back. "What the hell do you think he's going to do? Be suddenly persuaded to let me out?" I picked up the chicken with my fingers and bit into it. Flavor rushed into my mouth, and I almost groaned. "Either this is delicious, or I'm desperate for food."

"Are you hungry, Kezia?" Nikan asked.

I took another bite. "No, I'm feeling stuffed and content. Of course, I'm hungry. Your people have starved me."

"We're not starving you," he corrected gently. He turned as another man walked into the light.

He was tall and bulky, with bulging muscles to rival Cannon's. Short, reddish hair and deep brown eyes, his skin was deep bronze, making my pale skin tone look even more ghostly in comparison.

"Hi," I greeted, taking another bite. "What makes you come out of the shadows?" I saw Nikan twist his head to avoid his grin at my attitude.

"You will not talk to the alpha's brother."

Flicking my gaze between them, I ate the last bit of chicken. "Why?" I asked as I chewed, rubbing my hands on my pants. "Who said?"

The new guy narrowed his eyes at me, and I mock glared back before I rolled my eyes at him and turned my attention back to Nikan.

"Why can't I talk to you? Is this my punishment? Small temptations of food to remind me how hungry I am?"

"Your *punishment*," New Guy said, "has yet to be determined."

"Where's my brother?" I asked Nikan, ignoring Mr. Posturing and Huffing. "When does Pack Leader Bale get here?"

"Enough questions!"

"Luna's grace!" I shouted in exasperation. "Will you take a fucking pill and calm your ass down? You're giving me indigestion."

"I think that's more likely the speed at which you ate your food," Nikan jabbed with a wry smile.

"I'm hungry," I told him. "If there is any food to spare," I told him earnestly, "I would be very grateful if I could get some more."

"We have food," Nikan told me. "I'll speak to the Alpha."

"Thank you," I told him sincerely. I sat back on the cot. "Is he here? I haven't seen him for a couple of days. Is he bringing my brother?"

"No more questions," the other guy snarled. "Nikan, come."

"Royce, it's fine. She's in a cage, she's hardly a threat!" Nikan seemed to have lost his patience with the barked orders too. With a deep breath, he looked at me. "I'll get more," he said as he pointed at the plate. "I'll see you soon."

"Thank you." I looked at Royce glaring at me. "Bye, Royce." I wiggled my fingers at him and grinned when he turned abruptly and marched away.

"If you want out of the cell, Kezia," Nikan said so softly his voice almost too quiet to hear, "try not to antagonize the ones who have the key."

When I went to speak, he gave a slight shake of his head, turning away from me. The door opened and closed in the darkness, and once more, it was just me, a bottle of water, and an empty plate.

No one returned, and I sat for a long time wondering if Nikan had been warning me against the others in the pack or telling me he was one of those who held the key.

Either way, a scrap of chicken was not enough for me or my wolf, and to take my mind off the gnawing hunger in my belly, I exercised. I'd taken the bedsheet they gave me off the cot, and with a lot of maneuvering and grim determination, I had hung it so it cut off the toilet and hose area.

I may be a shifter and wasn't precious about nakedness, but I was determined to have privacy when I was on the toilet.

Days were long, so I passed the time not by counting the

minutes until I got food but by doing exercise. I was midplank when I heard the door open. I felt him before he came into the light, and I refused to let Cannon see he bothered me, so I stayed in my plank.

"Why are the clothes on the floor?"

I kept my back straight, my attention on a point ahead of me. "I smell. I don't like smelling. The clothes smell too, so I took them off."

"Which is why you have a hose. Use it." His voice was firm, and I really wanted to ask him if he was the monster he appeared to be. His next words almost made me lose my composure. "Do you think you can entice my pack with your naked body?"

Pushing up with my hands, I rested back on my heels and turned my head to meet his stare, knowing I looked as stunned as I felt by the accusation. "I don't give a damn about your pack. If they're enticed by this"—I waved a hand down my front—"then I will definitely know starvation is key to your pack." I stood gracefully, facing him in only panties. My long hair covered my breasts.

"My pack are well fed, pup."

I looked him over. "Pity I can't say the same about me." Looking past him, I searched the dark. "Where have you been? Have you brought my brother?"

"Your brother is with his pack." Cold green eyes watched me as I tried not to react.

"Did you tell him you took me?"

"Took you?" Cannon folded his arms across his chest—a favored pose of his, I noted. "We caught a rogue wolf as is the right of pack law in the mountains."

I knew I was gaping at him. "I'm not a rogue wolf!"

His head cocked to the side. "Really? No pack makes you a

lone wolf. Danger to humans? A heightened risk to packs by bringing exposure to them?" He ticked off the items on his fingers as he spoke. "Sounds like a rogue to me."

I was at the bars, glaring at him, my fingers curled around them as he watched me impassively. "I am *not* a *rogue*," I snarled.

"You're not in control either," Cannon snapped tersely with a look at my claws which had pushed out. "Your eyes have changed, pup."

With effort, I stepped back, forcing my wolf down. "I'm in control."

"No. You're not." His look was as cold as his tone. "And until you are, you stay in the cage."

I screamed as I launched myself at the bars, my body jarring against the immovable steel. My arms reached through the bars, claws extended as I reached for the arrogant alpha in vain, swiping futilely at the empty air, inches from where he stood watching me impassively, unbending like the bars that surrounded me.

Panting with fury and feeling powerless, I yelled out in frustration as I took an angry step back. I kept my focus on the floor as I willed myself to calm down.

Sweat dripped from my brow onto the canvas, my arms were limp at my sides, and my hair was hiding me from his gaze like a curtain.

"Why won't you shift?" Cannon asked me calmly. When I didn't answer, I felt him move closer. "Because you know as well as I do, if you shift, as out of control as you are, you won't come back. Your wolf will take you, and then you will be everything you swore you weren't. *Rogue.*"

I fought the tears as he spoke the truth that I was too scared to admit out loud.

"And that is why you remain in the cell, pup," he said softly.

I heard him walking away from me, the door closing behind him, and the light turning off as he left, leaving me in darkness. It was only then that I let the tears fall.

I was everything my pack had feared me to be.

Wild and feral.

CHAPTER 17

Kezia

CANNON STAYED AWAY FROM ME FOR SEVERAL MORE days, and when Nikan came in, he was always accompanied by Royce, who, thankfully, had decided to stop hiding from me.

Nikan had reverted to saying little, but they had put slightly more food on the plate, and for that I was grateful. The more they left me alone in the cage with one meal a day to see me through to the next day, the more she paced in my awareness.

Some days, I tried to reason with her, but other days, we stared at each other in silence, neither of us willing to break first. I knew I had to address it. I needed to shift. The uncomfortable itching beneath my skin that had been starting to surface all those months before Bullet attacked me was back. I did not want a repeat of my heat taking over as I was locked in a cell with Cannon watching me again.

Nikan and Royce came into the barn—I recognized their scents now. Nikan was fresh pine and citrus. He smelled clean, and it was almost addictive to inhale deeply when he was near, almost like his scent was cleansing me. Royce smelled of rainwater and cotton. He was so grave and stern it confused me that he smelled of comfort.

And with them came the tantalizing smell of meat, juicy sauce, and delectable spices. My mouth watered in anticipation.

As they crossed over into the light, Royce's arm shot out, pulling Nikan back, causing Nikan to almost lose his grip on the tray.

"Careful!" I yelped, lurching to my feet from the cot. "That's my only meal," I added quietly, wondering why Royce glared at me. "You okay there?" I asked him warily.

He gave me a long look of consideration and then turned to Nikan. "Give me the tray. Get the Alpha."

Nikan looked between us both, his confusion clear. "Why?"

"Nikan, I gave you an order."

Nikan's cheeks flushed, but he gave a stiff nod and hurried out of the room, leaving my not-so-number-one fan and me alone.

"If you've spent all this time starving me, only to kill me now, I'm going to be so pissed off if I don't get to eat what's on that tray first."

"You are insolent."

I returned his hard look with one of my own. "I probably am, but you have given me no reason to show you anything else."

"I feed you."

The tray was placed on the floor, and I looked between him and it with mounting suspicion. "You're not giving me it, are you?" I watched him step back. "What do you mean you feed me?"

Royce's stance widened slightly as he folded his large arms across his chest. He remained quiet as my frustration grew at my food being so near to me but still too far from reach.

"Are you the jailor?" I asked with derision. "How many barns are there with cells in them? You do this a lot?" Royce gave nothing away as I began to pace. "Okay, I get it...you hate me. I understand I've been a snarky bitch, and you've been a grumpy dick." I nodded as I paced. "We met under really shit circumstances. Were you there the night your alpha kidnapped me?"

"Kidnapped?" Royce drawled skeptically.

"He took me against my will...that's kidnapping." I ignored his sneer. "Anyway, whether you were there or not is irrelevant, but since I've been here, we've been...okay? Right?" I stopped pacing. I was more or less in line with the tray, and I pointed to it. "Why can't I have my food, Royce?"

"Wait."

"I've been waiting. I've been waiting since yesterday. I'm so fucking hungry that I'm ready to chew off my arm, so I think I've waited long enough, you sick, twisted asshole."

He said nothing, but I noticed his shoulders eased slightly. Had he been tense? What had happened to relax him? And then I sensed him.

Alpha Dick of the Century.

"Ooh, goody." I retreated to my cot and sat. I'd stripped it of its remaining sheet yesterday and shoved it through the bars. No one had commented on it. Or removed it. I guess Royce only did cooking, and laundry must be up to someone else.

"You can go," Cannon murmured to Royce as he came to stand in front of the bars. His gaze swept over me, the frown I thought I saw was so brief I was sure I imagined it. "Pup."

"Asshole." His eyes narrowed, and I dramatically slapped my forehead. "Oh right, I forgot. *Alpha Asshole.*" I looked past him, searching the shadows for Nikan, the only shifter I'd met here I liked. Kind of. "Where's your brother?"

"Not here," Cannon answered tightly as he bent and picked

up the plate from the tray. Uncovering the food, he sniffed it deeply. "Mm...don't you love the smell of meatballs?" He picked one up, popped it in his mouth, and chewed slowly. "Delicious."

"That's mine."

"No," Cannon corrected me as he took another meatball from the plate. "Nothing here is yours." He popped it in his mouth and grinned at me as he chewed. "Your demands are quite annoying."

"Then let me go, you irritating asswipe." I watched, transfixed as he swirled his finger in the sauce before licking it clean. Closing my eyes against his obvious amusement, I willed myself to stay strong and not show him weakness.

"I can't let you go because you're a danger," he told me bluntly. "We discussed this."

My eyes snapped open, and I fixed him with a glare that would have had my brother battening down the hatches. "*We* discussed nothing. You like to hear your own voice. I am being held here against my will." The plate was in his hand, his hold on it almost careless in appearance. "That food is mine," I bit out, and when he went to speak, I hurried on. "That food was *meant* for *me*."

Cannon placed it on the floor, and I wanted to kill him. I felt her behind me, straining against my hold to keep her back. Licking my lips, I raged the silent battle within while he stood in front, not knowing I was wrestling her back.

Cannon's sigh echoed in the barn. "You aren't beating her," he said with a shake of his head.

It appeared I hadn't deceived him like I thought. He knew too much, this alpha. "I don't know what you mean."

"Do not *lie* to me, pup."

"Then don't speak in riddles," I snapped back.

"I don't know why I come in here," he muttered as he turned away. "I'm going to—"

"What!" I yelled. "You *do* nothing! You *say* nothing! I've been here for weeks. Either let me out or do what you keep *fucking* muttering about. But just for the love of Luna, do *something*!"

He was at the bars in two steps. It should have frightened me to see the rage in his eyes, but instead, it made me step closer.

"*Do* something? You want action from *me*?" He snarled, his eyes tight with fury.

No. "Yes."

The air escaped him in a rush. Large hands curled around the bars, fingers long and strong, locked tight on the bars.

"Your heat is coming," Cannon told me, his eyes holding mine. "Tell me, little pup, do you want me in there with you, or do you want me out here as a reminder to the pack that you are not to be touched?"

I swallowed nervously. "You can tell?"

"Your scent is quite potent," he growled, stepping back.

"Oh." I tore my gaze off of his. "I didn't know it was at that point yet," I admitted, wondering how I was yet again in a situation where Cannon was experiencing my heat.

"Because you're clueless about most things," he answered curtly. "Royce!"

I jumped in surprise as the order was barked, not at all surprised to see Royce coming quickly to his alpha's side. Cannon stooped and picked up the plate, handing it to him.

"She'll need fresh meat, not this," he told him. "I saw her last time...deer sates her."

"How recently slain?" Royce asked with a questioning look at me.

"Still breathing," Cannon grunted. "She needs the kill."

"I'm still here," I reminded them both sharply. "Let me out, and I'll come back." I ignored Cannon as he turned his head to look at me, but for some reason, my attention was on Royce only. "I'm a complete security issue. You know the men go wild and stupid, and it's just a complete nightmare for you to handle. Really, do you want to fight your own pack over the likes of me? No, it's stupid. If you let me out, I'll run it out of my system, and then I'll come right back."

"You'll come right back?" Cannon asked dryly.

I kept my eyes on Royce as I answered the sarcastic twat beside him. "Yup. You won't even miss me."

I saw Royce's lips twitch as he looked away. "I'll get some of the pack on the deer. How many? One or two?"

Cannon gave a small nod, and my instinct to run was overshadowed by the thought of two juicy deer being my next meal.

"Two?" I asked him, hating how hopeful I sounded.

"Two," he confirmed, his face once more unreadable. "You need to do one thing first."

"No."

His head cocked to the side, a sly grin playing about his lips in a challenge. "Chicken, pup?"

"Fuck you."

"We can do that if you prefer."

I gaped at him. "Wh-what?"

Cannon gave a careless shrug. "It makes no difference to me if you eat first or fuck first. Either way, you still need to do one thing."

"I'm *not* having sex with anyone in this pack. I'm definitely not having sex with you!" When he said nothing, I stepped back, my knees hitting the cot as I put as much distance as I could between the alpha and myself—a tricky thing to accomplish when trapped in a cage.

"You need to shift," he spoke as if he hadn't witnessed my retreat.

"No."

"Pup, you need to shift. You need to regain control, and the only way to do that is to shift."

"I said no. I'm in control."

We were locked in a stare-off.

"You're weak," he told me calmly.

"You starved me," I answered back, just as coolly.

"You have not been starved," he answered. "She needs to come forward."

And I realized what they had been doing. What *he* had made them do. "You thought by keeping her hungry, she would take over?" I gaped at him. "That's barbaric!"

"You killed three men!" he growled back. "*That's* barbaric!"

"They were going to rape me! And then kill or torture me or both. That fucker shot me three times." I was so angry I was gasping for air. "If I killed Bullet, then he deserved it."

"So you did know them?" Cannon asked me, his look shrewd. "Who were they to you?"

But I was too angry to talk to him. I was too angry at being in this cage. I was too angry he had tried to force the shift this way. It was cruel and unnecessary.

"I want you to go," I told him, purposefully sitting on the cot, my back to him, staring at the darkness.

"You are not in charge here, pup. You're not even in charge within yourself," he added with a scoff.

"Just *leave*," I whispered, but I knew he heard me. I could feel the pain starting in my gut. "I can't let this happen with you here."

"Your heat will come on quicker if you are hungry, angry, or with need," he told me flatly as he stayed behind me. "You're all three, pup."

I heard others come in, and the scent of blood filled my nose. I don't know if they heard my moan, but I heard the sound of the cell door opening, and when I turned, he was in the cell with me.

Cannon appeared bigger than before. His muscles were more defined, his hair longer, and his eyes a deeper green that held me captive.

"The only way out is past me," he told me, pulling off his shirt, and I hated how quickly I drank in his naked flesh. I felt an uncomfortable throbbing between my legs, which only intensified as I watched him toss his shirt behind him.

His feet were bare, and his dark jeans hung too low, showing off his every sculpted muscle. His body was such a distraction that as he walked toward me, I didn't even register that a deer was being dragged into the cell behind him. A different hunger rode my needs now.

The cell wasn't big when I was in it alone, but with him in it, I couldn't get enough air.

Somewhere deep inside me, rational, sarcastic Kezia was reminding me I was in an open-bar cell, and suffocation was the least of my worries.

All I could see was the alpha male in front of me, who my body was burning for.

"Leave us," he murmured, and I heard the sound of the cell door closing as he stood over me, my heart racing as he looked down at me with hooded eyes.

"Get on your knees," he commanded me softly, and I scrambled into position on the cot, the mattress firm enough underneath me.

Even on the cot as I rested on my knees, he towered over me.

"How many heats have passed since you left the peak?" His finger ran along my jaw, dipping under my chin, tilting my head back farther to look at him.

"I don't know," I answered truthfully. "My first one was when I was there, then I missed one, maybe two, so this could be my third...maybe my fourth?"

His thumb rubbed over my bottom lip gently, a flare of heat in his eyes as my tongue darted out and licked it. "You don't know?" he asked, withdrawing his thumb, his knuckles tracing over my cheek before his fingers slid into my hair, tightening there as he held my head firm. "You haven't had a full heat yet. That's why they're coming so quickly to you when you're in your human form."

That made sense. Each time, I had shifted to my wolf, and then when I was human again, the pain and desires were gone.

Cannon leaned down to me. "How many men have you let fuck you?" His grip tightened slightly. "How many humans have been between those legs?"

"None," my voice was a whisper. I was completely enthralled with him as he stared down at me, and I once more saw the heat in his eyes at my confession.

"And in the wild?"

I shook my head slightly. "Never." I swallowed against the lump in my throat.

His mouth claimed mine. He didn't hesitate or ask permission, and I didn't want him to. My mouth opened as he kissed me, his tongue sliding against mine as I scrambled off my knees to meet his kiss. With my hands digging into his shoulders, I hardly noticed when he effortlessly lifted me off the cot, my legs wrapping around his waist as he pushed me against the cell bars.

Cannon's hands gripped my ass as we kissed, his lower body pushing into where I desperately needed to feel him. His lips left mine, trailing hungrily along my jaw, down my neck, nipping at my shoulder, and then he pushed my shirt open. The flannel shirt had been cleaned and returned, but I heard his growl as he ripped it open more with one hand. His mouth covered my breast, his teeth and tongue finding my nipple effortlessly, and my groan as he stroked over it had him murmuring his approval.

My heat was untamed.

My body was on fire, and every stroke of his tongue, touch of his fingers, and kiss of his lips only fueled the flames.

He switched to the other breast, and the fire burned hotter within me. "Luna," I whispered hoarsely as he sucked on my breasts.

I felt his hand glide along the inside of my thigh, reaching the apex of my thighs, where no one other than me had ever touched before. A light stroke over my sex had me gripping him tighter. The fire within me burned hotter as my blood felt like it boiled through my veins.

"Cannon!" I groaned as his finger stroked over me again. A touch so light had me crying out for more, my moan quickly smothered as he kissed me again. Strong, sure fingers brushed over me skillfully as his mouth claimed me.

Cannon drew his head back, his eyes meeting mine. I saw the heat and desire, so it confused me when he pulled away as I tried to capture his lips with mine.

"What?" I gasped, squirming as his fingers slowed, then his hand was on my thigh. "No, I need—"

"Shift."

I'd let my guard down.

I'd let my control slip.

In my state of arousal, I'd lost my hold on her.

My wolf knew it.

When he commanded me to shift again as he lowered my legs to the cell floor and stepped back away from me, I knew I'd lost as she broke free.

CHAPTER 18
Cannon

As she lay on the cot, I watched her sleeping.

Thick blonde hair so light it looked white made her skin appear paler, sicker. The girl looked like a day in the sunshine would kill her, like the vampire myths humans liked to invent.

She'd been sleeping for hours, and had I not been able to hear her breathing, I would have checked her pulse a long time ago. It didn't help she hadn't moved from where her wolf had relinquished control.

I knew shifters. I was an alpha, for Luna's sake, but her wolf... I grit my teeth as my jaw clenched hard. Her wolf was as wild and untamed as she was. It barely acknowledged an alpha command—I'd had to put my Will on her three times to yield to me.

Three fucking times.

And still, I could see the defiance in every movement as she submitted.

My wolf was restless within me. I hadn't let him come forth as I battled the defiant fighter in front of me. I was an alpha. I was strong, and my Will in human form was enough.

It was a cruel thing to force another to do something against their will. My father had abused his power in the pack, which is why I didn't do it, and I sure as hell never broke my pack's will as a wolf.

My pack respected me as their leader. Their alpha.

But the girl in front of me, who couldn't weigh more than a hundred and ten pounds soaking wet, had pushed me further than anyone—man or wolf—to wanting to bring my wolf forth and crush her defiance with my will.

I heard Royce come into the room and walked up to stand beside me. I didn't need to see his face to feel his worry. We were pack.

"She still out?" he asked in surprise. I felt him turn to look at the remains of the two deer. "At least her belly is full."

Royce was my beta, my second-in-command. For all his size and brawn, he was a huge softie. Being a husband and father of two girls, he had struggled the most with my plan to weaken Kezia.

"She's going to be louder and shriller when she wakes," I reminded him. "Don't be too pleased she's finally full just yet."

He gave a soft grunt but said nothing further. We'd both witnessed the white wolf devour the deer. Her coat had been half red by the time she was sated. The overriding hunger had taken precedence over her other needs. When I commanded her to shift and stepped back to show her the deer, I'd taken a gamble.

Thank the Goddess it paid off.

It was not my desire to bring harm to either of them. Had the wolf still been riding her heat, it could have turned violent. As it was, all I had to prepare for now was Kezia's fury when she woke.

And she would be furious.

"You're smiling," Royce said beside me. "You're anticipating the fallout?"

"She's quite vicious with her words," I told him with a low chuckle. "I think she swears more than I do."

Royce snorted in answer. "Your brother is glaring at everyone who looks at him," he changed the subject.

My smile faded. "He doesn't understand."

"Because you never told him why."

"He doesn't need to know." I heard him inhale and knew he was about to start lecturing. "Beta..." I spoke softly. "This is my choice."

Royce rolled his head on his shoulders rather than answer, and I knew he was fighting back his frustration. I understood why he was pissed, but just because I understood didn't mean I would change my mind.

"Did you link with her?" he asked, changing the subject again. It was a reason why he was my second—he knew what battles to fight and what ones to leave alone.

"She resisted complete surrender," I told him, checking over my shoulder to make sure we were alone. "She's so fucking strong," I added with a frown. "Too strong for an eighteen-year-old girl."

I felt the side-eye this time. "Her age didn't stop you from almost bedding her in a cell," he reprimanded me.

I knew I'd taken it too far. I didn't need his reminder that I'd almost fucked her then and there. She was like the sweetest nectar. Her scent was intoxicating, and her heat...*fuck*...her heat made me want to rip off her clothes and pound into her untouched body until we were both exhausted and spent.

"I needed her to lose control," I reminded him coolly. "Once the control went, I knew the wolf would surface."

His *harrumph* spoke volumes. "She didn't submit, but did she at *least* communicate?"

I nodded slowly. "She did. She's protective." I looked at him with a grin. "She's not a fan of either of us." Rubbing my forehead, I sighed. "She's been hunted by men, which we knew. Fighting for money, which we knew." I watched her sleep. So peaceful. So innocent-looking. "She said nothing about the men she killed."

"Nothing?" Royce asked in a sharp whisper.

"Nothing. When I asked, she shifted back to Kezia," I admitted. "I made her shift two more times, but each time, she shifted back."

"Then you need to use your Will on her."

"I did." I anticipated his protest. "No. I will never use the wolf's Will on an innocent. I am not *him*."

"Cannon? She took three human lives."

"There's more to the story," I told him. "I know there is." I was sure of it. I just didn't know what. "She said to me in the cell earlier, before I made her shift, that *if* she killed Bullet. Why *if*?"

"She's trying to place doubt in your mind?" He nudged my arm for me to look at him. "And from the sound of it, it's working."

"I don't think she was aware," I told him my suspicion quietly. "*If* her wolf did it, I don't think she was conscious of it."

"We aren't separate entities," Royce reminded me gruffly. "We exist as *one*."

"What if *she* doesn't?" I countered. "What if they *are* separate, and they coexist?" I gestured toward her still-sleeping form. "What if she's never melded to her wolf?"

Royce gaped at me. "That's insanity. The mind and spirit

combine at the first shift. She's eighteen years old. They can't exist apart."

"I know," I said with a nod. "But I think she's different." I glanced at him, seeing my oldest friend struggling to accept the possibility. "I need the human here."

"Are you insane?"

"She was with a man the night we caught her. He runs the fighting rings. He knows more than he let on when we questioned him the first time. Bring him to me."

"I am *not* bringing a human into packlands."

I turned to face him head-on. "Do you want me to leave her while I go down and get him myself? She's newly fed, her wolf's hold is back, and she's going to be livid when she wakes up. And her heat is bound to come back." I held my hands up in mock surrender. "I mean, I'm eager to avoid the conversation about kissing her, so if that's what you'd prefer, to fight off the pack as they fight to get to her, then, just say…"

With narrowed eyes, he took a step back. "You owe me for this. *Huge.* And when I come back, you better have another cell ready, because no human is seeing where my children live."

"Take Nikan."

Royce opened his mouth to protest, but instead, he turned on his heel and marched out of the barn.

I *would* owe him. Probably huge.

My focus returned to her, and I stood leaning against a wall and waited for her to wake. Then, hours later, her arm moved, and her hand was raised to scratch her cheek.

"Cannon…" she murmured as she moved slightly on the cot.

I almost choked in surprise at the wistful sound of my name on her lips, hating how much I wanted to hear her murmur my name that way again.

Her head turned toward me, her eyelids fluttering open as ice-blue eyes found me immediately, pinpointing me effortlessly as I stood in the dark. "Cannon, you dirty bastard...what the fuck did you do to me?"

CHAPTER 19

Kezia

WHY WAS I SO AWARE IF I WAS SO DEEPLY ASLEEP? Curled in a ball, my hands tucked under my face as I lay there, I could feel her moving as I remembered what happened.

He stood back, away from her, giving her room. The alpha was backing away from her? Then I saw her see the deer at the same time as I did. Her focus shifted to the blood trickling from the wound, and puncture marks on its neck that were not hers allowed blood to spill.

Wasted.

Her hunger took over. She would have knocked the alpha aside if he hadn't been quick to move. Blood filled her mouth as she fed. I could feel her satisfaction as she took her fill of the fresh meat. He'd starved her on purpose. Not to make her weak, *us* weak, like I had thought. He'd done it so I would be closer to losing control.

What had he said?

Your heat will come on quicker if you are hungry, angry, or with need.

I'd been all three. He had engineered it so I was all three. Even buried deep in my wolf's mind, I knew why he had tricked me. He tricked me with his body and *lured* me in with his scent. I'd heard tales that an alpha's scent could be just as potent as a female's in heat. I had never believed it. Of course, that scummy bastard would use his alpha power to seduce me.

When I got control back, I was going to rip his throat out.

Sitting up, I watched her as she fed. She'd taken as much as she wanted from the first deer. The second was dead but still warm. She moved onto it, using the wounds from the kill to tear the hide away from the flesh. Her savagery as she fed told me how hungry she was. As I watched her eat her favorite parts first, I was reminded how fierce my wolf was. I wasn't squeamish—I was a shifter—but something was nauseating me as I watched her eat the heart, liver, and lungs.

I turned my head away. The blood, the ripping of flesh from bone, and memories that weren't mine surfaced. I saw the terror in their eyes as she dismembered them and the snaps of their bones as she killed them.

Sleep.

My awareness jerked me around, and I saw her looking back at me. Golden amber eyes watched me, her muzzle thick with blood, her nose shiny and wet.

You need to shift. I tried to sound forceful to convince myself I was in control. *He tricked you.*

He tricked you, she said with a huff. *I waited.*

Well, now I felt all kinds of stupid. Even my wolf had known what the good-looking asswipe had been doing. *It doesn't matter,* I snapped angrily. *You're letting him win!*

Her eyes held an ancient wisdom I knew I didn't possess. *Sleep, child,* she commanded. I was already lying down becoming less aware. *No harm will come to you.*

THE ALPHA WAS in front of me. He'd covered all the toned muscle the human liked to look at and then pretended she wasn't. He was in control of his Will. I could see the wolf behind his eyes, but he wasn't using his true *alpha Will. The man was strong. Not just in muscles, but his brain was sharp. His wolf was stronger, and* him *I wanted to see.*

"Why did you kill the humans?" he asked again.

He asked mundane questions, questions the child would have answered had he asked her better. He kept questioning about the males we'd killed. He didn't need to know that it was over. Done. We would do it again. Each time he made me submit, we'd done it. But in this, he wasn't strong enough without his wolf's Will too.

He never called his wolf forth. A weakness?

Why would he show me his weakness? It didn't matter why. We would remember. All weaknesses were ours to exploit.

Luna, it felt like I'd been asleep for days. My belly was full, and as I slowly awakened, I rubbed my cheek absently, remembering the feeling of his knuckles over my skin.

Cannon.

My body remembered how I'd responded to him. The way he touched me, kissed me, used his mouth and hands. My wolf huffed, and I glared at her.

You were no use, I scolded. *You seemed to enjoy it.*

She'd shifted. I was back in my human form. How? Warily, I eyed her, but her head was on her paws, her eyes closed. I needed answers, but she was quite obviously telling me I had to wait. I wanted to press, but then I caught the scent of him.

Cedarwood and nutmeg.

How dare he smell like that. Opening my eyes, I found him in the darkness. I couldn't see him clearly, but I knew where he stood.

"Cannon, you dirty bastard. What the fuck did you do to me?"

"You're finally awake," he drawled, walking forward. He wore the same jeans as before, his feet were still bare, but a long-sleeved T-shirt covered him. I had a fleeting pang of disappointment he was no longer shirtless until I remembered he had purposefully seduced me.

Sitting up, I swung my legs over the cot's edge, pausing when I saw the fresh sheet on it. I was in another pair of sweatpants and a white tank.

"Who dressed me?" I demanded as I stood.

"You're complaining that we put clothes *on* you?"

The sly smirk on his face made me want to punch him. Repeatedly.

"I hate you, you know that, right?" Pushing myself off the cot, I didn't expect my legs to feel weak, and as I tried to catch myself from swaying, I overcompensated, causing myself to stagger instead.

"With your heat gone, I thought you'd be over wanting to fall at my feet," he taunted, and my look of anger was met with one of amusement.

"You tricked me," I bit out. Smoothing my hands over my hair, ignoring my momentary panic about what it looked like, I met his stare with a calm coolness I wish I'd woken up with.

"Did I?" He relaxed his stance. For him, that was legs wide

apart, arms crossed, and shoulders dropped, free of tension. To anyone else, he looked like he was standing at attention, but I knew he was at ease.

How did I know that? Maybe my wolf did, but when I checked in with her, she was asleep, probably overstuffed from all that deer meat. *Hog*. An eyelid opened, and she fixed me with an amber eye before closing it again.

You're still a hog.

"Pup?"

My attention snapped back to Cannon, my eyes already narrowing in a glare. "Don't call me that." Looking down at my clothes again, I tugged the hem of my shirt. "Whose is this?"

"Pack."

"Did you trick *her* out of her clothes too?"

A lazy grin appeared. "You sound jealous, pup."

"In your dreams." We stared at each other as I struggled to control my body's reaction to him. "So?" I avoided looking at him, my attention on anything but him. "Did you get what you wanted?" I crossed my arms over my chest, mirroring his pose, and hastily adjusted my stance, my arms dropping to my sides. "I shifted, I'm back, all is good. Can I get out now?"

"No."

I kept my focus on his bare feet. Why were his feet bare? Why did I think he looked sexy with jeans, a T-shirt, and bare feet? Feet had never interested me before.

"Do my feet interest you that much?" I could hear his laughter, and what's worse, I could feel my wolf snuffle with laughter too.

"I need answers," I opted to change the subject. "You tricked me, you used me, and you did it in a shitty way."

"Again, with the tricking accusation? How did I trick you,

pup?" He moved closer to the cell, and I knew I couldn't look at him. "Tell me."

"You know you did, I know you did, so just tell me why."

"I kissed you." He was closer. "You kissed me. There was no trick." He was now in front of the cage. "I can come in there and demonstrate how quick you are to kiss me, pup."

I jerked my head up to see his cocky smirk. "Stay away from me." With as much dignity as I could muster, I gave him my back as I went to the cot and sat.

With me sitting and Cannon so tall, he towered over me. That had not been my intent, but now I was committed to sitting, and standing would only amuse him.

"You said I was scared to shift," I spoke reasonably. Calmly. "I shifted. You fed my wolf, and I'm human again. Now you see I'm in control. Let me out."

"No."

He was equally calm and reasonable, and I had a nagging suspicion he could maintain this façade a lot longer than I could.

"Why?" I even forced a fake smile. "I'm no threat."

Cannon snorted, and I watched as he shook his head slightly. "You're dangerous."

"Are you scared of me?" I mocked him. "I think your thigh is thicker than my waistline."

Cannon gave me a flat stare. "You are a trained fighter, you are a hunter, and more importantly, pup, you are a killer."

"We're all hunters," I snarled. "We're shifters. If we don't hunt, we don't eat. Shifters are *killers* by nature."

"The blood on *your* hands is human." He saw my wince as he spoke, but carried on regardless. "The shifters in my pack *are* hunters and fighters, but no one in my pack has killed three men and has a national manhunt searching for them."

"I told you I was defending myself." I stared at my hands. "Is your pack not allowed to defend themselves against those who would cause them harm?"

"Yes. They can. And any shifter who was in *control* would have fought their way free and *ran*."

Lifting my head, I met his glare. "So you encourage cowards in your pack?" I challenged him, holding his stare.

His sneer was ugly. "A coward is someone who uses their speed, strength, and supernatural powers to their advantage over a weaker opponent."

My brother would say the same, and the thought of Kris knowing what I did filled me with a heavy sadness. He'd be so disappointed in me. Would he understand? Would anyone?

"He shot me three times, then he kicked me in the face, knocking me out," I whispered, breaking his stare. "I came to in the back of a truck. The guy they had me with, he was going to..." I swallowed past the lump in my throat. "He was going to use me. They said..." I took another breath as I remembered my fear.

"They were going to rape you," Cannon finished for me, and even though he had gentled his voice, the tone was still hard. "I believe you. I know what men can do." His heavy sigh made me glance at him, staring at the far wall, his expression unreadable. "But you are not just a woman, pup." He turned his head to look at me. "You are stronger than them, quicker, and you are *more* than human."

I dropped my head from his stare. "I was hurt and scared." I felt the tears fall. "I was alone. There were three of them, and I'd fought Bullet. I knew he was strong and fast." Angrily, I wiped my eyes. "I was weak. I wasn't healing, I had blood loss, was *weak* in a corner, and I didn't know how to get out."

"So you shifted? When you know pack law expressly forbids it."

My eyes closed against his words. Wearily, I lifted my head and met the cold stare of an alpha. "Pack law?" I asked, my top lip curling upward. "As I lay in that back seat with a filthy man's hand on my jeans button and their intent obvious that they were going to use me until I broke, you know what I remembered, *Alpha*?"

"What?"

I stood slowly, wiping my eyes dry as I stepped forward, looking up at him through the bars. "That I was no longer *pack*." He didn't react. "So I let her come forward, and I ripped out his filthy throat."

"His? What did you do to the others?"

I looked away. "The same."

"Did you?" I heard him move. "Pup?"

I turned away from him. "I ripped out their throats."

The cell door opened, and I stiffened as I heard him enter the cage. Large hands landed on my shoulders, and I was gently turned to face him.

"Look at me," he commanded softly.

Reluctantly, I raised my head. "Come to try your seduction tricks on me again?"

"Stop that." His finger pressed against my lips. "Tell me how you killed them, Kezia." I jerked my head away, but he grabbed the nape of my neck, holding me firm. "How did you kill them?" he pressed.

"Painfully."

I saw the reprimand in his eyes. "The truth, pup."

"Why does it matter?" I asked, searching his stern eyes for a sign of understanding. "It was me or them. Would you rather it be them?"

"Never," he answered quickly. "But you need to tell me what you did."

We stared at each other, the heat between our bodies a distraction I didn't need. I didn't need him so close to me, touching me.

"I told you, I killed them. I ripped out their throats."

"And dismembered them."

I gulped. "And I dismembered them." I nodded firmly, hating the burning in my eyes as I waited for his judgment, remembering the strewn body parts from where I'd ripped them apart.

"Who did you kill first?"

"What does it matter?" I shouted, breaking free of his hold, my temper snapping. "I killed them! I ripped them apart, right? I did everything you judge me for!"

"Who did you kill first?" he insisted, his voice even and tempered.

"Bullet."

"You're lying." He gave a heavy sigh, taking a step back. "Why? Why lie? You admitted you killed them, so why are you lying about how you did it?"

"What kind of sick freak are you that you need the details?" I bit back, my defenses raised as I returned his glare.

"What kind of sick freak am *I*?" He scoffed. "I'm not the one who tore them limb from limb, pup! I'm not the one who *toyed* with them as I prolonged their deaths."

Toyed with them? I flinched at his angry words.

"Just...stop it." I turned my head away so I couldn't see the condemnation.

"Stop it? Why? You don't want to hear it? Why, Kezia? Why would I...unless..." I heard him take another step back, and I turned to look at him. "That's it, isn't it?" His hands curled into fists, his attention on the darkness beyond the cage. "You don't know, do you?" Cannon cursed, and I watched as he rubbed the back of his neck. "Were you aware?"

I blinked, not understanding. "What?"

He looked at me in resignation. "Were *you* aware, or did you black out completely?"

My throat closed, and I took a step back.

I couldn't tell him.

I couldn't admit it.

I would *never* admit it.

"For fuck's sake, Kezia, *tell* me."

"I have nothing else to say." I sat on the cot. "Keep me in this cell. I don't care."

"If you don't let me help you, I have to report it. You'll be tried in front of Pack Council."

Drawing my knees up to my chin, I turned my head to look away from him. My wolf raised her head, and watched me steadily, her amber eyes glowing with a strength I wasn't feeling.

"I don't need help. Not from you." She looked at me, strong enough for both of us. "We never did."

CHAPTER 20
Kezia

IT HAD BEEN TWO DAYS SINCE I SAW MR. MEAN AND Moody. After our confrontation in the cell, he had left when I refused to say anything else. I knew I pushed him, but he never forced it from me.

Why would he? He knew as well as I did that I'd lost control of everything that day in the clearing. I wouldn't be surprised if he knew more than I did about what I had done, what she had done.

No. What *we* had done.

Cannon wanted me to say it out loud. Admit I lost control, blacked out, and gone rogue.

Well, he could want. I would never admit it. They would need to force it from me.

I was also missing my normal servers. Royce and Nikan were conspicuous in their absence too. Instead, I had a new guy—older, gruffer who refused to make eye contact with me as if I was some form of demon that could entrap him with a single look.

Because I was a petty, moody teenager locked in a cell, I took great delight in taunting him, making strange noises and babbling in gibberish just to mess with him.

He lasted two meal trays, and then Cannon was back. He crossed the floor, his look telling me he knew exactly what I'd been doing. He opened the cell door and unceremoniously dumped the tray on the floor, the soup spilling over the sides of the bowl.

"Asshole," I hissed, racing across the floor to grab my dinner before he tipped the tray over just for spite. Picking up the bowl, I drank from it, grabbing a spoon, watching him watch me as I backed away with my dinner. The thick broth was delicious.

"I'm the asshole?" He scoffed. "Wyatt is refusing to come into the *possessed shes den*."

I stopped drinking, my head bent as I picked up the spoon, my hair hiding my grin. "Who's Wyatt?"

"You're being a brat."

I lifted the heavy-loaded spoonful of broth and winked at him as I ate.

"Anterrio Pack should be ashamed of themselves if this is the caliber of their young," he muttered, slamming the cell door shut. He turned to leave, and I realized I didn't want him to go.

"You've been gone?"

Cannon turned to look at me over his shoulder. "Have I?"

I gave him a look that told him exactly what I thought of his subterfuge. "Where's Nikan? Royce? Where've you been?"

Turning, he adopted his usual stance. I felt a thrill of pleasure as his biceps bulged. *Thank you, Luna.*

"What are you looking at?" Cannon looked down at his shirt in confusion.

"Huh?" I drank from the bowl, hiding my horror at being caught. "Eating," I told him as I chewed the chicken in the broth.

"I don't believe you."

Snorting, I finished my soup and went back to my tray. "Tell me something I don't know." When I lifted the lid off the plate, I grinned when I saw the roast meat and mashed potatoes and eagerly grabbed a stalk of broccoli. "Ugh, I never thought I would be so happy to see vegetables."

"You're one of the strangest creatures I've ever met."

"Thanks." I cut into the meat, taking a huge forkful. "This is so good," I told him as I chewed.

"Whoever made this, tell them I love them."

"Love?" he asked in amusement. "We only kissed once."

I stopped midchew, staring at the food on my plate and then at him. "You made this?"

His head tilted to the side as I cautiously sniffed my meal. "If I wanted to poison you, pup, I would have done it weeks ago."

"You cooked?" I really wanted to put the plate down, but the smell of it had me salivating. My hand moved of its own accord as I scooped mashed potatoes onto my fork. "Are you shitting me?"

"No."

I squinted at him as I ate more. "I've never seen an alpha cook."

"Then you've known some shitty alphas," he said dryly, turning to leave.

"Bale is decent," I blurted. "He runs a good pack."

"The pack that turned their back on you? The pack that never accepted you? The pack who never looked for you once when your brother helped you escape?"

He was at the door.

"The pack that took us in when our parents were *murdered*," I said to him, the food souring in my stomach. I hadn't said one word of my brother's suspicions since I had been here. Let's face it, I had a lot on my plate, but as he taunted me about my previous pack, I couldn't stop my tongue from blurting out things I knew I should keep to myself.

"Murdered? Ever asked yourself *why* they took you in?" he sneered as he stepped outside. The door was closed before I found my voice again.

I spent the night pacing my cell. The question turned over and over in my head, and no answer was forthcoming. Why would he imply my old pack had something to do with this? Is that what he was implying? I was lying down on my cot before I even noticed the spotlight was off.

I stood and looked around. I could see the whole barn. My wolf came forward, and we shared a look.

It's been like this since you woke up this morning.

It had?

Why hadn't I noticed? Why was I so blind to what was in front of me?

"What's he playing at?" I asked her out loud.

The hunt for him is over.

"Oh." He had what he wanted? He knew what had happened, so he didn't need to hide anymore. That made no sense. "I don't understand."

Males are confusing. She tossed her head. *Alpha males are worse.*

I couldn't argue with *that*.

"I should have noticed I was no longer under a spotlight," I griped. "I'm supposed to be on my guard, and I didn't notice the lights were on?" I gave her a reproachful look. "You could have told me."

Why? I was aware. You are blind to much when he is in the room or when you are thinking about why he is not in the room.

Stating the obvious wouldn't help either. "Shut up."

She shook her head again. *I wish to run.*

"In case you haven't noticed, we're not in an open space."

Get the male. Give him what he wants. Let us out.

"No."

She huffed as she lay down. *You did not mind his taste before, do it again.*

My cheeks flamed red. "I am not kissing him again," I hissed at her. "Where's your pride?"

She kept silent, but I knew it was different for wolves. My attraction, *bleurgh, I hated saying it,* but my attraction to the arrogant alpha was very much a human thing. She wouldn't understand that the possibility of Cannon rejecting me was a crippling fear. That he only kissed me the first time to trick me.

What was I saying? I didn't want to kiss him. He was gorgeous. No, he was insufferable, *not* gorgeous. It was bad enough he was my first kiss—he didn't get to be any of my other *firsts.*

Ever.

Looking around the barn, I noticed something I had been blind to all day. There were no windows in this barn. The walls weren't wood. They were steel.

I wasn't in a barn.

I was in a room.

I inhaled deeply. The air was slightly stale.

"We're underground?"

Stop seeing the male when you close your eyes. You'll see more with your eyes open.

Suitably reprimanded, I turned in a circle one more time. "Does his pack know I'm here?" I wondered out loud. I bet my dinner they didn't. I sat on the bed with a heavy thump.

He was hiding me from them?

To protect them?

Or to protect me?

The thought surprised me.

Why would Cannon protect me? He thought I was a murdering rogue. He threatened me with the Council. But he had never said they were coming. He never told my brother he had me.

If the alpha of the Blackridge Peak Pack had reported me for my crime, my brother would know. Kris would be here. My brother would find me. I had no doubt.

Which meant Cannon was keeping him from me. Did he think Kris would insist he free me into his guardianship? He was blood. Blood *could* trump pack. All my brother had to do was take responsibility for me.

Biting my lip, I looked at the door in the corner.

The issue of whether my brother would take me until my trial wasn't even a question. I knew he would. Kris would never pass up the opportunity to berate me for the mess I got myself into. I also knew my brother wouldn't be as quick to condemn me for the deaths of three humans.

They weren't innocent. I had smelled the evil on their bodies.

Everything Cannon had said to me was true. A shifter could have gotten away from them. But they had shot me. Three times. Once in each leg and once in the shoulder.

"Wounding me where I would feel it most if I shifted." My bitterness said out loud made me look down at my legs, and then I *heard* what I had just said.

Pushing the sweatpants down, I looked at the white scars on my legs from the bullets.

"You bastard," I whispered in the quiet of the room. I was on my feet, at the bars, yelling for him.

"Cannon!" I felt my wolf stir, but I ignored her. "*Cannon!*"

I screamed myself hoarse until finally, the door opened, and he walked in, irritation flashing across his face. I wasn't surprised to see Royce with him.

"Are you trying to wake your ancestors?" Cannon snapped at me. "I swear to fuck, if you tell me you're hungry, I will smack your ass myself."

"They shot me with silver."

He came to an abrupt halt as he looked at me, the question in his eyes.

"They shot me in the calf, then they shot me again in the shoulder, the opposite side. Bullet shot me a third time in my leg." Pulling my shirt to the side, I pointed at the scar on my shoulder. "I'm a *wolf*. I don't scar." Turning, I pointed to my legs, not caring I was flashing my ass at them.

"Look," I spoke over my shoulder to them. Cannon stepped forward, his stare intent. I turned to face them both. "The aim was to make me *lame*, so even if I shifted, the silver would slow me down." I didn't realize I was pressed up to the bars. "Cannon, they knew what I was."

"How?"

"I don't know. I didn't fucking tell them!"

"Stop screeching, pup. I never said you did," he barked back at me.

"Do you believe me?" I demanded, looking between them. "Also, where have you been?" I asked Royce.

"One thing at a time," Royce grumbled. He looked me over. "Turn again."

I did as he asked, this time pulling the shirt over my ass as I felt them both approach. I ignored Cannon's huff of amusement at my not-so-subtle attempt at modesty.

"Make sure the door is locked," Cannon spoke to Royce, and I heard the cell door open. He was in the same space as me again. Not that the room wasn't the same space, but there were usually bars between us.

My heartbeat picked up. I saw his knowing smirk, and I dropped my gaze as I tried to calm myself. This was stupid. He was just a shifter. I'd been around shifters all my life.

"Lift your leg," he instructed, and I did as he asked, my teeth biting hard on my lip when he stroked his hand over my calf.

With a light touch, he circled the wound. *Luna help me, my legs felt like jelly.* I breathed out slowly when he lowered my left leg, but when his hand gripped my upper thigh, I had to bite back a moan.

"She's right. Look," he said. "Don't touch her," he scolded Royce sharply.

I turned my head to look down at him, my lips parted in surprise. Cannon glanced up at me but said nothing.

"Why didn't you mention this before?" he asked me, his thumb pressing into the circle-shaped scar left by the bullet hole.

"I didn't realize until just now," I admitted. "You believe me?"

"Turn."

I did, quickly. His face was level with my panties, and I almost swallowed my tongue as I felt his sharp exhale against the thin material. Cannon pushed to his feet, his chest rubbing across my breasts. I stepped back reflexively, but he grabbed my arm and held me still.

"Stay," he commanded softly. I couldn't hide the shiver when his fingers trailed over my skin to my shoulder. "This is small."

I went to speak, but the sudden dryness in my mouth made me cough. "Sorry," I spluttered. "Exit wound. He shot me from behind."

"Chickenshit," Royce grunted, and I'd completely forgotten he was in the cell with us.

Cannon moved me slightly, his body pressed against mine as he half twisted us so he could see the wound. "Fuckers," he hissed, his finger rubbing over my skin.

"I've never seen it myself," Royce spoke to his alpha. "Thought it was one of the crazier myths humans made up." He glanced at me. "Did it hurt any differently?"

I shook my head. "I've never been shot before," I told him, lifting my hand to rub my shoulder. "It burned and was hot. But that could be normal?" I shrugged. "When I came to in the truck…" My voice dropped as I spoke to him, ignoring the male who stood beside me, pressing into my side, supporting me as I leaned into him reflexively. "I was drowsy and not healing. I could feel the blood loss and knew how weak I was."

Royce's eyes flickered with sympathy. "Why didn't you notice this?"

I thought he was talking to me, but I felt Cannon stiffen. "I thought it was her." I almost interrupted when he carried on. "She's so pale skinned, she looks like sunlight would kill her."

"You are very pale," Royce told me with a slight smile. He let out a loud sigh. "I know little to nothing about silver bullets," he admitted. "Should I get Doc?"

"No."

I looked up at him and saw him staring down at me. "How many times were you shot, pup?"

It felt wrong to be called pup when I was half naked in his arms, and I tried to move free of his hold, but Cannon merely tightened his grip.

"I just told you," I answered with a glare. "Three times."

"In the leg."

"Why do you do that?" I demanded. "Why make it like I lie? You heard me quite clearly tell you once in the calf, once in the thigh, and once in the shoulder."

He held my stare. I knew he knew I was strung too tight as his fingers caressed my skin, his actions in contrast to the hardness of his stare.

"Three times," Cannon murmured, and my head dropped with heaviness when his fingers massaged the back of my neck. Deft fingers pulled my hair over my shoulder, his breath on my neck causing me to shiver once more.

"Should I, um…leave you two?" Royce asked, stepping back.

"Stay." The alpha command was sharp. He turned me so quickly I would have stumbled had he not pressed my back against his chest, his arm circled my waist, holding me in place. I felt him push my head down. "Three times," he repeated. "You sure?"

"Humans have things called hearing aids…you should get one," I snarked at him, the fogginess of him holding me clearing.

"I hear you just fine, pup," he said with amusement. "You had no other wounds when you woke?"

I hesitated. I didn't know. I had been out of this form for so long after the attack I could have been black and blue and wouldn't know.

"Kezia?" he demanded sharply.

"Why?" I snapped back. "What are you looking at?"

"A scar," Royce told me, trying to ease the tension between us.

Cannon let me go, and I turned to face them both. "A scar?"

He was angry. I could feel his temper riding his emotions. "They shot you three times? You're clear on that?" I nodded. It wasn't good enough for him. "Ask her."

How many times? Three?

She nodded.

"Three," I confirmed.

Cannon stepped back, hands on his hips as he watched me. "Then who the fuck shot you first?"

"First?"

"Lift your hair," he demanded. I automatically complied. Even my sassy self knew not to push him right now. "Royce, come here."

The other man walked closer, reached out, and I jumped when Cannon snarled. "Don't *touch* her."

"I'm not contagious, asshole," I hissed at him, my cheeks flaming.

"Shut up," Cannon growled at me, but I felt the gentle sweep of his fingers against my shoulder.

"This one is paler," he told Royce, stroking the back of my neck. "Older?"

I felt Royce at my back. "Turn her to the light. I need to see her shoulder."

"I can move," I grumbled when Cannon moved me slightly. They both ignored me.

"It's definitely paler, but I don't know if that means older. You would miss it if you didn't know to look for it." Royce stood back. "Doc might know."

"Go."

I lowered my arms, my hair falling down my back as I turned to look at the alpha. He was watching me, his face closed off, his arms at his sides, his fingers curled into fists.

"Why are you mad at me now?" I asked, bending to pick up my sweatpants. My cry of alarm caught in my throat as he moved with speed only a shifter possessed.

I was pushed up against the bars, his head in the crook of my neck.

"Whoa," I choked out, my fingers digging into his biceps. "What's going on?" My heart was thumping in my chest, and every nerve in my body was on red alert as he pressed his body into mine.

"Your scent," he told me gruffly. "Your arousal is...a lot."

Holy Luna. I was going to die of embarrassment.

"Um, sorry?" I couldn't deny how he affected me. We were shifters.

Cannon's lips skimmed my neck, and his teeth nipped at my earlobe. "Tell me to stop," he breathed, his hand sliding down my side, cupping my ass cheek. "Tell me," he whispered. His plea made me weak. He lifted his hand from my ass, sliding under the elastic of my underwear, gripping bare flesh.

"I..." I couldn't think. I didn't want him to stop.

His mouth hovered over mine. Deep green eyes looked into mine. "Stop me, pup."

I lifted onto my tiptoes, deciding for him, but he jerked back, releasing me suddenly.

"You good here?" Royce asked suspiciously as he approached the cell.

"No," Cannon growled, stepping back. "I need a minute."

He barged past Royce and the newcomer, leaving me red-faced, out of breath, and incredibly horny, which every male in the room could scent.

Fuck my life.

CHAPTER 21

Kezia

"Hi."

The older man looked at me and then over his shoulder at the door the alpha had just stormed out of. "Hello," he spoke with a slight accent. He looked at Royce and jerked his head to the open cell door. "Shall we?"

Royce looked at the door, and then with a sigh, he looked at me.

"I won't bite," I promised.

"I don't care if you bite me," Royce said with an eye roll. "You try and shift, and I'll defend myself."

I blinked back the sudden wetness in my eyes. "I've never..." Clearing my throat, I grabbed my composure, dragged it up from the depths of my soul, and held my head high. "I've never attacked a shifter. I've never fought pack."

Royce nodded once, and he and the guy named Doc entered my cell.

I stepped back immediately, my hands held up in warning. "You smell weird," I told the newcomer. "What are you?" I sniffed the air. "You're...*human*?"

"Eh, no. Kind of." He grinned at me. "Are any of us in this room human?"

I sniffed again. "Right now? I don't know what you are. What are you?"

Mutant.

"My wolf says you're a mutant." I flinched at the harshness of my voice. "Sorry, that's...really rude." I glared at her, and she sniffed in return.

"Mutant?" He grinned. "Says the wolf shifter?" He was older-looking than Royce, and I put Royce at mid-thirties in human years. In shifter years, he could be anywhere between fifty and two hundred. His hair was dirty blond, and his goatee was weird but suited him. A slight frame and no visible muscle that I could see, he looked harmless.

He didn't smell harmless.

What is he? What's a mutant?

Half-breed.

I looked at him again. "Oh."

"Yeah, oh." He took a step forward. "I'm Mal," he told me, offering me his hand. "Most people here call me Doc."

I reached to take his hand when Royce knocked his away. "Hey!" I protested.

"Just don't touch her," Royce mumbled, his eyes flicking nervously to the door.

"Oh, for the love of the Goddess, I am not contagious."

"You don't unders—"

The door slammed open. Cannon strode back into the room, determination on his face. "Stand back!"

Royce and Mal jumped at his command, but I was frozen in place as I watched him raise his right hand, and I couldn't believe what I was seeing.

He fired twice—once in the leg and once in the arm.

Crashing to the floor, I screamed in pain. "You absolute cock-sucking motherfucking asshole!" I yelled at him as I rolled in pain. "Why the hell did you shoot me?"

He was standing over me. "Shift."

"*You* shift, you dickwad," I growled. I pressed my hand over the wound, and my wolf moved within me, restless.

He shot *me.*

You're healing.

I was. Quickly, I dug my fingers in and pulled out the first bullet. "I really, *really* don't like you." I glared at him as I tossed the fragments aside.

"Where did you find a gun?" Royce asked in bewilderment.

Cannon ignored him as he crouched beside me. "Give me your arm."

"Fuck off."

"Pup! Give me your fucking arm before Doc has to cut you open to get the bullet out."

"Now you want to show concern?" I inched away from him as I tugged at the open wound. He'd hit me high up on the arm that it was difficult to reach. "Here's a tip, *Alpha*. Don't fucking shoot people!" Cannon moved toward me, and I bared my fangs. "You even *think* of coming closer, I will *gut* you," I hissed.

"Can I help?" Mal asked behind me. "You're making me nervous the way you're digging in there, girlie."

"Leave me alone."

"Pup," Cannon warned.

"Fuck you."

"Pup!"

Turning, I looked up at him as he towered over me. "Fuck. You."

Royce shoved his alpha backward and stepped in front of him. "Kezia, let us help you. Please."

"Your alpha is a fucking lunatic."

"He has his moments," Royce agreed. "Please, Kezia. You're bleeding badly."

I looked at my arm. "I thought I was healing?"

"The second bullet was silver."

All three of us gaped at him.

"What is *wrong* with you?" I demanded incredulously.

"We need to see it for ourselves," he said gruffly. "To figure this out."

"I'm not a puzzle," I snapped at him. "I'm not a fucking experiment, you crazy asshole."

Mal touched my arm, and when Cannon growled, he snatched his hand back. "What's happening?" he asked, looking between the three of us.

"Cannon, leave."

I stared open-mouthed at Royce. Was I hearing properly? Cannon huffed out a sigh but stayed exactly where he was.

"Cannon, *leave*. I won't ask again."

Holy shit. The beta just gave his alpha an order.

Cannon looked at me and my arm. "Fuck." He turned and walked away. I watched in amazement as he crossed the room, the door shutting firmly behind him.

Royce held up his hand as Mal reached for me. Doc halted, and when Royce cocked his head, listening for Luna knows what because I couldn't hear anything except my blood dripping onto the floor, then he gave a sharp nod to Doc.

"Now."

Mal grabbed my arm, and I flinched in pain. "This is going to hurt, Kezia," he warned me.

"Does it feel different?" Royce asked as he watched me. "From the leg wound?"

I shook my head, and then I was nodding as the shock of the last few moments wore off. "Yes, yes, it…" I hissed in pain. "It's burning."

"The metal is reacting to the blood," Mal murmured. "Knife?" Royce handed him a switchblade wordlessly. "Brace yourself," Mal whispered.

I screamed as the knife cut into me. Royce was already running across the room when the door opened. He threw himself at it, forcefully pushing the door shut against *whoever* was on the other side. With a grunt, he shoved it closed and then quickly turned a large lock. He jumped back when the door was thumped from the other side.

Royce walked backward, his attention on the door. "Why aren't you getting it out?"

Why? Because Mal, like me, had been absorbed in what was going on with Royce.

"Your flesh is scorched," Mal explained to me. "It's literally burning you," he said with fascination. "A delayed reaction, it looks like. Fascinating."

"It *is* literally burning me, like you said, so can you stop being *fascinated*?" I asked him through gritted teeth. "Can you fix it?"

"Of course, sorry. This is gonna sting, girlie."

Sting? It didn't sting. It was *agony*. Gut-wrenching, pure agony.

My scream erupted, and I heard Royce asking me to keep it down. I think I told him to go do something physically anatomically impossible to himself in reply. Mal tried to soothe me, and I clenched my teeth. But the pain. I'd never felt anything like it. Or I had and didn't remember it.

The rhythmic thumping against the door finally penetrated as my sobs lessened. My body was curled up in a ball as Mal held my arm up and bent away from me.

"I got it all," he told me quietly.

"Good, I can't thank you properly," I told him as I hiccupped through tears. "Not yet, that fucking hurt."

"You did well," he said, patting my shoulder. "Let him in."

"Get back," Royce warned.

Their voices were distant as the pain still radiated through my body. I hiccupped again. I didn't care what I looked like, knowing the floor was wet with my tears and blood. I sniffled, curling into a tighter ball, holding my arm protectively close to my body.

I felt Cannon as he lowered behind me.

"I hate you."

"I know," he said softly, running his hand over my tangled hair. His touch was so different from Mal's. He pulled me into him, curling around me and spooning me. He gently lifted my arm, ignoring my hiss of pain as he pulled me closer. "Why didn't you shift?"

"What?" I was choosing to ignore the fact I was soaking in his comfort, even though he was the reason I was in pain. "Shift?"

"You're in pain. Why didn't you shift to heal?"

Why didn't I shift? Turning in his arms, I looked up at him in confusion. "Why did you shoot me?"

"Pup," he scolded softly, the look in his eyes gentle. "Don't change the subject."

"You shot me with silver!"

"Why didn't you shift?" he asked again. "Ask her the question, Kezia."

"Her?" I heard Mal ask, and Royce shushed him.

Frowning, I searched his eyes but saw nothing hidden there, no answers either. "Cannon?"

"Ask her." He rolled me gently onto my back so he was above me, but he was still holding me.

I turned to my wolf. She was waiting.

Why?

The burning binds us, we cannot shift form.

Shift now, I commanded. *We need to heal.*

In the wolf form, the urge to bite the alpha was stronger. We snapped our jaws at him, but he merely laughed as he stood. Shaking our head, we felt the power heal the last of the hurt, but we were still weak. We were tired. We relinquished control to the child.

Cannon handed me his shirt as I rose, waiting until I had covered my nakedness before stepping back. "Better?"

"Yeah." Shaking my head to clear it, I spun and punched him. It didn't matter that he barely moved. I got the hit in. "That was unnecessary," I added with a glare.

Cannon rubbed his jaw, his eyebrow arched as if to say "really?" "Show me the scar."

I held my arm out and felt like an experiment once more as the three males crowded me.

"Silver," Royce murmured. I looked at him in question. "Your scar, it looks like silver."

I strained to look, and sure enough, I saw the silvery-white wound against my pale skin. "Good job. I don't tan," I muttered in disgust. "I can't *believe* you shot me."

He ignored me. Lifting my hair, he showed Mal the other scar. The scar I never knew I had. "Kezia, hold your hair," he ordered roughly.

"Why?"

With a huff of impatience, Cannon grabbed my hand and forced it into my hair. "Hold."

I was too tired to argue. When I was holding my hair, I felt him tug at the shirt he had just given me. "I think she was shot here first. This was a few months ago," he spoke quickly. Clinically. "Then this is tonight." His fingers were softer as he skimmed the most recent scar. "Am I right?"

"Does it matter if you're not?" I grumped tiredly. "You only listen to yourself anyway."

"Not talking to you," he chided, pulling me into his body. "Doc? What do you think?"

"Am I allowed to touch her?"

"You already touched me," I told him irritably. "I already told His Dickishness I'm not contagious."

"Quickly," Cannon said tightly. His hold on me got tighter as Doc pressed and prodded my three scars. "Not there," Cannon said sharply when Mal bent to look at my legs.

"Okay."

My head was resting against his chest, my eyelids drooping. "It's not right," I muttered. "The only person who shouldn't be touching me is you." I nuzzled into his chest more. "I'm so tired," I told no one in particular. "I need to sleep."

"We need to clean this up," Royce spoke for the first time in a while.

"Kezia?"

Tipping my head back, I looked up at Cannon. "What?" I asked him sleepily. "What else can you possibly want?"

His hand cupped my cheek. "Why didn't you shift?"

"She said the silver binds," I mumbled, yawning widely. I slid my arms around his neck, trying to climb his body like a tree until

Cannon bent and scooped me up. "I think it stops the shift," I told him, yawning again.

"Did she say anything else?"

I felt the cot beneath me, and I curled onto my side. "No. I made her shift to heal the rest of the way." I flung my arm out, waving an accusing finger at him even though I couldn't see him since my eyes were firmly closed. "Dick move, by the way. You don't shoot your hostages." I paused, thinking of some of the movies I'd seen. "Okay, sometimes the hostages get shot, but *you* shouldn't have shot me."

I heard someone snort out a laugh, but I was too tired to look to find out who.

"This place looks like a battlefield," I heard Royce murmur. "You made it happen...you clean it."

"I'm your Alpha."

"You're a shit, that's what you are. She's right. You know that, right?" I heard him asking. "You shot her, for fuck's sake. You could have killed her."

"I knew she'd heal."

"Did you?" That was Mal. "You didn't seem so certain about ten minutes ago."

"My wolf isn't happy with me," Cannon said, his voice gruff. "She survived three shots before, so I risked it."

I wanted to tell them to shut up so I could sleep, but curiosity at their openness when they thought I was sleeping kept me on the brink of consciousness.

"She said the wolf told her she can't shift with the silver in her body...it binds?" Royce asked quietly.

"Sounds like it," Mal agreed.

"What does that mean?" Royce asked. "How is she alive?"

Because I healed. Duh.

"She healed," Mal said what I was thinking. *Thank you, Doc. I knew I liked you.*

"She would have bled out," Cannon told him quietly. "She was in a truck with them. She told me she could feel how weak she was when she regained consciousness."

"And she shifted?" Royce asked dubiously, and I somehow felt like they were all staring at me. "How? If the wolf says it binds them to the human form."

"She never shifted tonight either," Cannon said softly. I felt the cot dip as he sat down, a warm hand soothing my hair back. "I thought she would shift," he admitted, his voice low. He let out a slow breath. "That would have been irony in itself if I killed her."

I didn't find it ironic. Massive dick. And he needed to understand what irony was.

"If she can't shift," Mal spoke slowly, "and she was bleeding out...how is she here?"

"That's what we need to find out," Cannon told him. I felt him leave the bed. "She won't tell us."

"Does she know?" Royce asked doubtfully. "Her wolf is... *different.* What if there is more of her that is different?"

"I can give her a full examination."

I'm not different. Old sadness welled as I thought of my old pack and how they had never welcomed me fully because I was different from them.

"She's not different," Cannon corrected them both. "She's..."

I waited, my awareness struggling to stay awake. *Special? Was I special? A freak? Oh crap, was I a mutant too?*

"Unique," he told them.

Huh. Unique. I liked that.

I heard a rumble of laughter. Royce? What was so funny? I

could be unique. I moved restlessly as I tried to wake up and tell them I *was* unique and also to fuck off so I could sleep.

"Shh," Canon whispered, his hand smoothing my hair again. "She needs to rest," he told them. "I need to clean this mess."

"You need to clean more than this mess," Royce scoffed as I heard them move away. "You need to speak to her brother, you need to speak to your brother, and you need to find out who the hell gave her attackers silver bullets. How did they even know that was a thing when we didn't know it was a thing until about an hour ago? Well, obviously, you knew. Where in the Goddess's name did you get it?"

"I sent you to the fighter," Cannon said, his tone sharper. "The fighter who's no longer where we left him."

Fighter? What fighter? Did he mean Vance? Why would he want Vance?

I tried to ask the question, but my tongue was heavy. Getting shot with silver sucked hairy balls.

"Did she just say hairy balls?" Mal asked, and I could hear his amusement. "Maybe she's dreaming."

"Of hairy balls?" Royce laughed.

"Not if she wants to get out of that cell," Cannon growled.

"It could be *your* hairy balls she's thinking of," Royce teased.

"Can we please stop talking about anyone's balls and my mate in the same sentence?"

He was such a grump.

Wait.

What?

My eyes opened in alarm.

Pushing myself into a sitting position, I looked at three very guilty faces. I locked eyes with Cannon. "What did you just say?"

CHAPTER 22

Kezia

"I THOUGHT YOU WERE ASLEEP," CANNON SAID, looking flustered. It was a weird look on him. Stoic, cold, expressionless, I was used to. Seeing him flustered was strange.

"Are you *blushing*?" I squinted at him in suspicion. "Wait, am I awake?" I looked at Royce who was half-turned away from me, biting his lower lip to stop from laughing. I pinched myself hard and flinched. "Ow."

"Did you just pinch yourself?" Mal asked with a grin.

"I need to know if I'm awake," I grumbled, trying to sit up properly. "They always say pinch yourself to see if you're dreaming."

"*Who* says that?" Royce asked curiously. "Wouldn't dream-you be able to pinch anyway because it's a dream, right?"

I thought about it. That made sense. Dream-me didn't want real-me to know it was a dream, so real-me would be fooled. "Shut up!" I shouted at everyone, myself included. Royce and Mal were both laughing at me now.

Pushing myself up and swinging my legs over the cot, I tried to stand and immediately sat again as a wave of dizziness swept over me.

"You should get some sleep," Mal said, walking back to the cell. "You lost a lot of blood. You need to recuperate."

Taking a deep breath, I pushed my hair back, and with determination, I stood. Ha! My eyes found him. He'd been suspiciously quiet, and that in itself would make *me* quiet if he wasn't the reason I was awake right now. Or that I had suffered blood loss because he shot me.

"What did you say?" I asked him, my voice firmer than my legs right now, and I tried to make it casual as I reached for the bars for support.

"Sit down before you fall down," Cannon ordered me gruffly. "You need to sleep." He was walking back to the cell, and for the first time, I noticed the cell door was open.

"You left it unlocked?" I blurted in surprise.

He shrugged as he got back in the cell with me. "There's a lot to clean up," he answered without looking at me. When he reached me, he didn't ask but picked me up and carried me the three steps to the cot. "Sit."

"I can walk. You don't need to carry me around all the time."

"Trust me, it won't become a habit." He grunted at me as he stepped back. Cannon turned to look at the others. "I've got this," he assured them. Royce hesitated, but whatever message his alpha sent him made him dip his head, and he led Mal out of the room.

I didn't know why I waited until the door was closed, but I did. We both seemed to be transfixed by the door. Weariness pulled at me, but I was also strangely alert and nervous. *Really* nervous. Maybe I wasn't alert but just nervous. I licked my lips as I waited.

"I'm thirsty."

"I'll get you water."

"No."

"No?" Cannon looked at me briefly before looking back at the door. "You want to dehydrate too?"

That earned him a glare. "Dick." Shimmying up the cot, I leaned against the bars as I watched him. "So? Mate? Are you for real?"

He turned his full attention to me, and I swallowed hard at the look in his eyes. "I am very much real, pup. This isn't a dream. Unfortunately," he added bitterly.

"I know you're real, asshole," I mumbled. My throat was so dry. "I really do need a drink."

He said nothing as he left the cell, the door still open, and had I had more energy, I might have relished getting out properly, stretching my legs, but I'd been shot with silver, lost a shitload of blood, and was weaker than a newborn foal. So instead, I leaned my head against the bars and closed my eyes. Just for a minute until he came back.

LATER, I woke up curled in a ball on my cot, in a cleaned cell, and wearing fresh clothes.

Groggily, I lifted my head and looked around. There were two bottles of water in front of me and a sandwich. I drank a bottle of water in one go before I half staggered to the corner of the cell and took care of the pressure on my bladder. I ate the sandwich in about three bites and washed it down with another bottle of water.

The door opened, and Cannon walked in. The pause in his

step was his only tell that he wasn't expecting me to be awake. "She lives," he joked lightly.

My eyes narrowed as I watched him. "No thanks to you," I said under my breath, but his stupid alpha hearing heard me perfectly because he grinned at my sullenness. "How long was I asleep for?"

"Two days," he told me, coming to stand in front of me. He looked at me and then at the floor. "On the one hand, the experiment worked because now we know more than we did..." he began. He must have known I was about to tear him a new one because he hurried on, "But it was risky, and I...I shouldn't have."

I gaped at him. "That's it? You *shouldn't* have?" His eyes flicked to mine, and he grimaced. "*That's* your idea of an apology?"

"I said I'm sorry."

"No! You really didn't say anything of the sort. To say you're sorry, you say, hey, Kezia, I'm sorry I'm a dick, and I'm sorry I shot you with a silver bullet."

"I'm not a dick."

We glared at each other.

"I'm not sorry I'm a dick," he amended. My glare got harder. "Fine. I'm sorry I shot you. Twice. Once with a silver bullet." Cannon let out a dramatic sigh. Okay, it was just an expelled breath, but to me, he was acting like a diva, so "dramatic sigh" fit. "It was helpful, though."

"Not to me."

"You're fine."

"Two days later."

"Still fine."

Arrogant and hateful jerk. "I need the bathroom."

"We need to talk."

"Want me to pee on the floor?"

"For fuck's sake, pup, I didn't mean you couldn't go to the bathroom."

"You should say that." I stood and walked to the corner of the room. "We'll talk when I'm done." But I'd already been to the toilet, and I didn't want to admit I just didn't want to *have the talk* with him, even though I knew I had to *have the talk* with him. So, I stood behind my sheet and thought about what the fuck I was doing.

"You okay?" he asked me.

Fuck.

I started to brush my teeth.

"Are you stalling?" Cannon asked, pushing the sheet aside, seeing me sitting on the toilet lid, brushing my teeth. "Really?" His smirk earned him a tube of toothpaste being thrown at him, which he dodged easily. With a shake of his head, he dropped the sheet and left me to it. Using the hose, I poured water into my hand to rinse, lifted the toilet lid, spat, and flushed.

With no reason left to hide, I stepped out from my sheet again, my eyes wide when I saw Cannon sitting on my cot, facing me, a pillow at his back against the bars.

"Comfortable?" I asked him with a pointed glare at his boot dangling off the side of my bed.

"It's got potential," he answered.

"How am I your mate?" I blurted.

He stared at me steadily. "Because the Goddess has a twisted sense of humor."

I waited for him to say something else, and when he didn't, I felt my temper rising. "That's it? Luna thinks she's funny?"

Cannon shrugged. "I don't know, pup. Why do you think you're my mate?" he asked with exasperation.

"I don't," I snapped back. "Having a mate has never entered my mind. And if it did, it would never, *ever* be you."

Cannon's face twisted into a bitter smile. "Right back at you, pup."

We stared at each other, and I had no idea what to do. He remained on my bed, watching me, his face blank, his eyes void of emotion. How was he so cold? How could Luna do this to me?

He was infuriating.

He was hard and cruel.

He was my jailor.

"This isn't right," I mumbled. "Mates are..." I floundered.

"Destined," Cannon said with a snort.

"Stupid," I blurted at the same time. He raised an eyebrow, and I flung my hands up in despair. "You detest me. I don't like you either. Mates are supposed to be in love and stuff."

"Says who?" Cannon asked curiously. "How many mates have you known?"

I stared at him blankly. "What? You know I haven't been with anyone."

Cannon tutted as he sat up farther on the bed. "Sit." He pointed to the end of the cot and caught my dubious look. "Just sit, Kezia," he said with a low growl. "You don't need to fight me on everything."

I sat on the cot's edge as far away from him as possible, a fact he noticed and one that made his smirk more irritating than usual. "Now what?" I snapped at him. "I'm sitting."

His flat stare wordlessly reprimanded me for being a brat, but I decided my inner brat had a lot to feel pissed off about, and I refused to feel guilt.

"I'll ask again, how many mates have you met?" He saw my frown and clarified. "Not partners but *mates*."

"I don't understand." Turning to face him properly, I considered the question. "I mean, there's Bale and the twin's mother, Claire. Um...there's Doug and his wife, and—"

"Not wife. Not husbands. Not partners. I told you that. How many are mated? Actual mates." He saw me struggling, and he sat forward. "Mates are rare. Anyone, any pack member can be married and call each other mate, but to be mated, *true* mates are said to be selected by Luna herself." I hadn't realized I'd leaned forward until he reached out and pushed my hair behind my ear. "True mates are a gift from Luna for her alphas. Her pack leaders."

"That's not true." Jerking my head back, I got up and moved away from him. Kris knew Cass was his. "That's some superior alpha bullshit or something."

Cannon laughed at me as he leaned back. "Really? And you know this how?"

"Kris." I started to pace, my fingers rubbing my temples. "My brother, Kris." Looking up at him, Cannon still looked unconcerned, and I opted not to share about my brother. The less this alpha knew of my pack or my brother, the better I would feel. "He never mentioned this."

Cannon drew up his knee, resting his arm across it, his chin dropping onto it as he watched me pace frantically while he remained the epitome of calm and collected. "Mm-hmm?" His tone was lazy, and his upper lip was curled in the semblance of a smile. "You're right...your brother never having mentioned it is why I'm wrong. You convinced me," he deadpanned.

"Don't be an insufferable dick," I grouched at him, making him smile fully, and I turned my head so he wouldn't see me fighting my smile. "Does Luna also tell alphas to shoot their mates with silver?" When I looked back, he'd lost his smile. "Thought not." I sat back on the cot.

"Mates, true mates"—he had turned serious again, but his posture was still relaxed—"they cannot fight the pull to one another. Luna picks her alphas. You at least agree with that, right?" I nodded without making eye contact. "Alphas are selected for their strength and ability to lead, provide, and protect the pack." He must have seen my eye roll because he was grinning again. "An alpha also needs a strong female who will balance them," he added. "A mate who will compliment her alpha's strengths as much as she nurtures and cares for their young and the pack."

I was frowning, and he reached out, his fingers grazing my arm. "What is it?"

"You keep saying alpha, like only an alpha can have a true mate."

"They can," he said easily. "Not everyone gets their mate, but from what we know, and I've searched for the last few months, it's more likely to happen to an alpha. We can find no record of it happening to a beta or any other pack member. An alpha has a mate."

Chewing my bottom lip as I looked down at my hands, I thought of what Kris said to me when he let me go. *Cass is my mate.* I thought he meant fireworks and destiny and all that shit, but had he just meant that Cass was the one he wanted to be with? He let me go alone because he had a crush?

"Kezia?"

I jerked my head up to look at him. "You've been searching about true mates?" I asked instead of admitting the hurt I had at my brother's deception. "You've been trying to find out if you can break it?"

Cannon lost his casualness, leaning back, his face once more a mask. "Yes."

I nodded, surprised that his admission hurt too. "I understand."

"It wasn't personal."

"Feels very fucking personal," I snapped angrily, frustrated with myself for showing him any emotion. "So how does it work? Let me guess, a silver bullet?" I was on my feet again, putting distance between us. Well, as much distance as I could in my cell.

"How many times do we need to talk about that?" he asked, getting to his feet, his irritation showing.

"Hmm?" I pretended to think about it. "Until you say sorry and mean it?"

"I said sorry, and I meant it."

I looked him up and down as he stood a few feet away. "And yet I don't believe you. Shocking." Turning away from him, I faced the sheet that separated my cell from the toilet. "I don't believe anything you say. This shit included."

I felt him step up behind me, his warmth surrounded me, and his touch caused me to jump as his hands skimmed down my arms. I felt goose bumps erupt wherever he touched me, and my throat was suddenly dry. I stood frozen as he pushed my hair aside and gathered it over one shoulder, leaving my neck and throat exposed.

I swallowed hard when his fingers traced over the scar I had at the base of my skull, his lips pressed against my shoulder.

"Do you feel that?" he whispered against my skin.

I could feel him, every inch of him, behind me, pressing into me. Cannon's tongue flicked out, and he licked right under my ear. My legs turned to jelly.

"Do you feel it?" he spoke to me, desire tightening his voice with need. His nose skimmed my jawline. "Your body is burning, your nerves are strung too tight, and you feel like you're going to snap." Soft kisses were peppered down my throat, along my collarbone. I heard my moan, and so did Cannon, his arm wrapping around my waist and pulling me into him tightly. "Do you feel how fucking hard I am for you?"

My ass ground against him, and it was his turn to groan.

"And you're wet. I can smell it," he carried on, his voice low and guttural. "Your pussy is soaked, weeping for my cock." He thrust his hips into me slightly, and my knees buckled. His thumb flicked over my nipple, and my head dropped back onto his chest. "Your body was made for me, Kezia. It's mine, and you know it."

I couldn't think. I couldn't breathe. My senses were heightened, and my need was primal. Turning in his hold, I reached up for him as his mouth claimed mine. We kissed with a ferocity and wildness that neither of us was willing to think about. We didn't hold back. My shirt was pulled off, and Cannon's hands and mouth covered me with kisses and caresses.

My fingers were already on his jeans button, fingers clumsy with desperation, tugging at his zipper.

"Up," he commanded gruffly, and I jumped into his arms, my legs wrapping around his waist as he lowered us both to the cot. He kissed me thoroughly as his hand smoothed over my thigh, hitching my leg up onto his hip as he ground into me.

He kissed his way down my body. My eyes were closed against the bright light, my hands tangled in his hair as my back arched, feeling his fingers hook into the band of my pants. My hips lifted eagerly to help him, desperate for him to reach his destination.

The sudden blast of cold water made me yell out.

Cannon roared as he leaped off me, his hands up to guard his face as we were both drenched.

"What the fuck!" I heard his angry yell even as I rolled away from the icy deluge, landing on the floor.

"Stop it!" I shouted, shaking my head as my hair plastered to my face, momentarily blinding me.

The water was turned off, and I looked up, panting for a whole different reason, looking at Royce's grim expression. I looked between him and Cannon, who was as soaked as I was, but he had collected himself a lot quicker than I had. He looked away from me and angrily wiped his face free of the water, his face stern.

"You good?" Royce asked his alpha with a hard look.

"Yeah. Thanks." Cannon nodded curtly. Glancing at me, he looked away with what appeared like disappointment. "Cover yourself, pup."

I watched in disbelief as he stalked out of the cell without another word. Pushing my wet hair off my face, I turned to Royce, who was putting the hose down. He gave me a guilty look.

"It's for the best, Kezia," he mumbled, following his alpha out of the room.

I watched the door closing in a daze, turning to the wet bed. "What the fuck is happening?" I asked the empty room. My shirt was on the floor, soaked. My sweatpants were wet too. "What a mess." Squinting upward, I glared at the ceiling as I pushed my pants down. "You have a lot of explaining to do, Luna."

With hands on hips, I turned to glare at the door. The *open* door.

"Forget I said anything," I whispered as I edged to the open cell door. "I need your blessing, Goddess. Just this one time, don't let me fuck this up."

I shifted, and we prepared to run.

CHAPTER 23

Cannon

"WHAT THE FUCK WERE YOU THINKING?" ROYCE demanded angrily as he followed me out of the bunker. "She's a child!"

"She's eighteen," I snapped back at him. "Trust me, she's no child." I could still feel her. Taste her. Hear her moans. *Fuck.*

"She's too young," he amended furiously.

"For me?" I asked him, sending him a scathing look. "Is that what you're going to say? I can't fuck her because I'm older than her?"

He grabbed me by the arm and pulled me to an abrupt stop. The follow-up shove to my shoulder meant I was turned to face him. "Don't speak about her like that," he told me angrily. "She's young, inexperienced, and isn't some pack whore you can use and discard."

He was right, and he was pissing me off. "I've never used a pack whore," I told him, my jaw clenching because as much as he was right, he was also *really* pissing me off. "I might need one for the blue balls you just left me with."

I should have expected the punch, but I didn't. That was on

me because my head, both of them, were still underground where my mate was—my mate who drove me to madness with her scent, temper, and terrible attitude. Rubbing my jaw, I looked at my best friend. Stretching my neck to release some tension, I rolled my shoulders.

"I'm going to give you that one," I told him quietly. "I may have deserved it."

Royce had been prepared for my counter punch, and I saw him relax slightly as he watched me with suspicion. "Ya think?"

"No," I told him honestly. "I can't think when she's near me." Shaking my head, I looked toward the town. "How many times before I don't leave the room? How many times before you're not there to stop me?" Clasping my hands behind my neck, I bowed my head. "It's impossible to ignore," I admitted to him. "This itch, this need to take her, claim her. Own her." I frowned at the floor. "I'm not in control when I'm in the same space as her. It's...it's terrifying how much control she has over me."

"I'm sorry." Glancing up, I saw his sympathetic look. "I don't know what it's like," he added gruffly. "Do I know lust? Of course I do. When Hannah and I got together, I was consumed with wanting to spend every single moment of the day with her. It's what attraction is...chemicals in our brain. I know it's not the same for you, it's more. Right?"

Licking my lips, I nodded. Checking the clearing to ensure no one was nearby, I lowered my voice to barely a whisper. "It's like that. Lust...but multiplied. It feels like my brain is short-circuiting. Every molecule in my body wants her. I can't think straight. I need to be inside her."

Royce winced. "Who said romance was dead?" Royce muttered. "Look, we're no strangers to sex. We've both been with females while they're in heat and know how crazy it can be. Do you think it's worse because she hasn't had a full heat?"

We started walking to my house. The alpha's house was in the center of our small town. It was big and had too many bedrooms for a single male, but the idea was for the alpha to find his partner and fill those rooms as soon as possible with their children. Pack life was about family. Bonds of a familial nature and friendship made a good pack. A tight pack. A pack that was safe to raise your kids so your kids could have kids.

She was just a kid.

And here I was, thinking back to her again. I could still taste her toothpaste, for fuck's sake.

"I think it's that," Royce carried on, oblivious to the fact I was thinking about Kezia again, "she's extra..." He paused, struggling for a suitable word. "Potent!" he blurted out. "That's it. She's your mate—"

I grabbed his arm. "Do you want to tell the fucking pack?" I hissed at him.

"Sorry." He held his hands up in apology. "She's your, you know," he said with a look around. "And every time you seem to be near her, her heat starts."

"Does it?" I looked at him in surprise.

"Doc and I were talking about it earlier. It's what I was coming to tell you when I came into the bunker."

Royce was no saint. Before he met Hannah, he was a faithless dick who slept with anyone, so to see this blushing prude at my side earned him a hard jab to the ribs.

"What the fuck was that for?" he asked with a growl.

"You've seen worse, much worse. Fuck, you've done worse with many different women, so this holier-than-thou act is fooling no one. Least of all me."

"I've never fucked a virgin," he hissed at me. "I've never walked in on my best friend, my *Alpha*, about to fuck a girl half his age, either. She's a fucking innocent. What the fuck are you thinking?"

We'd reached my house, and I climbed the steps to the main door, opening it and pushing it too wide with anger, the door banging off the wall as I did. Taking the stairs two at a time, I strode into my bedroom, ready to be free of these wet clothes when I heard him at my back.

"Give me five minutes," I snarled. "I need a shower. Meet me in the study."

He didn't argue, and as I heard my bedroom door close, I went into the adjoining bathroom, my hands on either side of the sink as I stared at myself in the mirror.

"She's not half my age," I grumbled to myself. "I'm twelve, maybe thirteen years older." I was fourteen years older. I knew it, my reflection knew it, and my beta knew it. "She's not a child," I counterargued. "She's old enough, more than old enough. Age means nothing to shifters." It was true. After a female's first heat, no one cared what age they were in human terms. We stopped aging like humans anywhere between twenty-one and twenty-five. Age was simply a number. Pushing myself off the basin, I stood back. "This is stupid. You're talking to your reflection."

I could still taste her.

With mounting frustration, I grabbed my toothbrush and toothpaste and brushed my teeth, pissed off I was trying so desperately to eradicate the taste of her. But I knew, deep down, it was too late. The taste of her was imprinted on my soul. My very soul. Tossing the toothbrush aside, I started the shower.

I needed to stop this. I was an alpha. I had a rogue wolf locked in the bunker and only four of my pack and I knew, five if Royce had told Hannah. I snorted. Of course, Royce had told Hannah.

I had my mate locked in a bunker in my packlands, and my pack didn't know. Only three people knew she was my mate.

What the fuck was I doing?

Stepping under the hot water, my mind was racing. I'd worked hard to make our pack better. My father was a chickenshit tyrant and had run roughshod over this pack for too long. On my return from overseas, I couldn't believe the damage he had done in the few years I'd been gone. One morning, that was all it took for me to see how beaten the Blackridge Peak Pack had become.

I challenged him the same day I returned. On the dawn of the next day, I promised them I was an alpha worth following. My pack would rebuild, and we'd find our return to what we once were together. My door would always be open, and I promised them full transparency. We'd be a proud pack once more.

It only took us months, and we were back to that. My pack had pride once more. Fast forward twenty months, and I had my eighteen-year-old virgin mate locked in the bunker my father used as a jail cell.

Luna, what was I thinking? I was risking everything for her.

She was wild. She was a lone wolf. She was a killer.

She was my mate.

Squeezing my eyes closed, I fought to clear my mind. We'd find a way to break it. What I'd told Kezia was true. Most alphas had a true mate. My father didn't. Or if he had, he killed her like he killed others. That poor excuse of an alpha of the pack at Anterrio had no true mate. I knew it as soon as I met his wife.

But Kezia...

I bowed my head under the spray, my hands flat on the tiles as the water beat down on me.

Kezia was *mine.*

A flash of her white-blonde hair and ice-blue eyes that regarded me with loathing one moment and burned with lust for me the next crossed my mind.

My cock jerked.

"Even when you're nowhere near me, you drive me crazy," I muttered as I grabbed my cock, stroking it slowly. I'd brushed my teeth, but I could still taste her. Her skin was so white, utterly colorless, making her seem sickly, but she was so strong. Healthy. I stroked again. Her hair was thick but as soft as silk. It shouldn't be possible. She should stink. She should be filthy. I'd kept her in that cell for weeks. *Weeks.* Yet she was always clean with that scent.

Vanilla and spice. It fit her perfectly—a delicate sweetness with a sharp bite.

Still, she should be weak and *broken.*

I smiled as my hand worked faster as I thought of her. No, she wasn't broken. My mate didn't break. She thrived. She got stronger. So strong inside but so soft to the touch. I thought of her smooth skin and how fragile she felt in my arms, but her will was like iron.

She was perfect for me and so incredibly fucking wrong.

My head tipped back, my hand moving in rapid, smooth motions as I thought of the way her skin tasted, her light pink nipples hard as rocks as I sucked them. The smell of her arousal flooded my memory. I yearned to lick every drop from between her thighs...

"*Fuck!*"

Panting, I stood in the shower, my head bent, the water cooler now with my hand wrapped around my softening cock as I watched my cum get washed down the drain.

"What the hell are you doing?" I asked myself for the

hundredth time since I met her. "Fuck, I need to break this bond."

Finishing my shower, I got dressed quickly, jogging down the stairs to the office, hoping that Royce would keep any comments about me jerking off in the shower to himself.

He was talking with Doc when I entered.

"Took your time," Royce muttered as I closed the door behind me.

My office was soundproof. I promised my pack an open door and transparency, but I also needed confidentiality to run my pack.

"I have a lot to process." I didn't meet his eyes and pretended not to hear his muttered *I bet you do*. "Tell me more about me triggering her heat," I said to both as I sat on the couch.

My study was open and welcoming. I wasn't a prick who sat behind a big fancy desk that created a barrier between him and his pack. I had two soft couches, a nice armchair, a couple of other chairs, and a round coffee table. Along one wall ran a shelf that folded out to a workbench if we needed a workspace. Along the other was a wall of books. Some were about strategy, some were pack history, and some were thrillers and crime novels. I liked to read.

Doc spoke first as I knew he would. "You met Kezia just as she was approaching her first heat, right?" I nodded. "From what you've said and what I get from Nikan and Royce, her pack knew her heat was approaching but not when. She met you for the first time when the shaman was to...what was it again?" He turned to look at Royce.

"Lick her blood," I answered. Seeing Doc's quizzical stare, I elaborated. "Shamans are supposedly linked to Luna and our wolf spirit. Whether we're in human form or wolf form, our blood is the same. It connects both forms."

"Our blood enables us to shift," Royce spoke up. "It was a complete shitshow the day she went into heat, but when we asked about her, when they realized her brother lost her"—he used air quotes when he said *lost*—"it seemed she often got tested by the shaman to know if she'd shifted without permission."

"There is so much to unpack in that," Doc grumbled. "So this charlatan, sorry, shaman, licks her blood and can tell when a heat is coming?"

"Yes," Royce and I said together, sharing a grin.

"They thought it could be that week, and then she meets Cannon, and bam..." Royce slapped his hands together. "She goes into heat."

Doc tilted his head to the side as he considered me. "What did you do?"

"Absolutely nothing," I told him honestly, remembering her insolence even on the very first day.

"Nikan said you pissed her off," Royce reminded me.

"You've met her," I countered. "Everything pisses her off."

"She does seem to be more agitated with you," Doc mused. "Of course, that could be the mating bond." His fingers tapped on his thighs. "You followed her trail? When she left?" I nodded —he knew this. "How many times were you close to catching her?" he asked curiously.

"Twice, and then we did catch her."

"How many heats has she had, I wonder," he thought out loud.

"She thinks it's three or four." I cleared my throat. "I think it's three."

"Care to share?" Royce asked, leaning forward.

"The day we met," I told them. "The day we almost had her at that shithole diner she worked in, and then the day we lost her before her wolf went on a killing spree."

Doc sat back. "Each time you were closer to her, she potentially went into heat, and then something happened to her, she shifted, and you lost her trail." He sucked his teeth. "God, I'd love to run tests on her."

"You don't touch her," I snarled. The room went quiet. "That will never not be annoying," I told them honestly. "It just happens."

"It's the mating bond," Doc said. "It is fascinating. Until you actually, shall we say, mate?" He grinned at me widely. "Your wolf is completely and *totally* psychotically possessive. You're Tarzan, and she's your Jane."

"What the hell is that?" Royce asked in confusion.

"It means I'm more of an asshole than normal," I grouched. "Fuck." I glared at the bookshelves. "Fine. I'll stay away from her. Reach out to more packs. There has to be someone who knows how to break the fucking thing."

"*Can* you stay away from her?" Royce asked me dubiously.

No. "Yes." He gave me a flat look. "No." Hitting my fist off the couch's arm, I looked between them. "I'll try."

"So it's back to me feeding her?" Royce asked with a sigh.

"You're married and loyal. My wolf knows you won't touch her."

"I'm gay," Doc reminded me. "I won't touch her either."

I shrugged. "He doesn't give a fuck if you're straight, gay, or a corkscrew, you're unmatched, so you're a threat."

Pushing myself to stand, I walked over to the window, looking out at my community. The community I rebuilt.

"It's because she's still *pure,*" Royce whispered to Doc. "The primal urge to be the only one to ever touch her makes our wolves more territorial."

"I can hear you," I reminded him.

"Never thought you couldn't," he quipped back at me.

Pure. Was Kezia pure? Her body may be, but was her wolf? Her spirit? I could still see the burned-out carcasses of the men she killed. The limbs tossed carelessly in a heap, left to burn. The ground had been saturated with their blood and fear, not to mention their piss, vomit, and shit.

What had she done to them before she killed them? It went beyond any torture I knew, that was for sure.

My eyes narrowed as I saw Nikan hurrying toward my house. He was pissed off with me as well. I hadn't told him she was my mate, and I hadn't told him the extent of how she killed the three humans. He thought I was being unnecessarily cruel. He didn't think I was protecting my pack from a rogue. A shifter who was not in control of themselves.

That's what she was—a wolf with no control. Mate or no mate, she wasn't getting out of that cell until I knew one hundred percent that she was in control.

I would not risk *my pack*.

I would not risk *her*.

"Nikan's coming," I warned the other two, turning from the window and walking over to the study door.

"Cannon!" I heard him yelling as soon as I opened the door.

"I'm here," I told him calmly, wondering how he was already upstairs. "What's lit the fire under you today?" I asked him with a laugh.

"Where's Kezia?"

My laughter stopped abruptly, my eyes narrowing as I stepped closer, feeling my wolf surface. "What do you mean, where's Kezia?"

Nikan looked between the three of us. "Did you let her out? Put her somewhere else? I need to know what to say if someone asks me about her!"

I turned to look at Royce. "Tell me you closed the door when you left?"

He was frowning. "I could have left the cell door open," he admitted slowly, obviously thinking about it. "I closed the door."

"Are you sure?"

"What's happening?" Nikan asked quietly.

Royce met my hard stare. "I'm sure it was closed," he spoke quietly.

"How sure?" I pressed, walking toward my front door.

I heard his heart rate increasing. "Not one hundred percent."

"Fuck!" I was already running down the stairs toward the bunker.

"What's going on?" Nikan asked behind me. "Is she gone?"

At the edge of the bunker, I caught a faint trace in the air, and my head turned sharply as my wolf chased her scent in the breeze.

"She's gone."

CHAPTER 24

Kezia

I PACED OUTSIDE THE MOUTH OF THE CAVES.

I'd been here three days, shifting between wolf and human form, and still, he never came. My wolf kept us fed as she hunted freely in the well-known area to us, but I was getting increasingly restless as I worried about being in the same place for too long.

Cannon would know I was gone. I hoped he hadn't noticed until the next day, but while Luna gave me her grace to let me leave, I didn't think my luck would have been that good. No. *Alpha Asshole* would be looking for me.

He thought I had no control.

I thought *he* was full of shit.

Mates? I had more chance of being mated to that tree over there.

I resumed pacing as I hoped my brother would come. The caves had been a shelter for our family when we were young. It's where my brother took us after our parents' accident. *Murder.* I gulped. They had been murdered, and I'd had my tongue down the throat of the male who could tell me more.

"Goddess! You're such a useless female, Kezia. Big muscles,

nice abs, and skillful hands, and you become no better than a floozy."

I grinned. *Floozy* was a term Lottie loved to use. *Luna, I missed Lottie.*

I also missed my brother, and I thought the stupid oaf would have come at least once to this spot while he was out running. Kris always let his wolf run—his was as impatient as I was.

I resumed pacing, grateful my brother had left our hidden packs there. Shorts and a T-shirt were better than greeting him, after all this time, naked.

Rustling in the trees had me spinning in alarm, too close to hide but not too close that I couldn't shift and run like hell if anyone other than my brother came out of those trees.

When I saw the familiar tawny wolf approach cautiously, I immediately burst into tears. My legs gave way, and I sank to the ground. I felt Kris shift, and I heard a mumbled *"hold on"* as he was covering himself, and then my big brother was on his knees beside me, holding me as I sobbed into his chest.

"Shh, Kezia, it's okay. I'm here, shh," he soothed over and over.

The tears didn't stop immediately, although I was sure my brother wished they had. I clung to him like I had as a child when it stormed, and Luna, bless this man because he let me cling.

When I eventually sat back, Kris watched me carefully, his eyes misty. "Hey, little sis," he greeted gently, reaching out and touching my cheek. "How are you?"

"I've missed you," I blurted. "I fucked up. Cannon got me. I'm a mess, and I fucked up."

Kris sat back on his heels as he watched me, his eyes narrowed as he looked me over. "You smell of something strange. Is it him?" His look of disgust at the thought made me think

Kris would not appreciate all that I had learned with the rival alpha.

"No, it's just been a really long time since I had a shower," I told him honestly. "Are you okay?" I reached out to him, my hand clasping his. "Did you mate with Cass?"

His smile was all I needed to know. Sheer happiness shone from him, and I felt so guilty for the terrible stab of jealousy and resentment I felt at how much obvious joy his mate brought him.

"It wasn't easy," Kris admitted. "She fought it for a while, but"—he shrugged, grinning from ear to ear—"we're mates. You can't fight it."

Wanna bet?

He grew somber. "I don't want to talk about that...tell me what you meant. What about the murders?"

I knew my eyes were wide with fear. "You know about that?"

He nodded. "We got the news that a girl who looked like you had been kidnapped by an escaped criminal," he told me, his frown fierce. "Criminals, there were three of them. Cass showed me the report, and Bale and I looked into it, but she wasn't you, obviously," he added with a scoff. "They caught the guys, but the girl died."

"Died?"

He nodded, looking away from me. "I was so scared it was you," Kris admitted softly. "Bale let me go to their town so I could prove to myself it wasn't my little sister." Kris sighed. "I've never known such fear," he told me quietly. "Knowing I had let you run, unprotected, and they had killed you, I would have never lived with that guilt."

"There's a body?" I didn't understand. "Of a girl?"

Kris was watching me as I got to my feet. "Kezia? What is it?"

"Tell me everything. All of it," I demanded.

He took a deep breath. "Three human males, they stalked and kidnapped women, hurt them…you know what I mean. They were on some rampage across the states." He grunted. "I didn't look at the details of their crimes too much. There was a picture shown on the news channels, and it was a girl who looked just like you, but with dark hair and some other slight differences that I knew couldn't be you, but I still *thought* it was you. They caught the men, but the girl didn't survive."

"They caught them?"

"Yes."

"They're in jail?" I asked him.

"I don't know. I was only interested in her." Kris was also standing. "Kezia?"

"There was a *manhunt* for *her, she* was wanted by the police," I bit out in frustration. "How did that change? Is that *not* what happened?"

Kris was becoming more and more agitated. "They said they wanted her for questioning, but it was all misled evidence or something." He rubbed his forehead. "It was months ago, and I can't remember much of it. I remember the fear it was you, but it wasn't"—he took a breath—"because you're here."

"It *was* me." I stepped back from him. "It *is* me. They didn't catch the men…I killed them. I'm wanted for their murders."

"What are you saying?" Kris asked me, his face white with horror.

"My wolf killed them. They caught me, were going to kill me, she took control, and we killed them."

"Kezia, no," he whispered, and for the first time in my life, my brother looked unsteady. He sank to the ground, his legs too shaky to hold him, it seemed.

I knew the feeling well.

"I'm so sorry, Kris. I...they left me no choice. I defended myself."

Kris looked at me and then at his hands. "Start at the beginning. Tell me everything," he ordered, his voice firmer.

I told him it all. The fighting, the running, the thought I was being followed. The fight with Bullet, the new start, Maggie, Lottie, and then the night Bullet found me. I told him how I shifted in the truck and killed the guy in the back with me first. I told him how I cleared up the bodies and set the remains on fire, and then I shifted, and we stayed in the mountains for months. I told him when I shifted back, we made our way to Vance's and that Cannon found me. I told him how I'd been in a cell for weeks because Cannon caught me as a rogue.

"I'm so sorry, brother," I whispered, my voice hoarse with the tears I shed. "I..." I swallowed the lump in my throat. "I'm sorry."

"Why are you apologizing?"

I blinked in surprise as my brother paced. "Um...because I killed humans?"

"Humans who were going to kill you after they raped and tried to break you," he snapped. "I only want an apology if those fuckers are still breathing."

"They're definitely dead," I said in a shocked whisper. I yelped when he grabbed me and held me tight, but eagerly returned the hug. "Kris?"

"Do not *ever* apologize for defending yourself, Kezia," he whispered furiously as he held me. "I taught you better, didn't I?"

He wasn't mad at me. He wasn't disappointed in me. My brother believed me and was glad I'd done what I had. The relief was so overwhelming that I burst into tears again.

"Goddess, how is there still water left in you?" he grumbled, pushing me back playfully.

"I thought you would disown me," I confessed through my sniffles.

"Idiot!" He scoffed at me. Kris paced again. "Okay, I need to hear it all again, including everything that happened in the Blackridge Peak Pack."

"All of it?"

"Leave out nothing. We need to plan."

"As you know, I left and ran for a few weeks, but we shifted back. I quickly learned that the human world needs a lot of money, and a girl like me eats too much to never have any. I made my way, and then I found out there are fighting rings..." I didn't look at him as I spoke, even though this wasn't my first time telling it today, it was possibly the first time my brother was hearing it. *Really* hearing it. "I did okay in them...they pay well. I fought them as human, holding my true strength back as you taught me."

He was frowning but listening.

"I knew to keep moving, though, so every few weeks, I would take my winnings that would keep me going until I needed to find the next fighting ring. I was at Vance's. He runs good fights, and I made so much money on them, but I kinda, um, clashed with his emcee."

Kris gave me a flat look, and I grinned at such a familiar welcome sight of my brother being unimpressed with me trying to downplay a situation.

"Bullet, the emcee, accused me of sleeping with Vance and basically cheating, and we started fighting." I remembered the anger I had, but it was quickly replaced by the horror I felt when I realized that I'd killed him. "We fought, I won. Just." I blew out a breath. "He was strong and fast."

"Human?"

"Definitely human," I confirmed. "I healed myself too quickly, considering the fight we had, and it aroused suspicion in a guy I worked with. He accused Vance of rigging the fights. Later that night, I got chased through the woods, and in the morning, I left town. I saw Vance had Bullet strung up, and I didn't do anything. I found a new town. I met two women who might have cared for me, and I think I could have stayed there. But a few weeks later, Bullet caught me. Shot me three times with silver, and when I came to, I was in a truck, and they were going to, well, you know..."

"Silver?" Kris's eyes were wide. "They had *silver* bullets?"

"Yes, but I didn't figure it out until I was captured by Cannon." I showed my brother my legs. "See, I'm marked."

Kris studied the marks and my shoulder when I showed him. "You said three times, what's this?" he asked, pressing the skin on my upper arm.

"That's where Cannon shot me," I told him.

My brother was on his feet. "*He* shot you with *silver*?"

"He was experimenting—"

"He was *what*?"

"Calm down, I can explain." Taking his hand, I tugged Kris back down to the grass to sit with me. "I was weak. The silver made me slow, and healing took longer. I woke up in the back of the truck, and I... She saved me."

Kris was nodding. "You have the right to defend yourself. Being weak and injured, your wolf will panic and overcompensate."

"Overcompensate?" Studying my hands, I recalled the devastation she had caused. "She tore them apart," I whispered. "I burned the remains, but I shifted, and we ran, and we stayed gone for months."

"You lost control of her?" he asked me quietly.

I nodded once. My brother understood how close to the surface my wolf stayed, despite my many protests that she didn't.

"But she let you come back," he said, his voice gentle. "You are still *here*, Kezia."

Squinting, I looked at my brother. "You must be having *all* the sex," I said with a laugh when I saw his flush. "Who is this mellow guy in front of me?"

Kris grinned, but he still punched me squarely on the shoulder. "Respect my mate," he admonished, but his smile was wide. "Finish the story."

"I needed money, so I went to Vance. Stupid mistake really, going back to somewhere I've been before. It was Vance who told me I was wanted for questioning for the murders. I was leaving so I didn't get him in trouble, and Cannon was waiting for me."

"Your wolf was always better at hiding than you," Kris scolded. "He's an alpha and can follow your trail easily enough and would have been waiting for your shift."

"They caught me, I was put in a cell, and he told me he had the right to do so, as I'm a rogue." My voice dipped when I spoke the last word. "He said I am packless, a killer, and wild. As an alpha, he could detain me."

"Who said you are packless?" Kris demanded. "You are still part of the Anterrio Pack. You haven't been cast out. Your home is still on the mountain with me."

"I am?" *It was?*

Kris shoved me so hard that I fell onto my side. "You left the pack...you weren't exiled. I took a risk in letting you run with your heat, but your home is with *me*. *I* am your pack, and *our* pack is on the peak."

My eyes welled up again, and Kris looked at me in panic, his expression causing me to giggle. "I won't cry, I promise."

"You never cry, it's...alien." He scratched his jaw as he watched me. "I don't understand how you went from suspect to victim. I don't know whose body they found. Do you think Cannon and his pack killed a human? To cover for you?"

I was already shaking my head. "No, he would never. I've listened to several lectures about how I'm more than human and should have run away." Prodding my leg, I thought about the stern alpha. "It was after one of his lectures that I realized when Bullet shot me, he deliberately shot me to make me lame. As if he knew I wouldn't heal well and wouldn't shift."

"But you did shift."

My nose scrunched up as I thought about it. "I did..."

"What are you thinking?" Kris asked me.

"When Cannon shot me, it took a few minutes for the silver to react, and when it did, I couldn't shift."

Kris was focused on my arm and the silvery mark. "I'll gut him."

Turning my back to him, I lifted my hair. "And I have this. They compared the scars, the fainter they are, the older they are."

Looking at my brother over my shoulder, I saw his frown as he scooted closer to look.

"How did I get this one?"

He was already shaking his head. "It's not a bullet wound. It's a birthmark. We both have them. Look." Turning, he lifted his hair to show me a faint silvery scar running from his neck into his hairline.

"Kris? That's not a birthmark...that's a scar from a silver bullet."

We looked at each other uncertainly, the silence stretching

before my brother spoke. "I think I have more questions than answers," he admitted softly.

"Can Cannon take me back to Blackridge Peak?"

Kris was already shaking his head. "No. You've done nothing wrong."

"I killed them."

Kris scoffed. "Says who? Where's the proof? The humans caught three killers after discovering a dead girl. You're not dead, so how can it be you?"

"And the fact someone covered that up? And we don't know who or why? Won't they know the truth?"

He stood and stretched. "And when they appear, we'll ask our questions." He offered me his hand and pulled me to my feet, surprising me by embracing me. "I've missed your smart mouth, your *remarkable* ability to get into shit, and..." He squeezed me tighter. "I've missed my sister."

"I'm crying again," I warned as I hugged him back. "Just letting you know."

He pulled away from me, but he was laughing. "I need to take all this to Bale," he told me more seriously. "He is the pack leader, and we need him on our side. I think we need to do what Cannon was threatening you with too..."

My brain stopped, and I froze. *Had I let slip he thought I was his mate?*

"We tell the Pack Council. They're the only ones with enough power to make a wolf shifter disappear from human attention."

"They're scary."

"You haven't seen Cass at seven in the morning with no coffee," Kris said with a wry grin.

I'd been walking back to the hiking packs that we hid here in the cave, when he spoke. "Are you at the cottage?" I asked, trying to sound casual, but although Cass was my friend and I loved her, I didn't want to live with her.

"No, it was horrible without you," he answered truthfully. "We have one of the new houses on the opposite end of town now."

I turned to face him. "Am I to come back with you?" I saw his guilty look, and I was already nodding. "You want to break it to Bale first?"

"Yeah, I think that would be best." My brother suddenly looked extremely uncomfortable. "Plus, eh...shit! I don't know how to tell you this...Landon..."

Alarm swept through me, and I reached out to grab my brother. "Is he hurt? Did something happen to him?"

Kris looked guilty. "I may have punched him." He took a step back. "Three or four times." He held up his hands as if in defense. "No more than five. Maybe six...definitely not seven. Okay, it's been eight."

His behavior was confusing me, but he was making me laugh. "Why do you look bothered about that? Landon's a big boy. He can take a few punches."

Kris took a deep breath and then blew it out.

"HeisyourmateandhatesthatIletyougoandhepissesmeoffsoeverynowandthenIpunchhim."

The world was spinning. I sat on a rock, missed, and fell off onto the ground. "Say that slower..."

Kris looked like he would rather poke sticks in his eyes. "He's your mate."

"Bullshit."

Kris blinked in surprise. "He insists he is, and he has been insufferable ever since you left. He blames me for letting you go, and when he pisses me off, I...yeah, I punch him."

"Total bullshit," I told him, regaining my senses. "*Landon*?"

Kris nodded mournfully. "I'm sorry."

"How does he know? I didn't even go into heat properly!"

"The same way I knew about Cass, I guess. I haven't sat down and discussed *feelings* with *Landon*, Kezia!"

My mouth opened and closed several times. Landon was my mate. Not Cannon. I inhaled sharply. What was that? What was that uneasiness inside me? Was I...disappointed?

Hell no. I'd rather have Landon. I knew Landon. It made sense. Landon was my friend. Sure.

My *mate* was Landon.

Not Cannon.

Excellent. All my problems were solved.

Then why did it feel like a big fat lie?

CHAPTER 25

Kezia

"Cannon will be looking for me," I told my brother as I still tried to process that Landon thought he was my mate.

Kris frowned, watching me. "Then you come with me now and forget what I said." He looked away from me, his eyes focused to the west, where the Blackridge Peak packlands were located. "Let the bastard come get you," he said grimly. "Let him try."

"I thought you wanted to talk to Bale first," I reminded him. "I mean, it's a lot to take in..."

"The shaman will keep you safe," Kris said with a half shrug.

"Keep me safe?" I asked curiously. "Why do I need to be safe?"

Kris grinned. "*Safe* is the wrong word, but Landon will know as soon as you're back that you're within slobbering distance." I grimaced, and my brother laughed in delight. "For all that I hate the idea..." he said good-naturedly, "you'll understand when you feel the bond kick in."

I wouldn't bet on it, brother.

"Yeah, it's destiny, right?" I tried to sound jovial despite my sarcasm.

"It feels like so much more," he said wistfully, a faraway dreamy look in his eyes.

I was going to barf. If I ever looked at Cannon, or *anyone*, like that, I was going to shoot *myself* with a silver bullet. Right between the eyes.

Cannon. I bit my lip as I glanced over my shoulder in the direction my brother had looked earlier.

"We need to move. If he finds me, he won't let me go without a fight."

Kris's grin was vicious. "Then we give him a fight."

"All right, Mr. Feisty," I joked as I patted my brother on the shoulder. "Let's not get carried away. You ready to run?" I asked him, my fingers on the hem of my shirt.

Kris nodded, and I turned my back, then quickly undressed, packing the clothes away neatly so they were there for us to use again. My wolf came forward, and the tawny wolf was waiting when we turned.

Our wolves were delighted to be free together. My wolf charged at her wolf brother, and soon they were playing and running, making up for lost time. As we reached the border of the Anterrio packlands, my wolf caught a scent and swiveled swiftly, her paws taking a few steps toward the mountain peak in the distance.

Moonstar, come.

She hesitated, taking another step forward away from her wolf brother.

What is it? I asked her. *What do you smell? Is it him?*

Moonstar!

She jerked her head to look at the tawny wolf, her eyes narrowing.

Now! He commanded. *Come, we go home to the pack.*

It is not our home. They are not our pack.

I saw my brother's wolf's top lip curl at her thought. I didn't want him to be angry, so I came forward, her attention shifting to me.

I know it doesn't feel like home, but it will, although it might be different this time, I tried to persuade her. *He is our pack.*

This is not where we should be. She turned to look back again.

Please, I whispered. *We can't go back to him. You know that. He lies. He shot us with silver.*

We do not like this. But she turned back to the packlands we knew and walked forward. Kris, appeased she was following his orders, resumed his journey back to the pack.

At the rear of the shaman's house, we both shifted. The shaman always had clothes at the doors to his home for the more modest of the pack. Kris handed me a shapeless dress and grabbed a pair of shorts for himself.

My brother entered the house first, and I heard voices, one rising in surprise. As I prepared for the worst, Cass came rushing out the back door, throwing herself at me and knocking us both to the ground.

"Thank Luna! Kezia!" she cried as she hugged me tight. "I thought you were lost to us." I felt her tears through the thin dress, and as I hugged her back, I looked up at my brother, who was watching us both with unabashed happiness.

Cass pushed herself off me and looked down at me. "You've missed everything!" she scolded, taking Kris's hand as he guided her to her feet. I watched as she automatically stepped into his space, seeking his arms, which slipped around her easily as my brother pulled his mate close.

I watched as he dipped his head to kiss her cheek. A whisper too low for me to hear made Cass blush. She turned her head to look at him, and I looked away as he kissed her softly.

"What did I miss?" I asked, clearing my throat. "Also, are you always like this?" I asked, waving my hand between the two of them. "Because there are things I don't need to see."

Cass's peal of delighted laughter made Kris chuckle, and I was suspicious they were both laughing *at* me. "Did you tell her?" Cass asked him, letting her hand trail over his forearm.

"I did, but I think she's in denial."

"Oh, I cannot wait to see this," Cass said gleefully. Stepping out of my brother's hold, she embraced me once more. "It's so amazing to have you back, Kezia."

"I would also like to talk to you again," the shaman spoke dryly from the back door. "Come inside, please."

Kris let Cass go first, surprising me when he reached for my hand, squeezing it once. Looking up at him, I again saw his look of happiness. "You okay?" I asked him quietly.

"I don't think I've been better," he answered truthfully, his eyes landing on Cass again.

Briefly, my brother outlined the last year of my life to the shaman and Cass. He left out crucial bits like murder, silver bullets, being a prisoner, and I understood that was for Cass's benefit. She always was more delicate than most.

Cannon's words that mates needed to balance each other out popped into my head, and I hastily pushed them away.

When he was done, a thick silence hung in the air until finally, the shaman moved in his seat. "You need to tell the pack leader," he spoke slowly. "Take Cass too. Kezia will wait here with me."

"But Landon—"

"Can wait," the shaman said briskly. "Your father needs to know first, and I would like to speak to Kezia alone."

Kris started at that, but he nodded. He was always respectful of the shaman's wishes. Cass grumbled under her breath, but Kris soothed her by distracting her, pulling Cass to his side as he prepared to leave.

"Stay here," he told me as he left. "Leave for no one but me, understood?"

"Yes, Kristoff," I said with a familiar put-upon sigh.

"Ugh, I have not missed that attitude at all." But his good-natured laugh told me otherwise, and I returned his smile. Cass waved, promising she would see me soon. The door closed behind them, and I could hear their giggling on the front path.

"It's been intolerable," the shaman told me, turning to face me. His sight may be gone, but his other senses were sharp. "They giggle *all* the time."

"It sounds horrible." It did. My skin was crawling. The thought of me turning into a giggling, sunshiney person was truly horrific.

"You have changed too," he told me. "Your soul is darker."

"Wow. Straight in there, eh? What do I say to that? Thanks?"

"Your insolence has remained the same," he told me dryly. "Your wolf is angry."

"She's uncertain," I defended her, ignoring the feeling of disgruntlement she was sending my way.

"Taking a human life changes you," he said in understanding. "Taking three...well, I do not need to tell you." The shaman leaned forward, and I knew I'd not fooled him. "Tell me everything, pup."

Pup. The pang of longing sliced through me like a knife. What the hell was wrong with me? I did *not* long for Cannon. At all.

"I don't think I should be called pup," I said, hating how shaky my voice was. "I'm technically an adult now."

The shaman snorted, telling me exactly what he thought of that. "Enough whining. Tell me your story and leave nothing out."

I wanted to do as I was told. But still, there were some things I didn't share. Surely, a wolf was allowed some secrets. I knew I was holding back more than I should, but I was beginning to doubt I should have told Kris as much as I did.

The shaman had finally stopped asking me questions and had shared his dinner with me when Kris returned, Bale in tow. I then went through my third interrogation. Kris said nothing when I didn't mention that Cannon had shot me with silver, but I could tell it was a fact he had left out too.

It was almost, *finally,* at an end when the door burst open. Landon came to a sudden halt so soon after barging in, it was jarring. He was out of breath, his eyes darting around the room, taking us all in before he slowly walked toward me.

I stood, frozen, unsure what to do, looking at my brother for assistance, but he was staring at his feet. Kris had told me, but I didn't believe it. I still didn't believe it. It was obvious that Landon *did* believe I was his mate if the way he was looking at me was anything to go by.

"Kezia," he murmured when he reached me, and I let out a squawk of surprise as he embraced me tightly.

Panicked, I looked at my brother again, who still had his eyes averted. I guess he didn't want to see public displays of affection when it involved his sister. I'd remind him of that later. The shaman was calmly sipping his tea, but when I met Bale's glare, if

Landon hadn't been wrapped around me like a vine, I would have stepped back at the open animosity I saw reflected in the pack leader's eyes.

Landon broke his father's glare when he drew back and looked down at me. His face was suddenly all I could see.

"Kezia, I...I can't believe it."

I opened my mouth to make a joke, but Landon kissed me, taking me by surprise. When his tongue pushed past my lips into my mouth and I heard his obvious moan, I floundered as I tried to figure out how to make this stop. His mouth moved over mine as he licked at my tongue. *Would punching him send the wrong message?*

My stomach felt uneasy as my whole body wanted to recoil away from him. I may be inexperienced, and I may not know much about mates, but I was pretty sure my first thought when my mate kissed me was not supposed to be *yuck*.

Something was terribly wrong with me. I knew it. I hoped my face didn't show it because when Landon finally stopped slobbering on me, all I could think was that Cannon was going to be severely pissed off that I let another man kiss me.

I knew with absolute certainty, as Landon started talking excitedly about how glad he was his mate had returned, that I was *not* his mate, and from the look on his father's face, so did he.

I'D BEEN "HOME" for three days, and it felt like I had never left. Not in a good way, either. My wolf was restless within me, and I knew why. Bale had said little to me at our reunion. When he had tried to tell me I was welcomed back, but I would live as before—with my wolf contained—my brother had stepped in before I could tell Pack Leader Bale exactly what I thought of his idea.

Thankfully, my brother, the diplomat, was on my side. The fact I had been living unbound and in my human form for months with no alpha or issues—the killing of three men aside—proved that I was in control.

Bale had watched me for a long moment before his son pressed me to his side and announced his mate would run free with him. He then kissed me again.

Ick.

At our cottage, I had looked at my brother in panic when Landon lingered on the path, obviously waiting for everyone to leave us alone. Again, my brother saved me, suggesting how over-whelmed I was and how I would appreciate a night to reacquaint myself.

Kris then sacrificed his happiness when he opted to stay with me, sending the firm big-brother signal to my supposed mate that sneaking back wasn't going to happen either. Far too many times that day, my brother had reminded me how much I'd missed him.

Unfortunately, Cass had not been put off by Kris's warning, and I woke in the middle of the night to sounds no sister should hear from her brother's bedroom. Slipping out of the house, I let my wolf run in the meadow, and we fell asleep under the stars.

Landon had a supply run to go on with Grant, the other beta, and his father refused to listen to his plea to stay back with me. I didn't think Bale realized how grateful I was for the reprieve, however unintentional it was that he gave it to me.

The rest of the pack was the same as they always were—some hostile, some indifferent, and fewer than that were happy to see me. I found it easier in the cottage. Or I ran freely, staying close to packlands, just in case.

Several times, I caught myself staring west, focused on the mountain that housed Cannon and the Blackridge Peak Pack. The argument I had with myself that it was because he scared me would fool no one, least of all me.

I was in the kitchen making a seeded loaf when the door opened, and Kris walked in. He looked furious, and I racked my brain to think what I'd done this time.

"Look at this." He slammed a cell phone onto the countertop.

Wiping my hands on a towel, I picked up the phone and read the screen. Three days ago, a message was sent from my brother.

> Beta Kris: She is found and in good hands, with me and her pack.

Two days ago, he got a reply.

> Alpha Cannon: Kezia told me she has no pack. I am coming for her.

My tummy flipped in anticipation. I read on. This morning, my brother replied.

> Beta Kris: Kezia is MY sister. I am her pack. This is her pack. You have done enough. She is where she belongs.

Twenty minutes ago, Cannon answered.

> Alpha Cannon: We'll see.

I looked up at Kris, who was watching me with his old familiar suspicion.

"What? I didn't do anything," I protested weakly.

"I know, but what makes him think he can go against me? I am your brother!"

Picking up the cloth, I wiped my hands again, now hot and clammy with fear and, if I was honest, anticipation. "He's..." I coughed. I needed a drink. "Arrogant, right? You remember that?"

"He's a dick." Kris took a seat in his old armchair. "When you left, and I came back, he was on me right away. I got hauled up in front of all the alphas, and he asked question after question about where you were. Where would you go? Had you planned it? How much money you had?" Kris shook his head, glancing at me briefly. "To be honest, I didn't have answers to some of them because I hadn't thought of how vulnerable I had left you. I'd been rash, making you go with no plan. I panicked. I owe you for that."

"You owe me nothing," I told him honestly, moving the phone so I could read Cannon's messages again without bringing attention to myself. "I needed to go. I've learned a lot since I've been gone."

Kris grunted, and I hoped he agreed. With a sigh, he pushed himself out of the chair, coming over to watch me knead the loaf. "You do make the best bread," he told me. "Are you making this for Landon?"

I blanched, and my brother saw my reaction.

"What is it?" he asked with concern. "Talk to me."

All I'd done was talk to him, and yet I didn't know how to say these words to him. "It's nothing."

"You're scared?" Kris nodded thoughtfully. "Cass said you would be and that Landon would understand." Kris gave me a sympathetic look. "You've been gone a while...it was bound to happen."

"What was?" I asked in confusion. Cass thought I was scared?

Did she also know I wasn't her twin's mate? Did she think he would understand? Hope rose within me.

"Landon has been no saint, I can tell you," Kris said gruffly. "He has had sex with some of the pack, so he will understand that you have too."

"Had sex with some of the pack? I haven't had sex with any of the pack."

Kris flushed. "Obviously not," he said with an eye roll. "But he'll understand you are no longer a maiden."

My eyes popped. "A maiden?" I burst out laughing. "Oh my Goddess, a maiden!" I laughed harder as my brother became more uncomfortable. "Who says maiden?" I teased, wiping my eyes, feeling bad for teasing him, so I controlled my laughter.

"All right, all right. You've had your fun."

"Have I?" I waggled my eyebrows as I transferred my dough into a bowl, covered it to proof, and started to clean the counter.

"Kezia," Kris scolded. "You don't need to worry. Your mate will understand you have had sex with another. Others." He looked away. "I don't need details," he added hastily.

Only I *was* still a maiden, but if Landon thought I wasn't and I was ashamed, would he stay away longer before I had to tell him I wasn't his mate?

Kris let out a sigh, mistaking my frown of thought for one of fear. "How do you feel when you think of Landon?" he asked gently.

Sick.

I couldn't say that. "Sad," I blurted instead. "I'm sad my friend is gone."

Kris nodded in understanding. "It's a huge change, but that goes away because he will be your best friend. He will be your everything."

"Good Goddess, you make me want to hurl," I told him with disgust. "He will be my *everything*? What kind of greeting card rubbish is that?"

"Stop fighting it," Kris snapped irritably. "That prickly feeling you have when you see or think of him, it's a good thing. It's the bond wanting to connect. Let it do what it needs to do."

"Have you spoken to Landon?" I asked him carefully. "Does he feel like this?"

Kris shrugged. "No, but it's how I felt. Cass was the same."

I nodded, keeping my silence.

"I can't believe I have to say this," Kris muttered. "Give him a chance, and let your body tell you how you feel."

I forced a smile, and we chatted for a few more minutes before he had to return to pack duties. I thought about what he said. Let my body tell me how I feel. I already knew what it was telling me —I felt nothing at all for Landon.

Nothing.

CHAPTER 26

Kezia

Landon was due back to the pack today. He wasn't the reason I was making bread, but as I looked around the cottage, I realized I also didn't want to be here if Landon came calling. Getting ready, I had a shower while my loaf baked in the oven, dressing in simple shorts, a black sleeveless shirt, and my favorite boots as I waited for the bread to bake.

Letting it cool on a wire tray, I left the cottage and went to visit the shaman. The shaman was hosting a meditation group in his backyard, and as soon as I heard the brass dong of the drum, I turned one hundred and eighty degrees and headed into town.

On my way to the store, I met Cass. She looked radiant. There was no other word for it. My friend was glowing, and her happiness was contagious.

"Kezia!" She embraced me tightly and kept hold of my hand when we drew apart. "I am so happy you're home. Kris has been so worried about you, and having you here makes him happy."

I gave her a skeptical look, but she was genuine. "Don't tell me...what makes him happy makes you happy, right?"

I was subjected to another hug as she squealed with happiness.

Good Goddess, did having a mate turn you into an idiot?

Cass laughed when she saw my face. "All these months gone and you still have RBF down pat."

Nudging her with my elbow, I couldn't hide the grin. "I'm useless at diplomacy," I agreed. "If my mouth isn't saying it, guaranteed my face is."

Cass let go of my hand, choosing to link our arms together. "Want to buy a bottle of wine and get drunk?"

"Yes! One hundred percent yes." I glanced around us—a few were openly staring and the ones who were simply looking, were smiling at the ray of sunshine my best friend was. "Won't we get in trouble?" I whispered.

"I'm mate to the head of security and daughter to the pack leader." Cass had a mischievous twinkle in her eye. "Who's stopping me?" She headed straight to the store.

"Me?" I asked, hurrying after her. "I feel like it should be me?" I added when I caught up to her.

"Are you?" Cass asked me with a raised eyebrow.

"Hell no. I make terrible decisions."

"Then let's get drunk," Cass whispered. Pushing the door open, we headed inside.

We ended up buying two bottles—one fruity white for Cass and a nice red for me. We got a disapproving stare from the store clerk, but Cass was right, who would challenge her? Especially when she said in the loudest voice possible that we were hosting a dinner for her brother's return.

I accidentally stepped on her foot when she almost called Landon my mate, but no harm was done. We headed to Cass and Kris's house, which sounded weird, but even I couldn't deny they were mated. They just oozed happiness. And love. It was nauseating.

The house was one of the newer builds in the pack. With a nice open-plan kitchen and living room, there was a master bedroom and bath upstairs with a balcony looking out to the mountains. Another bedroom was situated off the family room, and it had a large, enclosed garden with a gate at the side of the house so you could go straight there without walking through the house. The main benefit of the garden for me was the recessed fire pit. I was a huge fan of a fire pit, which Cass knew, and as I arranged our chairs around the pit, Cass opened the wine.

Not ten minutes after arriving home, Cass was wearing short denim shorts like me and a white halter-neck top. Her feet were bare, and I contemplated removing my boots but decided to keep them on.

"All right," Cass announced as she sat beside me. We clinked glasses. "Tell me all the bits you haven't told your brother."

Which implied everything I *had* told my brother he had told Cass. I wasn't sure how I felt about that. "I don't know what you mean?"

"Kris told me you were evasive about, you know, sex—"

"Oh, for Luna's sake!" I growled. "Of course I was...he is my brother."

"I know," she said calmly. "Which is why you and I are here, alone, with wine. Talk."

Turning to face her, I narrowed my eyes, watching as she sipped her wine. "Are you trying to get me drunk so I will tell you details?"

Cass nodded enthusiastically. "Yes. And when you are super drunk, I'm going to tell you mine."

I was already shaking my head. "No, not happening. I do not

want to hear about my brother's bits and your bits, and no, not today. Not ever."

Cass started laughing again, and I took a large gulp of wine.

"Cass?"

We both froze as the voice got closer.

"Cass, you here? I'm back."

"I didn't know," Cass whispered quickly to me. "I promise." She shot me an apologetic smile and then shouted, "I'm out back with Kezia."

There went the idea of jumping the fence.

Landon paused at the patio door, his gaze wary as he looked between us. "Hi," he offered, his eyes locked on mine. "You're here?"

"In the flesh." My voice had more bite than it should, and I took another drink to hide my grimace. "How was your trip?" I asked, remembering right up until I left the peak, Landon had also been my friend.

"Good." Uncertainty made him hold back, but out of the corner of my eye, I saw the not-so-subtle nod from his twin, and Landon cautiously walked forward. "We got a lot of stuff, I..." He looked at the glasses and then over his shoulder. "Can I join?"

"Of course," Cass said, springing to her feet. "Red or white?"

"Beer?" he answered with an easy smile as his sister pushed past him on her way into the house. Landon's gaze rested on mine once more. "Can I stay?"

"Sure," I told him, hoping my voice was as bright and breezy as Cass's. "She's your sister, after all."

"And you are my mate."

It hung there between us, the awkward silence stretching until I cleared my throat.

"Do you really think so?" I asked quietly, staring at my now empty glass. Where did all the wine go?

"Yes," Landon took a few eager steps forward and then seemed to stop himself from coming any farther. "Can't you feel it, Kezia?"

No. "I don't know," I lied. Tilting my glass, I made brief eye contact with him. "I need more."

"I'm coming," Cass called from the kitchen. "Just getting snacks."

"Eavesdropping ho," Landon muttered as he sat opposite me.

"I heard that, jerk!" Cass yelled, and we both smiled at how predictable she was.

The easy familiarity of the siblings bickering relaxed me. "What did you get? Anything new? Phones?"

Landon looked surprised. "We don't need phones on the peak. Everyone we know is here."

How incredibly shortsighted. I knew he had a phone as did Cass. My brother showed me his earlier, but the rest of the pack didn't get technology. Bale didn't think we needed it. There was a common hall for mingling as pack.

We ate there.

We watched television there.

Together.

As pack.

But I knew Cass had a tablet. I never asked Landon if he had one but assumed he had. What his sister had, he had, and vice versa.

His sister had a mate. An *actual* mate.

My head jerked back in realization. *He wouldn't fake it, would he?*

Cass called for him to come help her, and he got up to do so. I watched him walk back to the house. He was so familiar to me, with blond hair like Cass and broad shoulders. He wasn't as tall as Cannon nor as muscly, but he wasn't unappealing.

Why was I comparing Landon with *him*? I needed to stop thinking about *that* man. Landon wasn't as tall or as broad as my *brother*. There, that was better. Healthier.

The twins came out whispering, and I strained to hear them, but they stopped. Cass set down my bottle of red and her topped-up glass of white. Landon had a tray with his beer on it and a platter of cold meats, cheeses, and grapes with some pretzels.

"Gone are the days of a bag of chips and some candy," I remarked as I looked at the artfully decorated platter.

"I'm mated now," Cass said as she sat. "I have a reputation to uphold. Oh, Landon, just scoot closer to Kezia so you can get some food. She doesn't mind."

She did mind. A lot. But Landon was already setting his chair beside mine.

"This okay?" he asked me.

"Sure." I forced a smile. "Why wouldn't it be?"

Like times before, Cass quickly took over the conversation, asking me where I had been, who I'd met, and what did I do? Had I really fought for money?

I noticed Landon's alarm at that, and I felt a quick sense of glee as I remembered I'd beaten his ass too.

"Yes, I did. It's good money," I told her, draining my second glass. "I need more." I refilled a little higher than was polite, but neither stopped me.

"Wow, you fought as human?" she asked me, her eyes wide.

"No, while they shit themselves in fear, I shifted to my wolf and fought them like that." Landon choked on his beer, and I absentmindedly hammered his back as he coughed. "Of course as a human, only as a human," I added sharply when I saw her about to ask more questions. "Talk about something else," I muttered, drinking more.

"How many did you kiss?" she asked with a gleam in her eye as her brother dropped his head.

"None." I felt them both staring at me. "I've kissed no human."

I heard Landon gulp. "And shifter? Have you..." He cleared his throat roughly. "Have you?"

"Yes."

He gave me a jerky nod. "I have, um...too."

I raised an eyebrow, enjoying watching him squirm. "I've heard," I told him. "It was a lot more than kissing too, wasn't it?"

Landon went bright red, looking to his sister for help in his panic.

Cass, like the slippery eel she can be, let out a forced laugh. "Well, this took a turn," she said. "Let's talk about something else." She suddenly clapped her hands in delight. "We should have a party."

"Why?" I asked.

"We should?" Landon asked at the same time.

The two of us exchanged a look because Cass was already on her feet. "Landon, you run to the store. I need more booze." She was already on her way into the house. "I need to talk to Kris, of course. Kezia, you—"

"Will stay right here," I said, pulling the bottle of almost empty red to me. "I'll have another one of these," I told Landon as he looked between the kitchen and me. "Cheers."

Settling back into my chair, I watched as Bale's two children created a party from thin air. As I ate my way through the platter Cass had made earlier, I saw them both work, and frankly, it was unnerving. Had it not been so repulsive a thought, and had I not seen my brother with her, anyone would think Cass and Landon were mates.

It must be a twin thing.

Later, when my brother came home, he looked surprised to see so many people in his backyard. He made his way over to me, where I was still hogging the fire pit with another bottle of wine.

"Do I want to know?" Kris asked, taking the bottle off me and taking a swig. I'd stopped using the glass a while ago—it had been slowing me down.

"At this point, I don't think I know," I told him honestly. "Am I drunk?"

He looked over at me and gave a nod. "On your way to wasted, I'd say."

I giggled. "Nice."

Kris kicked off his boots. "Let me catch up." He took my wine bottle off me, finishing it in three swallows. Minutes later, Cass was on his lap, and they were wrapped around each other. I may not remember much, but I knew I didn't want to see that.

Grumbling about losing my prime spot, I got up in search of more wine.

Landon cornered me in the kitchen, which was unfair. It was bright, crowded, and had no red wine.

"Did the wine get drunk?"

He grinned at me. "No, babe...you did, though."

"Babe?" I rolled it over my tongue. "Babe." I inhaled deeply. "Nope, I don't like it." I swayed slightly. "I did what?"

"Got drunk," Landon answered with a laugh. "Your lips are stained red with the wine," he added, moving closer.

"Really?" I leaned back, rubbing at my lips. "Weird." Looking around, I saw lots of pack, some in couples, some just hoping to hook up. I hated this scene. "I need to pee." Pushing away from Landon, I got free.

Shaking my head, I looked at him. "Did you hug me?"

He shook his head, his eyes dancing with laughter. "No, Kezia, I was holding your hip."

I looked down at my shorts, inspecting both sides, then looked up at him with a shrug. "Still got 'em." I made my way to the stairs, but Landon caught my hand.

"They don't like people in their space," he told me. "There's a bathroom this way." He led me by the hand through the pack that was in the room. I kept staring at our joined hands because I didn't remember him taking it or him ever wanting to hold my hand before.

It was weird, but maybe it didn't feel weird. Maybe it was nice to hold hands?

"Here." He pushed a door open. "I'll wait here, okay?"

"Yup."

Inside, I took care of my bladder and then stared at myself for a very long time. My lips were red. I tried to wash it off, but I think I made it worse. Then, I spent a long time looking at the silvery scar on my arm.

"You shot me," I told the scar. "You fucking shot me."

"Kezia?" Knocking happened, so I looked around. "Kezia, I'm coming in." Landon stuck his head around the door and saw me braced against the sink, my head turned to watch him. "You okay?"

I pointed at my lips. "Won't come off."

Landon moved closer. "Really?" His voice had dropped. "Let me try."

It was such an obvious line, but still, I didn't stop him when his intent was clear, and instead, I waited to see if it would be different this time. His lips were warm, a little bit dry. Maybe that was my lips, so I licked mine to wet them. I heard him groan and had no idea why, but when his tongue licked at the seam of my mouth, I opened.

Landon licked inside my mouth. It was weird, like he was licking a lollipop, but there was nothing there to lick, because I didn't move my tongue back. It tickled though, and I started to laugh.

I have no idea how he thought that meant go further, but when his hands cupped my ass, my knee met his balls.

Landon dropped like a stone. "Kezia," he grunted as he rolled on the floor.

"They called me Zia," I said as I watched him. "When I fought, I liked Zia." I stepped over him as I left the bathroom. "I miss her," I mumbled. Coming back into the family room, I saw the party was getting rowdier.

Kris would hate it.

I hated it.

It was time to go home.

There was no point saying goodbye. I dared not look outside in case I saw too much. Instead, I left and headed home.

I was halfway to the cottage when I knew *he* was there.

CHAPTER 27

Kezia

"Thought you'd be here sooner," I said to the night as I walked on, my pace steady, even if my legs were not.

"Are you drunk?" Cannon asked as he came out of the darkness and walked beside me.

"I think so." I thought about it. "I was... I think I may be losing it. I ran out of wine," I told him easily. "Have you got any?"

"I didn't come to party," he told me grimly.

"Hmm." Turning my head, I looked his way. Even in the moonlight, he was gorgeous. "Landon kissed me."

I saw his eyes flare briefly. "Is that so?"

"He says he's my mate."

I heard the scoff. "And what do you think, pup?"

"I think when I fought in the rings, they called me Zia. I like Zia. You can call me Zia." I reached my cottage. "You can't come in."

Cannon smiled. It had no warmth. No mirth. I felt sobriety rushing back.

"My brother's where the party is." I pointed behind me. "Go there. It's him you want to talk to." Without waiting for a response, I walked to the door, trying not to show him I was hurrying.

Closing the door behind me, flicking the lock, I didn't falter when it burst open moments later as Cannon let himself into my cottage.

"Kezia, are you running from me?"

"Nope." I staggered as I tried to get my boots off. "Floor's unsteady," I told him. "Kris isn't here. He's at the party. Go there."

"Your brother doesn't interest me," Cannon snapped, grabbing me by my hips and holding me steady. "Stay." The look in his eyes was firm and sure, the command natural. I remained mute as he waited for an argument or sharp response. With a quirk of an eyebrow, I saw some of his anger melt a little.

Stooping, he bent and started to undo my laces. I felt his breath on my legs, and I looked up at the ceiling, biting my lip against the moan as his fingers trailed over my calf as he unlaced the other boot.

"Lift," he commanded, his voice quiet, his breath tickling my skin.

I did as I was told, raising my leg as he pulled off my boot. When they were both off, I lost about two inches in height. But still, I felt tall as the alpha looked up at me from where he still crouched, poised on his toes, ready to pounce.

"So, did you let him kiss you?"

I blinked in confusion. "I didn't *let*, he just did." Pushing my hair off my face, I shrugged. "It was weird."

"Weird?" Cannon rose. He was in my space, his chest rubbed against mine, causing friction in places I didn't need to feel him rubbing against right now.

Stepping back, I lifted my hair off my neck. "I'm hot. I need water."

"You're hot?" he asked, and I felt him behind me as I ran the faucet. Fingers stroked over my bare shoulders. "You feel cool to me."

My body was burning. Either he was full of shit, or I had a fever. Filling a glass, I drank greedily. The longer I went without the wine, the quicker sobriety returned. Shifter metabolism made for expensive binge drinking. I felt his lips on my neck, and hastily, I refilled the water glass.

"Kezia," Cannon murmured against my skin. "Did you kiss him back?"

"I..." Why was my mouth dry? I had drunk some water. Thinking it wasn't enough, I swallowed several more gulps. "I don't think so."

I felt his fingers tighten on my upper arms, his lips still skimming up and down my neck slowly. Torturously. "You don't *think* so?"

I heard the bite. I knew I was on dangerous ground, but either wine or recklessness danced in my bones. "Nope."

Fingers bit into my skin as Cannon abruptly turned me to face him. Looking up into his anger-filled eyes, I smiled. "Miss me, *Alpha*?"

His eyes closed, and I heard his low growl. When he looked at me, the anger was gone, and something a lot more dangerous looked back at me.

Passion.

"I have *not* missed you, *pup*."

Raising myself on my tiptoes, my lips were a breath away from his as I looked deep into his eyes and smirked. "Liar," I whispered.

His mouth was on mine, his tongue moving against mine in artful synchronization as I clung to him. Cannon walked backward, turning quickly, lifting me, and my ass landed on the counter. He was already pulling off my shirt as I reached for his. His mouth trailed kisses over the curve of my breasts and, reaching behind me, I unclasped my bra, much to his moan of approval as his mouth covered my nipple, his tongue flicking against it, causing me to arch my back as he tipped me backward slowly.

The alpha raised his head to look at me, my breath catching in my throat as I saw the unbridled lust in his gaze. "Did he do this?" I watched in fascination as his tongue licked over my nipple slowly. His teeth, sharp and white, bit gently on the tender peak, and I cried out at the sensation. "Did he? Did he touch you here?"

Quickly, I shook my head, hearing his huff of approval as he returned to his task. My fingers tangled in his thick, dark hair as he shifted his attention to the other breast.

Good Goddess, that loud panting I heard was me. I was almost embarrassed, but Cannon's fingers were at my shorts button.

"How about here?" he asked me, his voice guttural. I shook my head. "Answer me," he demanded, teeth biting into the flesh at my hip.

"No." I groaned. "He touched my ass, and I kneed him in the balls."

The speed at which I was turned over caused me to cry out. My ass was in the air, and my body was pressed into the cold counter.

"He touched your ass?" Cannon growled. "This ass?"

I yelled out as he struck his palm on my cheek, closely followed by another smack on the other cheek. I tried to push myself up, but he pinned me down with his other hand. Two more smacks landed on each cheek.

"Let me go," I snarled, trying to get away.

"You let someone touch what wasn't theirs," he reminded me, and another two slaps hit my ass.

Suddenly, I heard the rip, and I cried out again as the jean shorts were pulled roughly down over my hips. The next two slaps were louder and more painful, with only the thin cotton of my black boy shorts between his hand and my flesh.

"Let me see how red this ass is," he murmured, his fingers gentle now as he peeled the panties down.

And I did nothing. I lay there and relished the feel of him smoothing my ass cheeks. First with his hands as he rubbed them and then with his mouth as he kissed over them.

"You smell so fucking pure," he growled, kicking my legs wide apart. "I need this," he muttered more to himself than me.

I felt the first swipe of his tongue over my sex, and I was so grateful the counter was holding me up. When he did it again, my hands were in my hair, my forehead pressed against the cold work-top, and my legs spread wider for the alpha's tongue.

Cannon kept licking, and I was getting closer and closer to the point of no return. My head tipped back, my hips moving to an ancient rhythm only they knew as his mouth and tongue threatened to bring me to my knees. He pulled me down, and I went as the alpha lay on his back, bringing my body over his mouth. Cannon feasted on me, and when I made eye contact, my body erupted into a million fragments.

Panting, I lay half on the floor, half of me still on Cannon as I struggled to catch my breath. I heard the door push open, and I didn't register there was someone in the cottage until they cleared their throat.

"Kezia, maybe put some clothes on." My brother's voice was gruff with embarrassment as my eyes flew open wide with alarm. "You too, Landon."

I scrambled to my feet in horror, my hair covering my boobs. "Kris, you need to leave."

Kris had his back to me, but he half turned when the low, dark chuckle sounded from behind me. I kicked out with my foot to stop him, but hit empty air. I wished I had closed my eyes, but instead, I watched my brother's widen in shock and horror as Cannon rose behind me like the ungodly demon he was.

"You?" Kris gasped.

"Me," Cannon greeted as he made a show of wiping his mouth. "Not Landon," Cannon spoke with a sneer. "It will *never* be Landon." Cannon handed me my shirt. "Cover yourself. I don't care if he's your brother. No one looks at you unless it's me."

My brother finally got over his shock, and his temper exploded. "What the *fuck* is going on?"

Maybe it was because I was still drunk or coming down from the high of the pleasure Cannon had just given me, but either way, I started to laugh.

My brother's look was full of outrage and disbelief. I even heard Cannon turn to look at me as my laughter filled the cottage. There I was—half naked, no fully naked, except for my socks—having just experienced my first-ever orgasm by someone who wasn't me, and not only did I get caught by my brother, but my orgasm was delivered at the hands, no the tongue, of the enemy.

The sharp slap to my ass cut my laughter off quickly, and I spun to face the alpha. "Enough with the ass slapping," I growled at him.

"I'm stepping outside," my brother said slowly, carefully. I turned to look at him and met his hard glare. "When I come back, I want you dressed," he told me. "And I want you..." Kris couldn't hide his anger as he met Cannon's cocky gaze. "As far away from my sister as possible."

The cottage was silent as he left with quiet dignity, and when the door shut behind him, I let out the breath I was holding when I saw the busted lock.

Spinning, I took one look at smug-as-fuck's face, and bending swiftly, I picked up my underwear and shorts, hastily trying to get dressed. I pulled the shorts up my legs before realizing Cannon had ripped them, and they wouldn't fasten.

"Shit." Pushing past him, I ran to my room to get dressed before my brother came back to lecture me and probably hand me directly over to Cannon.

I found a pair of black leggings and pulled them on. When I turned, Cannon was standing in my bedroom door, leaning against the frame, my bra dangling from his finger.

"You forgot this."

Snatching it off him, I turned my back, pulling off my shirt and putting on my bra. Warm hands slid around my sides, and they traveled upward smoothly as he cupped my breasts.

"Your heat is back," he murmured, thumbs brushing over my nipples. "Your scent is fucking with my head."

"Hold your breath. Hopefully, you'll pass out," I snapped, stepping out of his hold. "You...we..." Shaking my head, I put my top back on. "Why do you keep doing this to me?" Turning, I looked at him and saw the same animosity he usually looked at me with. "I'm still a virgin. Though I'm not too sure about the shades of gray involved after what you just did," I muttered. Moving past him, I went back to the kitchen where my boots were. "My scent is stronger when I'm aroused." My face was aflame, but I surged on. "You need better control."

Cannon barked out a laugh. "*I* need better control?" Running a hand through his dark hair, he looked me over once. "Says you?"

"Yes, yes, the irony is lost on no one," I muttered, trying to fix my hair. "Just keep it in your pants, okay?"

"*It* hasn't been out of my pants. Trust me, pup, you'd know."

My breath caught at his implication, and we stared at each other, frozen for a moment as the pull grew between us.

"And that's enough of that," Kris grumbled, entering the cottage. I wasn't surprised when Royce followed him inside.

"Hey, Royce," I greeted. Knowing he'd also have heard everything, my face would never not be red again.

"Kezia." Royce didn't look at me, but I could tell he was just as pissed as my brother, and the glare he sent his alpha's way wasn't hiding how he felt either.

"Um…" I looked around our small cottage—three large males didn't exactly fit well into the small space.

"Kezia." The door pushed open, and I knew my mouth was hanging open as I watched the shaman enter. "Let's take this to my house. I can seal us in there."

No one said anything, but the four of us dutifully followed the old shaman to his cottage. Kris refused to look at me, and I watched Cannon ignore every pointed look his beta gave him.

Inside the shaman's cottage, Cannon sat in the same chair he sat in the first day I met him, and Royce hovered near his side. I took my usual seat, my feet automatically resting on the coffee table, and I grunted but bit my tongue when my brother swiped my feet off the table.

"She has always been at home here." The shaman chuckled as

he took his own seat. "I do not know you well, but you may sit. No harm will come to anyone while in my walls." He was looking at Royce, and with a simple nod from his alpha, Royce took the remaining chair.

I heard the shaman mutter gently, and then I felt the privacy spell as he sealed us inside.

"You forgot Bale?" I broke the silence.

"Most do forget your pack leader," Cannon said with a dismissive snort. He was leaning back, one leg crossed over the other, his hands at ease over his abs.

He couldn't be sending a more relaxed *fuck you* to my brother if he tried.

"Will you show some respect?" I hissed at him. "We're not in your packlands now."

His gaze settled on mine, and I looked away from his heavy stare. Unnerved. I hated when he looked at me like he could see every secret I ever had.

"Well, pup, you managed to get yourself in a bind again," the shaman spoke, and I saw, with some small satisfaction, when Cannon's nose wrinkled in distaste. "I am two hundred and ten years old, Alpha...you are all pups to me," he added with a sly grin.

"Cannon means wolf cub," I blurted out.

I felt four pairs of eyes on me. Well, not the shaman's, but had he still had his full sight, I was sure they would mirror the other three's varying looks of intrigue or, in my brother's case, shock.

"You been looking me up, *Zia*?"

"Her name is Kezia," Kris bit out. "Or have you forgotten her already?" he sneered as he looked Cannon over. Cannon merely grinned at my brother's veiled insult, but I felt a wash of shame sweep over me.

"She told me she prefers Zia," Cannon replied lazily. He licked his bottom lip as he held my brother's stare. "And I remember her *very* well."

"Enough," Royce spoke to them both, his look hard. "Kezia." He glanced at me, his gaze sympathetic. "I apologize for my Alpha's disrespect."

Kris went to speak, but I spoke over him, "Royce, you are a true beta, difficult when one's alpha is such a monumental prick. Thank you." I inclined my head in respect.

Cannon grinned wider at me, but he turned to the shaman. "She comes with me," he told him bluntly.

"She stays here," Kris growled. "She's *my* sister."

"I don't give a fuck," Cannon told him pleasantly. "She was in my custody and is dangerous." He looked at me. "Plus, she's *mine*."

I was?

Hell to the no.

"I am *not* yours. I am not anyone's," I snapped. I ignored them all as I looked at the shaman. "I am in control," I told him quietly.

The old male raised his head as voices broke around me. "Quiet," he told them. "Come here," he asked me.

Nervously, I got to my feet and crossed the floor to the shaman. Habit made my moves smooth as I extended a claw and opened my wrist. I ignored the murmur of protest from Royce. Holding up my wrist, I took the bowl from the table beside the shaman, and I let my blood drop into it.

"Behind you," he murmured. Half turning, I refused to make eye contact with anyone while I grabbed the small pouch. "Half a pinch will do," he told me.

When I had blended the herbs with my blood, I raised the bowl to him. He sniffed once. A quick dip of his finger, and he tasted my blood. With a frown, he held out his hand, and I put my hand in his.

I heard a scuffle behind me as the shaman dipped his head, and his tongue flicked out over my wrist. Nodding, he sat back.

"Thank you, pup."

Only when I was back in my seat did I raise my head and was blasted with a look of pure rage from Cannon. Royce was at his side, his hands firmly on his alpha's shoulders. *Had he been holding him in place?*

Kris reached out and took my hand, squeezing it lightly as my wound healed.

"The wolf is very angry," the shaman told me with a faint smile. He turned toward Cannon. "Kezia holds control. Your fear is warranted, but in this instance, unneeded."

"She comes with me," he said stubbornly.

"No."

Cannon looked at me, the challenge in his eyes clear. "No?"

"I remain here with my pack. I am not yours. You have no control over me."

His eyes flared with challenge, but it was Kris who spoke, "We have called for the Pack Council. We need to know what happened with the humans and after the humans." His glare was hard as he looked at the alpha. "There is a lot to discover."

Cannon kept his eyes on me. "*This* is where you would rather be?" he asked as if we were the only ones in the room. "This pack, these wolves who spurn you? Treat you as less?"

"Enough!" Kris bit out. "She stays with me."

Cannon held my gaze for a long moment and then abruptly rose. "Fine. When the Pack Council comes, let me know." He gestured to Royce, and they headed for the door. Turning back to look at me, he ran his eyes over me slowly. "Be good, pup."

"Fuck you."

"Next time, if you're lucky." He winked as he turned away. He looked over his shoulder at Kris. "Ask yourself why *you* have a mate," he told him. "Ask yourself why he's called pack leader and not alpha."

Cannon opened the door, standing back to let Royce walk out. He looked at all three of us. "Ask yourself what the fuck is wrong with this pack." His eyes locked with Kris. "You don't need to look too far for the source of that bullet. Open your eyes." With a look of scorn, he left us.

CHAPTER 28

Kezia

My head was reeling. "What?" I felt the privacy seal us within the room. "What did he mean?"

"You need to leave," Kris bit out, surging to his feet. "Now. Tonight."

"I need to...*what*? *Why*?"

"You're not safe here," the shaman said in agreement, his head cocked to the side. "Had your brother allowed it, you would have been better with the Blackridge Peak Alpha."

"She's never going to be with them," Kris snarled. "What were you *thinking*, Kezia? *Him*? Really?"

"Cass? Really?" I shouted back.

Kris's eyes widened in horror as he realized what I was saying. "Him? *Him!*" He turned to the shaman. "*Him?*"

"It would appear so," the shaman said with a faint smile. "The Goddess does love her trickery."

"But Landon?" Kris struggled.

"Wants a mate like his sister has a mate," I snapped. "But only an *alpha* can have a mate."

Oh shit.

"Oh, shit, you're an alpha."

Kris looked at me as if I had lost my mind. "Be careful what you say, Kezia."

"Cannon told me, he *told* me only an alpha has a *true* mate." I sat down with a thump. "Why didn't we know?"

Kris was avoiding my questions and my look. I stared at the shaman sitting non-plussed. "You did know," I said with sudden understanding. "Kris?"

He shrugged. "I suspected," he said with a glance at the shaman. "And then we confirmed it."

"Why didn't you tell me?" I demanded.

"Because I keep you safe," he hissed at me. "And you have an *amazing* ability to make that very, *very* fucking difficult!"

"I..." I floundered. "I'm sorry."

He sighed as he rubbed his face. "It's not your fault." He glanced at me. "Not all the time." He smiled, and the shaman chuckled.

"This has been the weirdest night," I said to no one.

Kris sighed. "Yeah." He sat down tiredly. "What do we do?" he asked the shaman.

Looking between them, I heard no answers to all the questions I had unanswered in my head. "*You* could try to tell me what the fuck is going on?"

Kris yawned but shook his head. "It's so much, *too* much, and honestly, we"—he gestured to the shaman—"we don't have it figured out either." Kris leaned forward, resting his arms on his knees, but his head turned to look at me. "Cannon?" He was already shaking his head. "Luna, I do not need *that*."

I grunted in agreement, but my head was reeling. "It's why he's called pack leader and not Alpha Bale." I realized. "If Bale isn't the alpha, does that mean you are?" I asked quietly.

"No," Kris scoffed. "This is his pack." The shaman harrumphed, and Kris grimaced. "Some of it is his," Kris amended. "It's difficult to explain. The pack is divided...it's complicated."

"I'm not stupid. I can keep up," I told him. The sharpness of my tone caused my brother to turn his full attention to me.

"This is not the time or the place," he admonished me. "Have they left?" he asked the shaman.

The shaman held still for a moment before nodding once. "They shifted and have run straight west."

"He'll come back," Kris muttered. Rolling his neck, he stood. "Is it a true bond?" he asked the shaman. "Can we break it?"

"It *is* true. And it can be broken only if it wants to be broken," he answered.

They both turned to me, and I looked at them with wide eyes. "What?" I asked in a panic. "It wants to be broken." I pushed away the whisper of *liar* that echoed in my brain, as my mind immediately conjured up the image of Cannon crouched at my feet as he looked up at me. *Did I want to be his mate?* Luna, no. Not at all.

Liar.

"I didn't know it was possible to reject the mating bond," I said as I looked at the shaman.

"It is difficult. Both need to want it, really want it." His whole attention was on me. "Distance will help," the shaman spoke quietly, his expression thoughtful.

"Why are you helping Kris and not telling Bale everything?" I blurted, flinching back from my brother's incredulous stare. "I mean, you're Bale's shaman. I didn't think you would be... divided?"

"I am the pack's shaman. I serve the good of the pack," he

answered simply. "The alpha or pack leader, it means nothing. A shaman is loyal only to the pack."

"You could tell Bale everything," I said, unable to shake the feeling of alarm as I got to my feet. "Kris!"

"I am loyal to a pack, and I am true to the leader," the shaman's voice was crisper, sterner.

Which meant he thought Kris was the leader. "Oh. Well... good."

Kris was watching me tiredly. "Distance, you say?" he added with a smirk, earning a grin from the shaman. "And the people hunting her?"

"She handled them," he answered easily. "Keep your head low, your nose out of trouble," the shaman spoke only to me. "And for the love of the Goddess, keep your temper, pup."

"I have to leave again," I spoke, looking down at my hands. "Really?"

"You are too volatile," Kris told me brusquely. "The work I am doing here, it needs...subtlety. Bale knows a little and suspects a lot more. It's too close for comfort with you here and Cannon on the other mountain."

"He will not expect you to send her away," the shaman mused. "Protecting your sister, to him, would be to keep her close. It is a bold move." I watched the shaman rub his chin in thought. "I can give you something to stop the heat and mask your scent."

"I want to stay," I protested weakly. "You are my pack."

"I cannot risk you," Kris answered quietly. "Too much is happening, Kezia...too much and too fast. This Landon thing is a complete shitshow," he added grumpily. "Why is he such an idiot?" Kris looked between us both, and when no one answered, he sighed. "He's definitely not the mate?"

"Why are you asking the shaman? Shouldn't you ask me?"

"No, because at the moment, the alternative is Cannon, and I genuinely think you prefer him," he told me with an eye roll. "You must be drunk," he mused.

For once, I kept my mouth shut.

"I will call for the Pack Council." Kris rubbed his forehead. "I thought to hold off, but he's forced our hand." My brother stood to pace. "They can take months to gather though...years," he added thoughtfully. He looked at me with a gleam in his eye.

"No," I was already shaking my head. "Whatever *that* look is, no."

Kris ignored me and turned to look at the shaman. "It could work."

I gaped. "Are you communicating with him?"

"Shifter, remember?" Kris said with a huff.

"Asshole, you mean," I sassed back at him and was pleased when I saw his slight smile. "I can't talk to you like that," I told the shaman.

Few can. I like the sound of your voice, pup, so I prefer to hear it out loud.

Oh. I was smiling in happiness that the shaman had granted me that honor, and I saw Kris was pleased too. "Thank you." My head dipped in respect. "What did you mean, though? What will work?"

"Seclusion."

I looked between them both. "Excuse me?"

"We can tell them you are no threat because you have opted for seclusion to think about your actions."

"I thought I was innocent?" I told my brother. He gave me a flat look. "Okay, I thought I wasn't to *blame*?"

"You aren't." He walked to the table, taking the small bowl I'd offered the shaman. Sniffing it once, he pulled his head back sharply. "No wonder he's claiming you," he muttered.

I opted to ignore that. "What does seclusion mean?" I asked fearfully.

"You find somewhere safe. We tell no one. You stay there until I come back for you."

"No!"

"We aren't really putting you in seclusion, pup," the shaman told me. "It's an illusion. We give them all an illusion of what they want, and you live free from here until your brother comes for you."

"Am I really so bad that I need to be pushed away?" I asked Kris. "Look what happened last time."

"No, you are not bad," he answered solemnly. "But you are a magnet for trouble. Landon is going to push that he's your mate. Who's going to tell him differently?" He gave me a look I knew well. "Bale is watching every move you make. He isn't as pleased as he pretends that Cass is my mate, and he hates that you are back. Cannon...well, that's its own mess." He ran his hand through his hair. "The coverup, I don't know who that was, I don't know who else knows. There is so much that *I don't know*."

Everything was a mess. I thought coming back would be better. I didn't know it meant I was in even more strife than before I left.

"You will come for me?" I asked him softly.

"Always," Kris promised. "Go somewhere new, somewhere where no one will know you. *Blend*." Kris pulled me into his embrace. "You *have* to blend. No attention to yourself. I will come for you."

"How long?"

"The Pack Council moves slowly," the shaman spoke bluntly. "It could be months."

I nodded, fighting back tears. "Okay. I guess I can do this." Scrubbing my hands over my eyes, I looked around the room. "I assume you want me to go tonight? Right?"

Kris nodded. "It's easier." In his defense, he didn't look happy about it.

"Yeah, easier. Right." I heard my bitterness. "Tell Cass...nothing." I saw him flinch. "I know her, I know you do too, but Landon's her twin. As you do everything you can for *me*, she does it for him. Tell her I'm overwhelmed. It's too much to process. Tell her I left quickly." I gave a self-deprecating laugh. "Rashly. It's me, after all."

"She loves you very much," Kris said, his voice softening as he thought of his mate. "But I agree." He didn't look happy about it. "It's too much of a risk."

"Okay." Looking down at myself, I checked what I was wearing. "I'm practically ready to go," I said bitterly.

"The backpacks, at our meeting place, there's money in yours. Take it and go." He sighed. "There's a phone too. Only I have the number. Keep it with you. When it's time, I'll come."

I nodded, letting my brother engulf me as he hugged me tight. "One more hurdle, Kezia," he whispered. "Then you can come back, and it can be behind us."

"Unless I fuck up."

He blew out a breath. "Well, don't fuck up."

The shaman started to laugh, and I grinned ruefully at my brother, causing him to laugh too. It was bittersweet that I would leave them when I was just beginning to understand *more*.

"Don't shift," the shaman warned. "Hike to your safe place. Your human scent fades quicker than your wolf's."

"You want me to go now, right?" I felt sick. The last few days had been a roller coaster, and I was constantly bracing myself for the next twist and turn.

"It would be best if it was at night," Kris confirmed.

"Okay." Chewing my lip, I looked between the two of them. "Um...call me?" I joked weakly, but it made my brother chuckle as he hugged me one more time.

I even got a hug from the shaman. "Luna is watching over you, pup."

"Can you tell her to give me a break?" I asked seriously. The old wolf patted my cheek. I wasn't sure I liked his answer.

Sooner than I liked, I was walking through the meadow, heading southeast down the mountain, alert for any sound in the night that meant I wasn't alone.

I picked the pack up and checked it all. *Kris must have been planning this*, I realized as I tugged out a black hoodie from the tightly packed rucksack. I found the phone and the wad of cash. No fighting rings for me, not for a while anyway. Stuffing in the herbs the shaman gave me, I got ready to leave.

Shouldering the backpack, I inhaled deeply. With one last look over my shoulder to view Anterrio, my eyes flicked past it, focusing on the mountain that sat behind it.

Was he back on his mountain? A shifter like him had speed to spare.

Distance—that's what we needed until the bond was broken.

With a sigh, I turned my back on the mountains and headed south.

I WATCHED THE TWO MALES FIGHTING IN THE RING.

Both were big and brawny, their muscles tight and defined. It was an even match. I watched as I walked around the ring, my eyes searching the shadows as always.

A cheer rose, and I turned my attention back to the ring. The darker-haired one was on his knees. Impassively, I watched as he struggled to rise, and with speed, he ducked the roundhouse kick, and in retaliation, he punched his opponent's inner thigh. There was still a fight to be had in there.

I found another set of eyes in the crowd. With a slight nod, I let them know I was ready.

Walking out of the barn, I looked up at the sky. The faint pull in my belly that I tried so hard to ignore was drawing me tonight, making its presence known. The moon shone above, making the night bright and sharper.

Scents and smells were surrounding me tonight, confusing my senses or trying to. With a snarl, I shook my head. I needed to be clearheaded.

Fingers trailed lightly over my arm as I glanced at the one who had followed me out. "You seem lonely."

"Do I?" I scoffed, my head turning to look east. I looked back at them. "Go inside, there's nothing for you out here."

I heard more cheers from inside, and I knew I needed to go back to the ring, but my attention returned to the moon as she hung full and heavy in the sky. A familiar scent broke my perusal of the night.

"Well?" I asked.

"I found her."

Turning my head sharply, I looked at Royce. "It's definitely her?"

He nodded once. "Yes, Alpha, it's her."

The bond tugged at me once more. "*Finally*, let's go get my mate."

~

About the Author

Eve L. Mitchell is a USA Today Bestselling author who writes Contemporary Romance, and New Adult Romance but also dabbles in Paranormal Romance.

If you like a morally grey alpha-hole, then chances are Eve's got a male character for you to claim as your next book boyfriend.

As an avid reader from a young age, Eve still considers herself a reader first. She believes there is nothing better than getting that new book either on your e-reader or in your hands, and the fact she may bring that excitement to a fellow reader fills her with wonder. She writes under a pen name; otherwise, her Secret Agent status will be revoked.

Eve lives in the North East of Scotland, with her three coffee machines and her significant other, Mr. M. She enjoys NFL Football, music (played loudly), and having long conversations with the voices in her head, which sometimes turn into the stories she writes.

How to Connect with Eve:

Join my newsletter and keep up to date with the latest news and updates on my books and releases: http://bit.ly/Eves newsletter

Connect with me on Facebook: http://bit.ly/evesfacebook page

THE BOULDER SERIES

The Boulder Series is an interconnected series that explores the relationships between friends, family, and the family you choose... with some love, heat, and underground fighting along the way! The series covers tropes of forbidden romance (ex-boyfriend's older brother), enemies-to-lovers, friends to lovers, opposites attract and second-chance love.

The Boulder Series will take you on a rollercoaster of emotions. You will laugh, scream, feel the characters' excitement, and it's possible you may throw your e-reader (just make sure it lands somewhere soft).

A complete four-book series that has all the feels. What's stopping you from jumping into Boulder?

The series includes **Unbroken Devotion**, **Dark Heart**, **Unbroken Bonds** and **Dark Soul**.

THE DENVER SERIES

The Denver Series is a three-book mafia romance shared world series. Each book is a standalone, featuring cameos from the other books. Although it is recommended that the books be read in order, it is not necessary to do so.

The series covers tropes of opposites attract, enemies-to-lovers, and forbidden romance (stepcousins).

The Denver Series is a steamy contemporary romance series that dabbles in the mafia romance genre, with book one hinting at it and the other two exploring the darker side of this much-loved genre.

A complete three-book series where sassy heroines meet and fall for their dark alphahole heroes.

The series includes **Her Greatest Mistake, Beautifully Broken** and **Keeping Harmony**.

GET THE SERIES

THE RUTHLESS DEVILS SERIES

A college sports romance series following twin brothers and their cousin. Three football stars who have it all: looks, money, talent and the world at their feet. No one messes with the Devils. Each book deals with a different Devil and their love interest who will either make them or break them.

The series covers tropes of enemies-to-lovers, second-chance romance and forced proximity.

This is interconnected three-book series with an underlying story arc that carries through from book one to book three, and therefore the series must be read in order. The series deals with some elements that sensitive readers may find triggering.

This series includes **Ruthless Heart**, **Ruthless Desire** and **Ruthless Charm**.

GET THE SERIES
WWW.EVELMITCHELL.COM

The Torn & Broken duet is a duet with a twist. You can read either book as a standalone. *Torn by Grace* was written first and one of the female side characters in that book is the main character in *Broken by Faith*, however, you don't need to know what happened in *Torn by Grace* to enjoy *Broken by Faith*. There is a little bit of crossover, but no spoilers.

Torn by Grace is a second chance, enemies-to-lovers, brothers-best-friend romance.
Broken by Faith is an enemies-to-lovers, forced proximity, fake relationship romance.
The series includes **Torn by Grace and Broken by Faith.**

THE BLACKRIDGE PEAK SERIES

The Blackridge Peak Series is a wolf shifter series about rival packs, hidden secrets, a little bit of magic, and a girl who's trying to find her way amongst a pack that doesn't want her.

Kezia is an outsider, and when given the chance she leaves the pack that never truly accepted her. But trouble follows Kezia and she soon learns that only an alpha can protect her.

An alpha who may be her mate.

The series includes **Wolf's Gambit, Wolf's Betrayal, and Wolf's Endgame.**

THE AKRHYN SERIES

Creatures of evil roam the shadows - the Drakhyn. They may look like humans, but their taloned hands and razor-sharp teeth serve one purpose only; killing.

A Sentinel's purpose is to patrol and protect. They are highly trained soldiers with superior skills and abilities. Whether they be Vampyres, Lycan, Castors or gifted Akrhyn, their purpose is the same; hunt the Drakhyn and rid the world of their evil presence.

This fantasy trilogy covers tropes of chosen one, fated mates, good vs evil.

The series includes **Into Darkness, Lost in Darkness** and **From the Darkness.**

THE ORDER OF THE RAVENS SERIES
written as Ava Speirs

The Order of the Ravens Series is a traditional epic fantasy series where the focus is on action and adventure.

Bastian dal'Leif is a Knight of the Order, an Order that has fallen into distrust. The Order of the Conclave which were once seen as warriors of the Gods and a beacon of hope, are now cast in shadow.

Bastian and his men remain true to their Order but are forced to become mercenaries, selling their swords for coin.

In the halls of his Order, Bastian is entrusted with a mission. A mission he is reluctant to accept.

The mission is so dangerous and deadly only a fool would take it... and only a coward would reject it.

The series includes **Knight of Sword & Shadow, Knight of Sacrifice & Shade, Knight of Dagger & Darkness, and Knight of Trials and Twilight.**

GET THE SERIES

www.ingramcontent.com/pod-product-compliance
Lightning Source LLC
Chambersburg PA
CBHW051241210726

48287CB00002B/351